HOUR OF RECKONING

A DONATELLA NOVEL

DEMETRIUS JACKSON

I dedicate this book to Denise Jackson. You always taught me to follow my dreams and exemplified the definition of a strong woman.

PART I

Decisions

PROLOGUE

JUNE 8TH – 7:15 P.M

Marcellous Thompson gripped the steering wheel of his royal blue 2018 Tesla Model S as he weaved back and forth through the nighttime traffic. The performance model upgrade and the dual motors provided the torque needed to hurry past any traffic unwilling, or in many cases too slow, to accommodate his rapid rate of speed.

"Damn it, Marcellous. Hurry! This is all your fault! I will not forgive you for this," Jasmyn screamed from the passenger side.

"My fault. My fault? If I recall we were both there and fully engaged in this matter that now has us in this fine predicament."

"Well if you don't hurry up and get me to the hospital, I will have this baby right here in the front seat of your precious *Blue Ice*." If you don't want to see that happen, I suggest you press on the gas and get me to the hospital."

This car is fully electric, Marcellous thought, *so there is no gas to push.* However, he decided in the matter of self-preservation, he would be better off keeping that thought to himself.

The couple was now only a few moments from the hospital and the nurses would then be able to take over and he would be able to breathe again.

"No worries, babe," Marcellous said in a calm, reassuring voice as he reached his hand over to his wife's hand. "We are almost there."

"Don't you touch me." The words came in rapid succession. "Oh...the pain. Get this baby out of me. And why is it so hot. Turn on the air. You are roasting me to death. Me and the baby. Is that your plan? To make us bake in the car while you take your sweet time getting me to the hospital?"

Marcellous shook his head in disbelief. Though he knew this wasn't truly his sweet wife talking, he still felt himself holding his tongue from his natural inclination to retort. Nine months of pregnancy had turned into nine months and two weeks and those extra two weeks had Jasmyn at her wits' end.

Saved by the bell, he thought as he turned into the hospital and saw a nurse standing outside the entrance with a wheelchair holding a sign that read, "Thompson". *That's a new one. I had no idea that they offered curbside service.*

When Jasmyn began to feel continuous contractions, she was convinced that the baby could come at any moment. Marcellous contacted the hospital and they said that her OB-GYN, Dr. Prince, could not be located at the time but that they would let her know that the Thompson's were on their way to the hospital. They also contacted the on-call doctor as a backup.

Marcellous depressed the brake, reached over to the touchscreen and pressed the unlock icon to unlock the door. While the nurse began to help Mrs. Thompson exit the vehicle, Marcellous hopped out of the driver's side.

"Oh, thank you so much for being out here and ready to take her inside. Wait. Let me grab her bag and we will be all set to go."

"No worries, Mr. Thompson," the nurse said with a genuine smile, "We will take great care of your wife. Why don't you go park the car, grab the bag and then come on in when you're done. We will take her up to labor and delivery located on the fifth floor. You can meet us there."

"Oh right, the car. OK. I will go park the car and then come up to labor and delivery on the fourth floor."

"Fifth floor, Mr. Thompson."

"My bad! Fifth floor. Gotcha."

Marcellous took another look at his wife and thought to himself how utterly beautiful she is and how much he truly loved her. Reading his mind, Jasmyn looked at him with a smile plastered on her face and said, "I love you, Marcellous."

He looked back at his wife and said, "I love you too, Jasmyn. I'll go park the car and then I'll be right back." He watched the nurse wheel his wife toward the sliding doors as he settled back into the driver's seat.

As he pulled away from the hospital door to find a parking spot his phone rang. It was Donatella, the baby's soon to be godmother and a special agent with the Federal Bureau of Investigation.

He answered the phone feeling more at ease now that the professionals had his wife and they would ensure their first child would make it into the world safe and sound. "Hey Donatella, I was just about to call you. We –"

"Marcellous, are you still with Jasmyn?" she interrupted Marcellous in a huff. "Are you at the hospital?"

Alarms began to register in his head. "No, I'm not with her, I just dropped her off with the nurse at the entrance to the hospital. They are taking her up to labor and delivery."

"Shit!" she said in a panicked voice. "This has all been a trap. A well-orchestrated trap. Jasmyn is in dire danger and you need to find her immediately."

Marcellous, beginning to process that his wife could be in mortal danger, quickly rotated the steering wheel a full 180 degrees, pressed the accelerator and quickly made his way back to the entrance. Without taking any time to place the car in park, he opened the door and ran inside. He frantically scanned the lobby and didn't see his wife, but his eyes connected with a nurse who was eyeing him. The nurse began to approach Marcellous and as she did, she spoke.

"You must be Marcellous. I was told to expect you and your wife. Is she outside in the car?"

"What do you mean is she in the car? I just dropped her off with a nurse who was waiting outside," he stated in a high confused voice.

"Waiting outside?" The nurse stated, raising an eyebrow. "I only received the call mere minutes ago and I haven't had time to tell anyone else. I came right down so I could meet you both."

With panic in his voice he raised the phone back to his ear, "Donatella, they've got her. They've got Jasmyn."

1

DECEMBER 10TH – 6:20 P.M

The crisp cool air accentuated by the starlight filled night breathed frost on this December evening. The trees, bare of leaves during the turn from fall to winter, glistened from the melting icicles dripping from the branches. Adam Joseph maneuvered his 2018 Toyota Camry between the lines in the lot, parking underneath the tree as the melting icicle drippings landed with a splash on the hood of the car.

Adam rummaged through his leather messenger bag until he found what he was looking for. Running his fingers through his thinning jet-black hair, he popped two breath mints into his mouth. Chewing the mints, he removed the silk red power tie adorning his neck and unbuttoned the top button on his specially tailored, white presidential dress shirt. As he swallowed the last of the mints, he cupped his hand over his mouth and nose, blew his breath into his hand and inhaled deeply.

"Fresh like a new spring day," he said out loud. Satisfied, he placed the mints back into the bag and opened the door. The frigid cold air rushed into the car sending a chill through his core. He shivered and pulled his coat tighter as he exited the car. He cast his eyes down toward the ground as a gust of wind stung his pupils. He quickened his pace as he hustled to 631 Sapphire Ave. He arrived at his destination, for the moment, and knocked.

After waiting a full 10 count, he knocked again wringing his hands feverishly to generate friction and thus some warmth. *She knew I was coming*, he thought as he began to bounce in place. He reluctantly moved his right hand from his left preparing to rap on the door for a third time when he heard the deadbolt disengage seconds before the door swung open.

Samantha stood on the other side of the door with a Cheshire cat grin on her face motioning for Adam to enter into her two-bedroom apartment. Adam rushed through the entrance but not without giving Samantha the once over.

She wore a pair of slim fitted dark blue jeans ripped above the right thigh. The fit hugged her hips, while narrowing at the waist. Tucked into the jeans, she wore a white, fitted body shirt that lay flat on her stomach while exposing the nipples of her A cup breast.

Adam walked through the opening and Samantha closed the door behind them. Turning to face him, he pulled her close into his embrace, kissed her deeply with passion that sent a spark down her spine and a stiffening in his pants. He reached behind her running his hand down the small of her back, over the soft feel of her jeans and took a firm grasp of her bottom. She returned the gesture with a quick tug of his bottom lip.

Adam had known Samantha for years and only recently did she come back into his life. His heart raced every time he thought about going to see her and today was no different. As their lips pressed and their tongues wrestled, he could feel each beat of his heart in a harmonious rhythm with hers. He inhaled her smell and that nearly sent him over the top. The coconut and lime scent mixed with her body chemistry pushed pheromones into the atmosphere and had Adam under a spell.

He began to nibble her earlobe before making his way down to her long slender neck.

A knock at the door momentarily broke the mood, but Adam would not be deterred. Again, the knock came from the door.

"I should get that," she said. "Tina is dropping off a sleeping bag I need for my camping trip tomorrow. Go on, have a seat in the living room. I promise not to be long." She stretched out the last word as she ran her hand down the front of his trousers.

Adam turned reluctantly away and proceeded toward the couch. Samantha turned back to the door, straightening up her hair in the process. She pulled open the door and was struck in the abdomen with a vicious blow that sent her sprawling to the floor. She let out an ear screeching yell as her head hit the ground.

Adam heard the scuffle and sound that arose from the front and came to her aid only to find himself staring down the barrel of a gun as a woman calmly closed the door.

"Not so fast, Adam. Don't take another step," the newcomer said patiently while waving the gun in his direction. "Please take these and secure Miss Samantha." The intruder tossed Adam a pair of flex cuffs. "And please be quick about it. Time is running short."

"Who are you?" Adam asked in a trembling voice while Samantha clutched her stomach, writhing in pain.

"Who I am is not important. You following my directions is what's important. Now the cuffs, if you would. I don't like to repeat myself and I've already done it once."

Adam retrieved the flex cuffs from the ground and made his way over to Samantha. He pulled her left arm from her abdomen placing the cuff over her wrist. He repeated the task with her right wrist and then pulled the cuffs tight.

"See that wasn't so hard, we are off to a good start. Now if you would be so kind, please bring our dear Samantha to a seated position."

Without a moment's hesitation, Adam did as he was asked. Samantha sat with her legs stretched out in front of her and hands secured with the flex cuffs sitting on her lap.

"Again, a job well done. Lastly, take this duct tape, secure her legs and place a strand across her mouth. I wouldn't want her to interrupt the conversation you and I need to have."

Adam once again did as he was asked while Samantha looked at him with uncomprehending eyes.

The intruder pulled a tablet from the left pocket of her overcoat while she leveled the gun at Adam with her right hand. Wordlessly, she tossed the tablet underhanded to Adam. "Please, take a look."

Adam terrified to take his eyes off the gun and the woman holding it, begrudgingly did as he was bid. He had to turn the tablet over so the screen was facing him. For a moment, the screen was blank.

"Go ahead, tap the screen."

Again, Adam did as he was asked. When he tapped the screen, he realized he needed to turn the tablet to landscape orientation to enlarge the multiple sets of pictures displayed. While turning the device, he could tell the screen was split into three sections. Once he did, he was mortified into silence.

On the top half of the screen was a video of his wife, Evelyn, in the kitchen of their house preparing dinner. On the bottom, left-hand side of the screen was a video of his oldest daughter, Courtney (10), and his youngest daughter, Megan (5), sitting in the family room playing a game. On the bottom right-hand side of the screen was his middle daughter, Chasity (7) sitting in her room listening to her headphones.

"What the hell is this?" Adam exclaimed raising his voice.

"You mean to tell me you don't recognize your own family?"

She said mirthlessly. "You are indeed far gone."

"Damn it, I know it's my family. Why are they on this... this tablet?"

"The better question, Adam, is why are you here instead of being at home with your family? No need to answer the question," the stranger chided while shifting her eyes toward Samantha who was now staring back at the stranger.

"But it's time we stop with these trivial questions because as I said, we are on limited time. You have a very important decision to make. Will it be your family, or will it be your mistress? The power is yours. You'll notice a clock at the bottom of the tablet you hold in your hands."

Adam looked down to notice 3 minutes and 15 seconds on the clock. The clock was moving in reverse acting as a countdown.

"What decision do I have to make?"

"Someone must die," she said in a cold, detached voice. She reached back into her left pocket and extracted another handgun. She took a few steps forward, the gun in her right hand still leveled at Adam, she handed him the gun in her left hand. "You can do nothing, and when that clock reaches zero your house will be set ablaze. The exits will be bolted, your wife, and three daughters will be burned alive. Or you can take the gun I've handed you and put a bullet into Miss Samantha, ending her life. In ending her life, your family will be spared. Oh, and you have a third option. You can kill yourself, in which case, both Samantha and your family will be spared. But make no mistake, if you point that gun at me, I will put you down, fire another shot into Samantha, and set your house on fire. The choice is yours!"

Adam could not believe his ears. "Those are not choices. Why are you doing this? What have I done to you?"

"Oh Adam," she said in a patronizing tone. "You haven't

done a thing to me. But you have been an unfaithful piece of shit to your wife and your family. It's obvious to me you do not deserve them. But I decided to give you a chance to do the right thing, or at least something. And instead of making a decision you are squandering your time by asking me questions."

He looked down at the clock; 1 minute 33 seconds. His hands began to sweat and his heart, that 10 minutes earlier was pounding with lust, was now pounding even faster with fear.

His eyes shifted from the stranger over to Samantha. Her eyes were wide with fear as muffled words and muffled screams emanated from her bound mouth. She was now crying as she tried to undo her hands from the flex cuffs.

Adam's mind raced. He loved his wife, even though he had been unfaithful, he still loved her. And more than that, he loved his children, unconditionally. They are everything to him and his being. He furrowed his brows in deep contemplation. He loved Samantha as well. He loved her from the moment he first met her, and had it not been for his job moving him away and them losing touch, the two of them could be married. His eyes blazed as he stared at Samantha.

Although she could not speak, her eyes pleaded with him. The tears that rolled down her slender face and puddled on the tape pleaded with him, "Don't do this. Please don't do this."

He glanced down at the tablet, 40 seconds to go. He dropped the tablet to the floor with a resounding thud. He needed to decide. He raised the gun and the muffled screams turned hysterical from Samantha. He placed the gun to his temple. Horror and confusion spread over her face and also a look of love, mixed with relief.

Adam closed his eyes and said out loud, "Lord forgive me." When they reopened they were cold and resolute. He retrained his eyes on Samantha, snapped his wrist in front of him locking his arm and fired.

2

DECEMBER 10TH – 8:15 P.M

Detective Carl Sampson, five years from the academy and first case as a detective, pulled onto the scene at 631 Sapphire Ave. The frigid bellows of cold air thrust condensation onto the aging windshield of his detective vehicle. The defroster, blowing in spurts, could not maintain the clear visibility needed, thus Sampson wiped the window once again with his initial-embroidered handkerchief. The dull red and blue flashing lights materialized into a dazzling display of two distinct EMS vehicles and two CMPD patrol cars once the window was clear. Detective Sampson sat motionless recalling the moment this case was dropped into his lap.

"SAMPSON!"

"Yes, boss?"

"There's been a murder. Single victim, District 2 that has your name written all over it. Here are the keys to old Betsy." Detective Neil tossed the keys onto the desk. Sampson caught the keys before they slid over the edge. "The HVAC system is on the fritz, but she's the only fleet vehicle onsite. Dispatch will provide the necessary details while you're en route."

Betsy, a 2001 Chevy Caprice, was well past her prime. She had nearly 250,000 hard miles on her frame, though the engine had been replaced in 2012. The first two turns of the ignition were met with an audible dissatisfying click. Sampson slammed his hand on the dash, "Come on Betsy baby. Start up for me – please!"

Sampson, eyes closed and with a silent prayer, turned the key again. This time the engine coughed before rewarding him with the engine turning over. "Thank you old girl and sorry for hitting you so hard."

Allowing the vehicle to warm in the abnormally cold winter day in Charlotte, North Carolina, Detective Sampson completed his vehicle inspection before calling dispatch.

"Dispatch, this is Vanessa."

"Hey Vanessa, it's Carl. I heard you have a homicide for me."

"Hey Carl, sure do. 911 call received from a hysterical female. One DOA. Address 631 Sapphire Ave."

"Anything else?"

"Unfortunately, no. The caller became unresponsive. We think she passed out."

Some details, he thought. "Thanks Vanessa, I'll take it from here."

DETECTIVE SAMPSON OPENED the cruiser door with an audible screech and stepped into a fresh inch of snow swirling at his feet. The cool breeze from the night brought a tickle of frostbite to his earlobes prompting him to tug down on his skullcap. Even in the icy weather onlookers stood behind the yellow caution tape with anticipation. They chattered away softly as white puffs of vapor parted their lips with every breath. Sampson pushed his way through the crowd, passed through the diminishing voice vapors, and stepped under the tape searching for the lead officer on the scene.

As he surveyed the landscape, Sampson noticed a mid-40-year-old man in a grey waist length peacoat – collar straightened and tucked under his chin. The man had black, expertly creased trousers on with particles of snow attached to the outer cuff. His hands were encased in thin form fitting leather gloves. Several officers approached him, giving him a report, and exited the scene as quickly as they had arrived. Sampson approached.

"Detective Carl Sampson, Charlotte Metro PD," he said extending his bare hand into the frigid air. The immediate exposure sent trickles of pain through his fingertips that shot up his arm.

"Officer Lee," the man said pulling his hand from his glove before grasping the proffered hand. As they shook, Sampson couldn't help but notice the warmth radiating from the fingers of Lee, immediately defrosting his own cold fingers. *I certainly need to get me a pair of those gloves.*

"We've been awaiting your arrival," Officer Lee continued breaking Sampson from his trance simultaneously placing his hand back in his leather glove. "Inside the home we have the deceased, Samantha Taylor, 36 years old. She's the sole occupant of the residency and did not have a known boyfriend. She was found by," Officer Lee flipped a few pages searching for the name, "Tina Young at roughly 8:00 p.m."

"What was she doing?" Interrupted Detective Sampson.

"Ms. Taylor had a camping trip tomorrow and was in need of a sleeping bag. Mrs. Young stopped by to drop off said bag. When she arrived at the apartment, Mrs. Young knocked on the door several times. When Ms. Taylor didn't respond, she twisted the door handle, shocked to find it unlocked. Mrs. Young commented that Samantha always locked the deadbolt. 'It's the first thing she does when she closes the door – any door.'" Officer Lee stated, conferring with his notes.

He went on, "Mrs. Young entered the residence and flipped the light switch on to illuminate the dark room. Mrs. Young identified the form of her friend, Samantha Taylor, bound, on the floor with blood pooled on her forehead and matted to her chestnut brown hair. She immediately called 911 and during the call she passed out."

This last nugget of information resonated with what Sampson obtained from Vanessa.

"I was the first one on the scene and found Mrs. Young laying on the ground. Her torso was completely in the building; however, her feet were still outside."

Officer Lee, reading the questions forming on Detective Sampson's brow answered the unasked questions.

"My house is around the block. Today is me and my wife's 15th wedding anniversary. We were headed back from dinner when I heard the call. Yes, I know. When I'm off I'm supposed to be off. Kristen, my wife, gets on me all the time. I would have allowed someone else to handle the call; however, when dispatch said the caller dropped and was unresponsive, I immediately came over. I let Kristen drive the car home. The cold walk home will hopefully give me a bright idea of how to get myself out of the doghouse this time."

Detective Sampson smiled inwardly, "We've all been there buddy. Why don't you show me the victim and go spend the rest of your anniversary with your wife."

Officer Lee tilted his head in agreement as the final puff of cold air from Sampson's words evaporated. He turned on his heel and the two walked into the apartment.

December 10th – 9:00 p.m

"COME ON SAL, could you do it for me - pleeeease?" If the way the word please that teased from her tonsils wasn't enough, Jane gave him the puppy dog eyes. It's been said Helen of Troy had the face that would launch a thousand ships – well Jane Markowitz had the eyes that could set off a nuclear war.

Salvatore "Sal" Grandson, was a former journalist for the *New York Daily* prior to his migration to Charlotte, North Carolina. During his time at the *Daily*, Sal had an on-again, off-again relationship with his nemesis from the *Times*, Jane Markowitz. Their relationship took a sour turn which resulted in Jane hurling dishes at Sal. This was the last straw for Sal even though she would always have a place in his heart.

The two were reunited a few months ago when Sal reported on the kidnappings within the gated community of Driftwood Springs. A story he wrote as an independent online journalist. A story that got him noticed and provided instant credibility to his journalistic chops. Sal had done everything possible to avoid being snarled into her Venus flytrap, but in the end, she was his Siren's Lore. The truth – he loved this woman and he couldn't resist her.

"Going to the store for a gallon of 2% milk for some Cap'n Crunch peanut butter cereal. Who does she think I am, the Milk Man?" In typical Sal fashion he asked this question out loud to no one in particular. "Well this is the last time I change out of my pajamas to go to the store. You better believe that! She can just –"

The words hung frozen in Sal's throat as he noticed the flashing lights off in the distance. *Flashing lights typically means a story to be told*, he thought. "Jane and her Cap'n Crunch cravings will just have to wait."

Moments later, Sal arrived on the scene. He grabbed his hat

from the passenger seat, pulled it down over his ears and stepped out into the brisk air. "Ahh," he said breathing the cool air into his nostrils eyeballing the onlookers at the yellow caution tape. "Why are they so bundled up? It's not that cold. Southerners, a small dip into the 30s and they lose their minds." He kept the remainder of his comments to himself as he stood with the others who gathered behind the tape.

Sal astutely surveyed the crowd until he found, *yes she will do,* the person he was looking for. There is always someone in the crowd anxious to prove they know everything going on in any given situation. As a reporter, Sal always sought out this individual because they always wanted to talk – and in many cases their information, though spun slightly, had elements of truth.

Sal saddled up next to the woman and took in her features. She was average height, 5 foot 4 inches, with blonde hair pulled haphazardly into a quick ponytail. Her makeup, some blush, nude lip gloss, and purple eyeliner had recently been applied. "She made herself up just to stand out in this cold."

"I'm sorry, what did you say hun?" The woman asked.

Sal's habit of talking out loud coming to bite his rear again, "I'm sorry Mrs., I said, 'They better hurry up I'm out here getting cold.'"

"I know, right! Ain't it a shame what happened to Samantha. Pretty little thing came home from work and got blitzed by three men as she was opening her door. She was tied up, gang raped, beaten and left lying on the floor like a dog. I guess one of them didn't want to chance her pointing them out later, so he came back and put a bullet in her head." She said this with her eyes darting around undoubtedly looking for a news van.

Sal figured the woman had the name right, Samantha, as she likely lived close by. He didn't know of anyone who chased the cops around waiting on a story to break. At which point they could curry favor with the reporter on scene to interview her for the story. Then again, Sal wouldn't put it past someone to do just that. Sal also surmised the woman was dead but not from anything the witness had said – he spotted the Coroner's van as he pulled up. Everything else he planned to discount as gossip, or simply – made up, *like her face*, he mused.

Sal felt the phone in his pocket vibrate. He extracted the device and eyed the frosting screen – *Jane texting probably wondering what's taking so long. She'll have to wait.* Sal did his best to overhear any information being shared between the members of law enforcement. He realized his hearing wasn't the stellar asset he wielded in his youth, and his lip reading was even worse. For the time being, he would wait until the detective on scene emerged from the house. At that point he would be prepared with his list of questions.

December 10th - 9:00 p.m.

DETECTIVE SAMPSON STOOD stark still in the center of the living area with both eyes welded shut. Upon entering the room, he quickly surveyed all four corners, followed by the décor on the wall, and finally the room as a whole. After taking these quick mental images, he closed his eyes to construct the 3D image around him. 30 percent of the time, he would glean useful information. 65 percent of the time, he would look like a jackass to his fellow officers. The other five percent, well there was that one time he nearly fell asleep, he had his eyes closed so long.

However, he could feel this crime scene would settle snuggly into the 30 percent as something in this room fired questions in his mind. He rolled his eyes from left to right behind his closed eyelids visualizing the scene in the room. The coroner had not yet taken the body. Sampson could see her wrist bound with the flex cuffs. Her legs and mouth secured with duct tape – *why no flex cuffs for the ankles if the goal was to immobilize her*? The single shot to her head, left of center slightly between the eye and the bridge of her nose. *Is there anything else here to see?* Sampson pondered and decided to shift his attention.

As Sampson retracted his gaze from the deceased form splayed on the floor, he began to look at the walls. A circular black and white wall clock adorned one of the walls. Next to the clock was a frame. The frame consisted of a picture – two individuals smiling wanly at the camera. The woman on the left side of the photo was the deceased, Samantha Taylor. The other person, another woman, bared no resemblance to anyone else in the dwellings. Shifting his eyes from the picture frame, he noticed something white, rectangular, in the bottom left corner.

"Detective Sampson," Officer Lee interrupted, "Tina Young is prepared to speak with you."

Sampson slowly opened his eyelids, and gave Officer Lee a smile, "I'll speak with Mrs. Young. I think it's time you make your way home to Mrs. Kristen and salvage the remainder of your anniversary. I can handle things from here."

"Will do sir. Thank you!" Lee nodded to the officer at the door who led detective Sampson to the apartment next door.

Tina Young was a nondescript woman of average height. Her hair, brunette, lay flush to her shoulders while being suffocated underneath a functional knit beanie. She wore an expression mixed with shock, disbelief, and the feeling as if she was adrift in an unspeakable nightmare. She wore a yellow retro Denali North Face jacket fully zipped to her chin and a pair of dark blue jeans – they looked like Levi's. She walked with an unsteady gait resting most of her body weight onto the officer escorting her through the apartment.

"Hello Mrs. Young, my name is Detective Carl Sampson."

Sampson extended his right hand while fixing his gaze on her deep brown eyes. Tina limply took his hand and gave it a cursory shake while forcing a grimace to her pale lips.

"I understand you were the one to find the victim, Samantha. Why don't you walk me through what happened?"

When she spoke, her dialect was both unfamiliar and strong, "I already told the other cop what I seen." The words trembled on her lip as her lower eyelids began to puddle with tears. Her pupils looked like blank saucers as she observed Sampson.

"Officer Lee relayed to me your account; however, it would benefit me greatly if I could hear the story from your perspective."

During this exchange Tina had not blinked and the puddles verged toward spilling onto her sunken cheekbone.

Resigned to her fate, she closed her eyes. A stream of tears permeated down both cheeks racing toward the point at her chin. When she opened her eyes, Sampson was surprised with the hollow far away essence they had taken.

"Sammy, Samantha, called me earlier in the day."

"Hey Tina babe," Tina said interrupting herself and dropping into her Samantha impersonation. "I know it's last minute, but I need a huge favor. I need to borrow your sleeping bag."

Sampson began to ponder how Samantha knew Tina had a sleeping bag but decided he would not interject.

"I told her sure and chuckled inwardly. The last time I used the bag, me and my husband, Ricky, decided to lay out in our back yard under the stars. He swore he seen a shooting star but I hadn't. He said his wish was to make love under the stars and we'd done just that! I told Sammy that story."

The new tear stream formation on her chin was hanging precariously in a pendant shape waiting to descend weightlessly to the ground.

"I told her I would stop by after we ate dinner and I put the kids to bed. Cop sir, I did just that. I came right over after we ate. When I got here, I knocked. Sammy didn't open the door and I didn't hear any rustling inside. I knocked again. My fingers were getting cold. You know with this cold weather we are having, it's enough to drive me crazy. Sir, she still didn't answer."

Her hollow eyes appeared to grow colder. "I reached for the doorknob expecting it to be locked, Sammy always locks her doors. But it won't locked. Mr. Cop, the door won't locked. This is when I knew something was wrong."

"Sammy," I said slowly pushing the door open. "Sammy hun are you home?"

"The house was quiet. The house was too quiet. I walked into the apartment and flipped on the light. That's when I saw it. That's when I saw her."

She closed her eyes again, the action jolting the pendant tear from her chin. Gravity tugged the clear substance until it met the ground with a splash.

"She was laying there – dead."

Tina could hold back no longer. The tears flowed continuously. She swiped the back of her hand down and across the side of her face. She did the same on the other side with the other hand. Sampson reached into his pocket, extracted his handkerchief and passed it along to Tina.

"Mrs. Young, you've been so brave. Thank you for sharing. Do you recall anything else? Anything out of place, anything missing?"

Tina blew her nose into the handkerchief, folded it over once and dabbed both corners of her eyes. "I honestly don't recall much after that. In a panic, I dialed 911 and shortly thereafter I fainted. The next thing I remember is your cop friend waking me up."

Her stomach began to heave as she pulled her shoulders in on herself as if she was going to introduce the dinner she ate before coming to the apartment. However, she was able to keep it at bay, she was stronger than she gave herself credit for given the circumstances.

Composure regained, she continued in a raspy whisper, "There was a guy she was seeing. She didn't talk much about him, but I could see the glow in her anytime she spent time with him. Since she didn't talk to me much about him, I could only assume he was married. She knew I would not approve so we operated on the 'Don't Ask, Don't Tell' policy. Do you think he would do this to her?"

Sampson had not yet formed any opinion, "We are looking into every lead. We will do everything possible to locate who did this to Samantha."

Sampson stood, plucking a card from his pocket and handed it over to Tina. Some of the color had come back into her cheeks and that hollow, vacant expression she had been carrying was starting to clear.

"In the meantime, I'm going to have an officer drive you back to your home. Here's my card. If you think of anything else, regardless of how small you think it may be, I want you to call me."

He turned on his heel and headed for the door. As he did, he began to tug at a string holding together a thought he could not reach. He walked back to Samantha's apartment and once again stood in the middle of the room. As he stood there something had caught his eye.

"Sir, what would you like us to do with the witness?" The officer asked shaking him from his trance.

"She still seems to be in a state of shock, though she is coming around. Have the paramedics cleared her?"

"Yes sir. Nothing serious."

"Good. See to it that she's driven home. I want to ensure she arrives back at her house safe and sound. She can retrieve her car tomorrow."

As the officer walked away, Sampson began to pull at that thread once again. He stood back in the center of the room and closed his eyes.

The deceased, who had been removed while he spoke with Tina, still played vividly in his mind. He could see her restraints, her distraught eyes, the chilling wound above her eye. He could see how her body had been jarred by the impact of the bullet. But what he didn't see was the string. That element that bothered him during his first viewing. He decided to move on.

As he began to move from Samantha to the wall, it hit him. The white object in the picture frame. His eyes shot open and he took the four long strides it took to cover the distance. He immediately looked to the bottom left hand corner of the picture frame. There he noticed the same shape he saw in his mind. He reached into the inner pocket of his coat and extracted a pair of gloves. He slid his fingers into the glove, never taking his eye from the object.

With a snap, the latex glove was snug over his fingers and against his wrist. Not wanting to disturb anything else, he carefully slid the object from the picture frame. The object was a white 3.5-by-2-inch business card. At least it should have been a business card. The front was blank - later on he would debate with himself if it was the front that was blank or the back. However, on the back there was one solitary object. An object he recognized. And under the object was type written "Five Days".

December 10th – 9:20 p.m

Sal watched anxiously as the officers milled around outside the apartment. He watched as a young lady, maybe in her early 30s had been escorted from the ambulance into an apartment next to the crime scene – *a witness perhaps.* He would need to check into this later. For now, he and the crowd held their collective breaths as the coroner began to wheel the body from the apartment. Of course, the body has been neatly tucked away inside a heavy duty 36-by-94-inch body bag therefore onlookers wouldn't see anything of value. However, this didn't assuage the anticipation of the gathered assembly.

Distantly he could hear a woman sob into her gloved hands. Looking to his right to identify the origin of the sound, he noticed an elderly man in his mid-60s. With his right hand he tapped his fingertips to his forehead, then to the center of his chest. In a deft fluid practiced motion he finished the cross by tapping the front of his left shoulder followed by tapping the front of his right shoulder. He arched his hands together and concluded by whispering to himself, *Amen.*

Miss Makeup, who was still standing next to Sal exclaimed, "Samantha! Oh Lord, my dear Samantha!" The words were right, yet the actions were all wrong. She spoke the words without an ounce of compassion as her eyes danced around looking for the nearest camera. Sal had seen many horrible things in his life as a journalist, but this utter lack of human compassion made him sick to his stomach.

It took a few moments, but the pair wheeling the gurney secured Samantha's corpse into the van. Sal watched as the red lights dimmed and shrunk exiting the scene. With the coroner's departure the crowd began to disperse. The woman who had been sobbing was now being comforted by the elderly gentleman. As her shoulders bounced up and down with her outpour of emotion, he gently patted and rubbed her back in alternative motions. Queen Makeup left disappointed that she would not be giving the interview of her life this evening. *Good riddance*, Sal thought as he watched her walk away.

Movement from the corner of his eye caught Sal's attention. The detective, he assumed it was the detective as he was given deference by the others on the scene, was exiting the apartment next door and walking back into the crime scene.

"I need to find a way to speak with this detective," he said, smoke vapors dissipating with each word. His phone vibrated again in his pocket. *Jane*. He unlocked the phone, tapped the notification and read.

Sal! Where are you? You are not answering my text. Let me know you are ok... and don't forget my milk.

Sal knew if he didn't respond soon, things could escalate fast. Jane had come back into Sal's life earlier this year after they had previously called it quits. On the day they met for the first time in ages, Sal had been kidnapped by a psychopath – Terri Buckley. Sal was being used as a pawn in a horrible revenge plot hatched by Terri against her former partner in the FBI Donatella Dabria. Donatella was able to save Sal; however, Terri had never been located. Jane feared Sal was still in mortal danger from this woman, this Terri Buckley, but Sal didn't think so. Terri, wherever she was located at the time, was more concerned with her revenge against Special Agent Dabria, than ending the life of Sal Grandson. Nonetheless, he figured he better let her know that he was ok before she sent a SWAT team looking for him. Sal typed his message.

Following a lead. I'll be back shortly. I have your milk.

"That should cool her jets for a while." However, he knew he would hear all about how he stood her, and the Cap'n, up so that he could follow a lead on a story.

The witness was being led out of apartment 633 a tad steadier on her feet than she appeared when she entered the establishment. She was more or less walking under her own power, although the officer held a steady hand close to her person in case she lost her balance.

The scene was beginning to clear as the officer took the witness away in a squad car. Sal, accustomed to working in both crowds and alone, began to feel the first sensation of the cool weather with the absence of the collective body heat. He needed this detective to make an appearance so he could make his move.

His phone vibrated again. Without pulling the phone from his pocket, he was acutely aware who was on the other end. It was Jane, no doubt in his mind. Taking a deep breath he reached for his right pocket to retrieve the phone. At that moment, the detective emerged. He released his grip from the phone and instead fished his Mead notebook from his pocket along with his favorite pen.

"Detective. Detective! Sal Grandson from The Sal Report. Just a moment of your time if you would."

The detective didn't break stride.

"Come on, Detective. I already know the victim is Samantha, she lives at 631 Sapphire Ave., and it's a single homicide. I'm willing to fill in the rest if I must, but I prefer to have an accurate account of what has transpired."

The detective slowed but did not stop.

Sal, pressing his luck and playing a hunch, "It was the boyfriend. He is responsible. Am I right?" Sal didn't know if Samantha even had a boyfriend; however, he had a better than 50 percent chance of hitting the nail on the head.

To this last volley, the detective stopped. "Mr. Grandson, I remember you. You reported on the case of the missing kids from Driftwood Springs."

"Yep, that's me. Guilty as charged. How about you giving me a bit to work from." His New York slang crept back into his voice.

"Mr. Grandson, at this moment we have no comment."

"Do you know why Samantha has been murdered?"

"No comment."

"Are you going to apprehend the boyfriend?"

"No comment."

"Well at least tell me your name. There can be no harm in that, and it's bound to come out tomorrow anyway."

The detective paused, sighed, "Sampson. Detective Carl Sampson." With that he carried on in the direction he was headed.

For a mere amateur, one would think Sal had struck out; however, this was not the case. Sal confirmed the victim was Samantha – he could find her last name later. She was the only victim. This was indeed a homicide, otherwise the detective would have made a show of denying this fact. He was also 69 percent sure a boyfriend was a person of interest. Furthermore, the detective without realizing it was giving away signs to the truth.

In the book *The Body Language of Liars* by Dr. Lillian Glass, an FBI body language expert and behavioral analyst, the author lays out signs of deception. Things such as repeating phrases and words. Touching or covering one's mouth. Staring without blinking and several others.

These traits Sal realized can be used in questioning law enforcement when they do not want to answer any questions. When Sal asked the detective, "Do you know why Samantha has been murdered?" the detective quickly changed his head position shifting from right to left. The detective likely didn't realize he had done so. Nonetheless, Sal noticed it. Sal knew this slight motion combined with the "No comment" response, indicated that it was a lie. The detective was saying the rehearsed comments used by so many in law enforcement when they want to obfuscate the truth, "No comment." In reality he was saying to Sal, "Yes, she has been murdered."

The other question, "Are you going to apprehend the boyfriend?" was a little harder to decipher. Sal realized he asked a question that didn't lend itself to a clear-cut answer. The boyfriend was a hunch, one Sal still believed would bear fruit, but it was a lazy attempt and he knew it. Sal noticed the detective's breathing changes and the raising of his shoulders. However, both of these could have been attributed to the dropping temperatures surrounding them at the moment.

Nonetheless, Sal felt he gained some insight. Some insight that would help him – his phone vibrated again in his pocket. In response to the rhythmic vibration in his pocket Sal quit basking in his victory and headed for his car.

December 10th – 9:30 p.m

VERONICA KING REACHED her cruising speed of 72 mph as she headed north on I-77 from Uptown Charlotte to her home in Huntersville, North Carolina. She engaged the cruise control feature and began running through her presentation that she stayed late working on that evening. King, the Chief Operating Officer of Global Insights Security, was a rising star at the company. She began her career at GIS right out of college and never looked back. Her superiors saw that she exuded the aptitude not only for the intricacies of high-level security algorithms and techniques, but also had a sound business mind for both strategy and operations. Her stock continued to rise when she was asked to present her findings of a malicious bug working to infest their network, and thus the network of the companies they were being paid millions of dollars monthly to protect, to the CEO, Edward Stein.

The members of the senior leadership listened with rapt

attention as King outlined the threat they were facing and the aggressive approach she recommended to combat the threat. Stein; however, seemed to be in another world barely paying attention to the presentation at all. At the conclusion of the presentation, she received unanimous approval to execute her plan – a plan that succeeded without a hitch and a new star was born.

King went through a series of executive training classes, all organized and paid for by GIS, and within seven years she had elevated to the role of COO. She was well on her way to being groomed for the role of CEO in five years, but King's excitement had been tempered.

Meeting with her boss, CEO Edward Stein, late one fall evening as they finalized the next year's fiscal budget, Stein made a nonchalant comment that completely floored Veronica.

"You know Mrs. King, we will need to continue our expansion into the Midwest. Our market share in that region is what, 23%?"

"22% sir."

"22% right you are. To achieve the budget and growth we have planned for next year, we will need to obtain three more points in that region. Make sure that Mark has a solid plan to grow and maintain that growth."

"Will do. Anything else before I head out?"

"Just one more thing. I know the board has been grooming you to one day take my spot, to be my successor. To one day lead the company my granddaddy started as a security for the rich folks of this city. Then when my daddy took the helm, he saw the opportunity to add security to financial institutions. Once I took the helm, I saw an opportunity to move into the digital realm and that, Mrs. King, is where we sit today. I have no doubt that you will find some next avenue that we can take and the company will be successful."

King eyed him with gratitude and acceptance.

He lowered his voice and spoke sternly, "However, Mrs. King, it'll be a cold day in Hell before I allow a woman to run the company my granddaddy built, that my father nurtured, and that I've grown. As long as I draw breath on this earth, you will never sit in my chair. My daddy's chair. My granddaddy's chair."

He paused, looking Veronica square in the eyes. She was thunderstruck and felt her mouth had gaped as her jaw muscles gave way.

And as if he hadn't said anything remotely sexist at all, he finished by saying, "Make sure Mark's plan is on my desk by the end of the day tomorrow."

RECALLING that day brought disgust and hatred toward her boss. She recognized she had two options. One, she could look for employment elsewhere. She had been sought after by numerous security firms across the country. She knew she could pick up the phone, place a call, conduct the perfunctory interview and land the job. She knew that two companies had offered her just that. But Veronica was loyal. She was loyal to her team, her career, and her passion. But at the end of the day, those were not the things preventing her from picking up the phone.

Her main reason for not picking up the phone was simple - she would not run away from this son of a bitch. She would not, under any circumstance, let him and his old-school mentality win.

So, she was left with one other option. She would have to convince the board that now was the time. Now was the time for her to take the reins of GIS and lead them into the next quarter century. It was a risk, she knew, but if all else failed and she gave it the old college try, she could fall back on numerous other offers brewing.

Veronica King had no intention of failing. The board meeting would be held tomorrow afternoon. Since her encounter with Stein she marked her calendar for this day. The day she would make her play to usurp him from his position, in his granddaddy's company, and watch that smug look erase from his face when the board approved.

Veronica pulled into her garage and killed the ignition.

"Veronica, old girl, there is no turning back now. Once you play this hand you'll stand atop the mountain, or you'll be out on your ass."

At that moment Veronica did not realize the truth she spoke into the atmosphere. At the board meeting there would be no turning back.

3

DECEMBER 11TH – 7:45 A.M

The sun rays at dawn of this crisp winter day knifed through the still air illuminating the master suite at 1812 Garden St. The rays danced across the slender brown cheek of Jasmyn Thompson creeping desperately toward her eyes. The faint heat of the rays caused Jasmyn to stir, but once the light fell across her closed eyelids she turned away from the window. In doing so she wrapped her arm across the hairless chest of her husband, drifting soundlessly back to sleep.

However, Marcellous Thompson lay on his back staring at the daylight scrolling across the ceiling preparing to fully illuminate the room. For the last hour Marcellous lay motionless in this position thinking through the future. Thinking through the baby his beautiful wife was carrying in her womb. Thinking through the madness that gripped their community only a few months prior and how no child, or parent, felt safe until the ordeal had come to an end. He lay there thinking through the lengths he would go through to keep his child safe – to keep his wife safe. But through it all, he thought about how lucky he was to have Jasmyn and to soon have a little person calling him Daddy.

As the sun continued to illuminate the room and the band of sunshine crawled up Jasmyn's back toward the intersection of their tangled forms, it would only be a matter of time before she was fully awake. For the Thompsons, today was a big day.

The couple had an ultrasound scheduled with Jasmyn's OBGYN, Dr. Prince. Marcellous liked Dr. Prince. She had a warm engaging smile, cool caring eyes, and an excellent bedside manner that put her patients at ease. It's no wonder she was one of the most sought-after doctors in the area. A neighbor within the community brokered the introduction and Jasmyn bypassed the extended waiting list. *Sometimes it pays to know the right people*, Marcellous mused. This ultrasound would be *the* ultrasound. Jasmyn was now far enough along to determine the sex of the baby. The couple had gone through countless cycles of, *yes, we want to know the sex of the baby – to no, we want it to be a surprise when he or she arrives*. They decided they would sleep on it one more night and make a firm decision in the morning before the appointment.

Breaking away from his reverie, Marcellous looked down to the resting face of his wife as the sunlight bathed her in an endless glow. Moments later Jasmyn scrunched her nose in an effort to push away the sunlight – he always loved it when she did that. Once she realized this would not help, and she had nowhere else to run and hide, she would awake. Right on queue her eyelids began to flutter until they were completely open providing Marcellous a glimpse into her deep brown, enchanting eyes.

She smiled that sleepy, uninhibited smile of one who has recently awakened. "Hey honey," she said in a voice still filled with sleep. "Have you been watching me, mister?"

"Nah, babe, I just opened my eyes to witness you staring at me. Are you thinking about taking me out in my sleep again?"

"Depends, are our life insurance premiums paid up to date?

If not, I can hold off another month or two." She leaned forward to give him a peck on the lips. "By the way, don't forget we have our appointment with Dr. Prince this morning."

"Is that today?" Marcellous asked in mock surprise. "I'm scheduled to play golf this morning and the team needs me."

Jasmyn lightly jabbed him in his shoulder, rolled back to her side of the bed and stood up. "I'm going to take a shower," she responded with a wry smile, tossing her pillow at him. "You have an hour to be ready. You don't want to mess with a hormonal pregnant woman."

"Aye, aye, captain," he said bringing his right hand to his forehead and giving her a salute.

Jasmyn entered into the bathroom and Marcellous retrieved his smartphone from his nightstand. Entering the four-digit code, he unlocked the phone and pulled up his internet browser. With a few clicks, he acquired the site he was looking for, *The Sal Report*.

Marcellous, a novelist by trade, enjoyed reading the articles posted by Sal on a daily basis. He was introduced to Sal by his wife and their baby's soon to be godmother, Donatella Dabria. Sal covered the tragedy that took place in their community a few months prior. Had it not been for the heroic efforts of Donatella, he would have been another victim to perish in the senseless crime. Since that day, Marcellous made it a ritual to read Sal's site every morning. Once the page loaded Marcellous was shocked to read the headline,

HEADLINE: ***Woman killed in home invasion***
www.TheSalReport.com
By: Sal Grandson

. . .

LAST NIGHT at roughly 6:30 p.m. the residents within the Piper Stone apartment complex were stunned at the death of one of their own. 36-year-old Samantha Taylor was found murdered in her apartment at 631 Sapphire Ave. by an unidentified person. Detective Carl Sampson with the Charlotte Metro Police Department have been assigned to the case and thus far have remained tight-lipped concerning any particulars. Neighbors say Ms. Taylor was well-liked and never had a cross word with anyone. Some suspect she had a boyfriend, though they never saw Samantha out with anyone. When questioned about the search for the unidentified boyfriend, Detective Sampson gave a "No comment" response. However, after conducting additional research, it's believed by this reporter that there is a boyfriend, or at least a person of interest, and the police plan to speak with this person as soon as today.

MARCELLOUS SAT STUNNED with this news. This was the first murder Sal had reported on in quite some time. Also, the name Samantha Taylor seemed familiar to him. Normally surefooted with names, Marcellous was finding it difficult to place this particular name. *Samantha Taylor, Samantha Taylor*. The more he thought about it, the further the name moved into the recesses of his mind.

He heard the water pressure of the shower cease pushing its way through the showerhead and Jasmyn open the door for the shower. He knew this meant it was his turn to hop into the shower if he was to adhere to the hour deadline his wife had given him. Looking one more time at the article and the name, Samantha Taylor, he still could not retrieve from his memory why he recognized it. Nonetheless, he stripped out of his pajamas and headed to the bathroom to take his shower.

December 11th – 8:15 a.m

ADAM JOSEPH SAT, hands cradling his forehead, forefingers massaging the pounding behind his temples. Although he could hear the forced air pushing the heat through the vents, his body had broken into a cold sweat. A sweat that was now running over his palm, down the side of his arm. The vice grip tightness in his stomach would have him doubled over in pain if he didn't think his head would explode if he removed his hands. From the moment he pulled the trigger on the gun, ending Samantha's life, everything was a shaded haze.

"WELL DONE, Adam. I'm sure your family appreciates everything you've done here tonight. Now if you would be so kind, I'll relieve you of that gun."

Adam dropped the gun from his shaking fingers, "I think I'm going to be sick," he said pulling his hand to his mouth.

"I highly recommend you hold in your bodily fluids or the cops will be at your door this evening. Why don't you go to your car, drive to your house, and make animal love to your wife? Forget all about the slut laying on the ground. She is no longer any concern of yours."

"But, what will you do with her. Please, please do not –" Bile began to fill his esophagus putting a halt to his words.

"I thought I told you I do not like to repeat myself. Rest assured, I will not defile her in any way. I just have a few loose ends I need to tie up before I leave. Now get in your car and drive straight home."

Adam was still mortified that he took a life. Not just a life, the life of his love. The life of Samantha. He felt himself getting sick once again and decided he should leave immediately. He turned, slumped his shoulders and staggered toward the door.

"One more thing Mr. Joseph. If you decide to make any stops or make any calls before you arrive home, I'll make good on my promise – and I'll burn the house down with you inside as well."

Adam turned around silently, turned the handle, opened the door and walked to his car.

RELIVING the moment was worse than when he pulled the trigger. At that moment his adrenaline was spiking and the only thing on his mind was saving his daughters'. Even though he loved his wife, he would not have taken the life of Samantha by his own hands had it not been for his three daughters in the house as well. This sickened him even more. The fact that he would be willing to let his wife burn to save his mistress.

To add to his frustrations – the cops. The cops came pounding on his door at 8 a.m. His wife, Evelyn, was in the kitchen making coffee while he lay curled in the bed. The pounding startled his wife and woke his youngest daughter, Megan. While Evelyn made her way to the door, weary of the early caller, Megan perched behind the rod iron poles adorning the handrail of the stairs.

"We have a warrant for the arrest of Adam Joseph," the officer exclaimed pushing his way through the door and casting aside Evelyn.

Her scream, more like a wail, startled him from his sleep and sent Megan into tears.

"Adam! My God, Adam! It's the police!" Tears now flowing down her face.

Adam hurried out of the bed as he heard footsteps echoing on the hardwood steps. His mind was still in a haze yet he clearly recalls the feeling of expectation. After what he had done last night, he expected the police would come calling at his door. He didn't think it would be this soon, but he knew they would arrive.

The door to their master bedroom bursts open and he was staring down the barrel of three, no four guns. "Hands up, on the ground!" one of the officers demanded.

Adam dropped to his knees and placed his hands behind his head. One of the officers threw him roughly to the ground, placed his knee in his back, and wrenched his left, then his right arm behind his back. He dimly heard his wife downstairs sobbing in between gulps trying to regulate her breathing. His two older children were also awake and crying. Adam was yanked roughly to his feet while another officer began to mirandize him.

"Adam Joseph, you are under arrest for the murder of Samantha Taylor –"

"Murder!" Evelyn yelled as they walked Adam down the stairs. "Oh my God Adam, what are they talking about?" was the last thing he heard before his mind quit processing information.

The metal door to the interrogation room opened and Adam knew his nightmare was only about to worsen. Detective Carl Sampson lowered himself into the chair across from Adam and lay a file, closed, onto the table.

HIS TEAM WORKED FEVERISHLY throughout the night searching for clues, any clues. The CSI team scoured Samantha's apartment, only to find it had been scrubbed clean. No prints to be found anywhere within the living, bedroom, or kitchen. Of course, this registered as suspicious as there were no prints found for Samantha either. To Detective Sampson and his team this murder had all the making of a professional hit. The break they needed came from the coroner.

"What do you have for me, Miranda?"

"Good evening, Detective Sampson," she stated in her clip, matter-of-fact voice. "Upon undressing the victim and preparing to place her clothing into evidence, I noticed some gelatinous residue on the back of her jeans. I lay the jeans flat on the table and grabbed my magnifying glasses. Initial inspection of the garment yielded a surprising result – a palm print.

Detective Sampson raised an eyebrow, "A palm print?"

"Yes, a palm print. I made a call upstairs and Jennifer came down with the fingerprint dusting kit and her camera. She took a few shots of the palm print, you'll find those in the folder behind you on the table, and began the process of dusting the pants. After a few moments, the outline of a hand could be seen in addition to the perfect impression of the forefinger, middle finger and ring finger. They were radiated out from the crotch of the jeans, over to the left pocket. From what I can tell, the person was facing the victim and grabbed a firm handful of her bottom with their right hand."

"WHAT WAS the material on her jeans?"

"Yes, I was just getting to that. Once Jennifer had completed her work, I took a sample of the material and prepared the Isotope Ratio Mass Spectrometer. The sample included Carbomer, Triethanolamine, Benzophenone-4 and Glycerin."

"Come on now, Miranda, you know me and chemistry were not best friends."

With a stern, motherly look, she continued, "These elements are used in your typical hair gel. The person who touched, make that grabbed, her bottom had run their fingers through their hair shortly before making that impression. My findings are also in the folder. Jennifer is going to run the fingerprints and will likely have that ready for you by the time you darken her doorstep."

"Thank you, Miranda," he said while giving her a peck on the cheek.

"MR. JOSEPH, my name is Detective Carl Sampson. I've been assigned to work the murder of Samantha Taylor. Do you know Ms. Taylor, Mr. Joseph?"

Adam stared blankly at Sampson.

Unphased Sampson continued, "Ms. Taylor was murdered last night while in her apartment. Here's the thing Adam, it's ok if I call you Adam, right?"

Sampson didn't wait for the response and continued to plow through.

"There was no sign of forced entry into her apartment. You're a smart man, Adam, and I'm sure you know what that means. Buuut in case it's not clear to you, she knew the person who was last in her apartment. So, let me ask you again, do you know Ms. Taylor?"

Adam remained mute, eyes focused on Sampson – unblinking.

"Adam, what I think is you were at her apartment last night. In fact, I'm willing to bet my last paycheck that you've been to her apartment before. Does your wife –"

He looked down to consult his notes.

"Evelyn know about Samantha? Does she know the two of you have been sleeping together?"

Still speechless, a bead of sweat had begun to form on the tip of his nose. Sensing he had hit a nerve, Detective Sampson slowly and deliberately opened the folder, removed a picture and slid it across the table to Adam.

He pressed on, "What you have in front of you, Adam, is a

close up of the victim's jeans with a palm print on the ass." He pulled out a second picture, "This is a close up of the jeans once they had been dusted for fingerprints. See the full outline of the hand along with the fingerprints?"

Adam looked down at the picture and recalled the moment he walked into Samantha's apartment. She had closed the door once he walked in. When she turned to face him, he pulled her into a close embrace before deeply and passionately kissing her. He could remember how he had stiffened as her tongue wrestled with his. He recalled sliding his hand down the small of her back to her lush ass. He remembered the moment he firmly cupped her bottom, forefinger tantalizingly close to her sweet honey spot. In response she bit him playfully on his bottom lip giving it a tug. In abject horror, he also recalled running his hand through his hair before leaving his car and making the short jaunt to her apartment.

Detective Sampson could see flickers of recollection and pressed harder. He pulled a report from the folder and placed it on the table. "Adam, this is a fingerprint analysis performed from the fingerprint impression on the jeans. I'm sure you can guess whose fingerprints we found on those jeans."

Even though Adam had not spoken a word, he made an audible gulp as his Adam's apple bobbed up and down.

"What happened, Mr. Joseph? Did you want to break things off and she threatened to tell your wife? Did you just get bored with her like you had your wife and decided you needed to tie up loose ends?"

Pulling the crime scene photo of Samantha laying on the ground, he slammed it on the table. "Had she become pregnant and you decided you couldn't chance the truth of your indiscretions coming to light?"

He realized his voice had raised and he was now yelling, but he was not going to stop there. "Or are you just a sick bastard and killed her for no reason other than to get your kicks off? Answer me, damn it!"

In a meek, barely audible voice Adam finally broke his silence, "I loved her, and no she wasn't pregnant."

"If you loved her. IF YOU LOVED HER, then why in the hell did you do this to her?" He jabbed his finger three times into the photo of Samantha laying on the ground. If you loved her, why did you kill her?"

A vacant ghostly expression had overcome Adam's face, but he spoke no more words.

The blue light above Adam's head illuminated the room. Detective Sampson realized his breath had become shallow and his heart rate had spiked. Slamming his palms on the table as he stood, he simply said, "You killed her." He removed the last photo from his folder and placed it on the table. It was a picture of Samantha prior to her death. A picture of her with her broad smile beaming across her slender face and a sparkle that shone in her lively eyes.

On the other side of the interrogation room door Detective Sampson was interrupted by Officer Johnson.

"Sir, there is someone here to see you. It's, it's –"

Already at the end of his rope, Sampson snapped, "Spit it out Johnson!"

"It's the FBI."

"The FBI?" Sampson asked perplexed.

"Yes sir. It's Special Agent Donatella Dabria. She's insisting that she speak with the suspect."

"Oh, is she now? And under what grounds does she feel she can speak with our suspect?"

"She refused to provide me with any details – only that she speaks with you immediately."

"Where is she now?"

"She's waiting for you in your office."

Perturbed by the interruption when he knew Adam was on the brink of breaking, at least that is what he hoped, he mustered self-control and proceeded to his office. He was familiar with Agent Dabria. A few months prior she single-handedly put an end to the abductions taking place within the community at Driftwood Springs. In doing so, she was able to expose a crooked detective working for CMPD. A discovery she made only by way of him firing shots at her within her own home. This discovery was a shock to the force and Internal Affairs began to scrutinize each officer on the force more closely than they had in the past. Although the initial barrage of inquiries ceased, a close watchful eye was always nearby

Upon entering his office, he saw Donatella standing picturesque in the corner staring inquisitively at a framed photo on his wall. "Special Agent Dabria, I understand you wanted to speak with me."

As she turned ready to address him, the remaining words choked off in his throat, his mind struggled to regain coherent thoughts and he did everything he could not to stare – but he was severely failing.

Donatella Dabria stood six feet tall with piercing hazelnut brown eyes. Eyes that could simultaneously comfort and destroy without hesitation. Her complexion, a luxurious golden-brown, was smooth, flawless, and glowing from the ambient light within the room. She had long, silky jet-black hair that curled its way down to slightly below the top of her shoulders. She wore a simple yet sleek two button black blazer atop a white-collared button-down shirt. Her matching black slacks accentuated the seductive curve of her hips while the fabric continued to flow down the length of her long legs with the hem pausing just above the crease in her shoe.

"Ah yes, Detective Sampson," she spoke in her mesmerizing

southern drawl. "It certainly is a pleasure to meet you," she said extending her right hand.

The synapses once again fired in his brain and Sampson was able to respond, "It's a pleasure meeting you as well, Special Agent Dabria." He shook the proffered hand. "Please, have a seat," he motioned her to an awaiting chair. "What can I do for you today?"

"Yes," she said lowering herself in the visitor chair and crossing her left leg over her right. "I understand you apprehended a suspect in the murder of Ms. Samantha Taylor. A gentleman by the name of Adam Joseph. Is that correct?"

Detective Sampson regarded her curiously. This information, none of this information, had been shared outside of his department yet. How could she possibly know all of this? *Do we have a leak in our department?*

Sensing the dismay from his furrowed brows and hesitancy to speak she attempted to set his mind at ease, "Rest assured, detective, this information did not come by way of anyone from your department. I have my ways of obtaining information that you need not trouble yourself with at this time."

The tension that built within Sampson began to subside as his eyebrows returned to their resting state. "Agent Dabria, assuming you are correct, though I'm not saying that you are, what interest is this homicide to the FBI?"

"Detective Sampson, I believe I know the person responsible for this heinous crime and my belief is the man you are holding, Adam Joseph isn't entirely at fault."

"Isn't entirely at fault! Are you kidding me?"

"I assure you detective, I am not kidding you. In fact, I'm willing to wager Mr. Joseph hasn't provided much to propel your case forward."

Sampson began to speak; however, he was halted by the raised hand of Donatella.

"Detective Sampson, in no means am I hear to take over your case; however, if I'm correct this isn't a simple homicide."

"What do you mean?"

"Give me five minutes with your suspect. I simply need to ask him three questions. I'll have all the answers I need after that."

Amused at the absurdity of her claim he snickered, "And what makes you think he will answer your three questions after he's refused to answer any questions that we have asked him."

Donatella shrugged, "I guess we won't know how he'll respond until I ask my three questions."

Detective Sampson considered this for a moment. Allowing this FBI agent access to the suspect without cause was highly unusual; however, if allowing her to ask her three questions – knowing they would yield no results – would move her along so he could get back to business he just might chance it.

"Alright, Special Agent Dabria. I'll let you ask your three questions, but no more. When you are done, you'll vacate the premises. Agreed?"

In mock answer, she simply tilted her head forward and stood. Detective Sampson was slower on the response and scrambled to his feet. He led Agent Dabria to the interrogation room and motioned for the officer posted like a sentry to open the door.

Donatella turned and spoke, "I need to speak with him alone."

Sampson fuming at this request, "That was not part of the agreement. You are not speaking with this man alone!"

"Our agreement," she said in a cool voice "was that I would ask the suspect three questions. To ask those three questions, I do not need your assistance. Furthermore, as you have already stated, he has refused to answer any of your questions. Seeing you will only exasperate him further and he is likely to shut down completely. Three questions, detective, and then he's all yours."

Reluctantly, Sampson stood aside and allowed Donatella to enter. Once she passed the threshold he motioned for the officer to close the door and he walked over to the bank of monitors to view the interior of the room. He watched as Agent Dabria casually walked across the room, sat down in the chair and crossed her left leg over her right.

"Hello Adam, my name is Special Agent Donatella Dabria with the Federal Bureau of Investigation." She said this while pulling her credentials from her pocket and laying the wallet open on the table displaying her shield and her credentials. Adam continued to stare ghostly into space and did not acknowledge the badge or the woman sitting in front of him.

In the outside room Detective Sampson began to think this was a monumental waste of time. Nonetheless, he was willing to let this play out so this Special Agent could go about her day and he could finish building his case against this sick bastard.

"Adam," Donatella continued. "It's a terrible thing that happened to Samantha," she said in her cool, honey, southern voice. "It's a terrible thing you had to witness happen to Samantha. By all indications, and from everything I can tell, you truly did love Samantha. Mr. Joseph," she said lowering her voice now barely audible to the contingent outside. "I know you are not the one fully responsible for her death."

Slowly, the cloud that shrouded his eyes began to dissipate and the holes that had been his pupils began to glimmer with focus. Adam Joseph blinked his eyes rapidly to clear his head of the fog in an attempt to register the words that were spoken. Donatella watched in silence as Adam transitioned from his zombie-like state to a man with determination.

"Was it your idea to kill Samantha Taylor last night, Mr. Joseph?"

Sampson upon hearing one of her three questions frowned. *Of course, the answer to this question is going to be no. What person, guilty of murder, would say that it was their idea to kill the person they murdered? That would be an admission and one that would certainly have them tossed in jail.*

Adam stared at Agent Dabria for what, to him, seemed like an hour, but in reality, was only 15 seconds. "No" was the word that croaked from his dry throat. He reached purposely for the warm water sitting idly on the metal table. He raised the cup to his chapped and cracked lips and swallowed a mouthful of water with an audible gulp.

"Mr. Joseph, I'm going to show you a photo. I want you to tell me if you recognize the person in the photo. Do you think you can do that for me?"

Outside of the interrogation room Sampson could feel his temperature rising and though he had a dark complexion, he could sense himself reddening. Every fiber of his being wanted to rush in the room and put an immediate end to this questioning. First of all, she had not mentioned she wanted to question the suspect by herself, and now she is preparing to show him a picture that she didn't run past him. He wanted to burst in there and put an end to this, but he didn't. He hadn't walked through the door and called a halt to this interview for two simple reasons. She had asked her second question and she was 66 percent of the way through her questions. One more to go and she would be out of his hair. The second reason was those hazelnut eyes.

While in his office, she halted him from speaking when she raised her hand. The hand was not truly what caused him to halt, it was her eyes. Her deep, hazelnut brown eyes. Eyes that could hold you in a lover's embrace, and eyes that could dissect you like a skilled physician wielding a scalpel. In that moment, he decided he would wait out the final question, the last 33 percent.

Inside the interrogation room a sliver of hope began to rise within Adam. Hope he dared not lean on to heavily, for he was sure it would crumble underneath him, and he would fall back into the murky darkness that had been the last few hours of his life. He did not verbally respond to the question from Agent Dabria because his throat was still raw. Instead he nodded his head a couple of times urging silently for this nightmare to be over.

Agent Dabria extracted a cell phone from her pocket. Outside Sampson was livid because she had taken a phone into the interrogation room, but he stayed where he sat. She unlocked the phone, the picture was already queued, and held it for Adam to take a close look at the woman staring back at him.

In an abrupt shout, "That's her! Oh my God, it's her!" The emotion, pain, anguish he had been feeling exploded out of him in both fear and tears.

Sampson leapt to his feet and with three quick steps forced his way into the room. "What is the meaning of this Special Agent Dabria?" By this time Adam was holding both hands over his mouth sobbing uncontrollably.

Casually Agent Dabria pulled out the chair that sat beside her and in her calm, southern voice said, "Detective Sampson, please have a seat." Sampson's heart raced as a bewildered look overcame his face. Like prey being stalked by a cagey predator, Sampson wearily sat in the chair eyeing Donatella.

Sliding her attention back to the sobbing Adam, Donatella fired her last question. "Would you please tell me, and Detective Sampson, what really transpired in Ms. Taylor's apartment?"

Adam regarded her while wiping the snot flowing from his nose with the back of his left hand. He wasn't sure how much he wanted to tell them without a lawyer present. Anything he said would be treading on thin ice – and incriminating.

He began inhaling deeply through his nose and methodically through his mouth. "I arrived at Samantha's apartment at roughly 6:30 p.m. I popped a couple of mints from my bag, straightened my hair and stepped out of the car. I knocked a couple of times on her door before she answered and let me in. Per usual, when I entered her apartment, she closed and locked the door. We began to... um... fool around. We kissed and fondled a little bit. Then there was a knock at the door."

His face took on a grave sour look as he proceeded. "Samantha thought it was Tina at the door bringing her a sleeping bag for her camping trip. She asked me to go sit in the living room while she opened the door. I sat down as Samantha unlocked the front door. Once the door swung open, I heard a vicious thud followed by Samantha bellowing out in pain. I rushed back to see the source of the commotion and found myself staring down the barrel of a gun. There was a woman – that woman," he said pointing at Donatella's phone, "Pointing a gun at my head while she reached behind herself to lock the door."

Adam stopped to take a drink and then continued. "She told me to secure Samantha with flex cuffs and duct tape. She said she didn't want Samantha interrupting as we talked. Once Samantha had been secured and her mouth taped, that woman threw me a tablet. It took me a moment, but once the tablet had come to life," the instant horror had once again registered on his face, "there were multiple videos playing at once. They were live shots from within my house. Video of my wife in the kitchen. Video of my children, all three of them. And there was a clock. Not a clock. A timer."

"That woman," he said subconsciously looking back toward the phone, "told me I had a choice to make. Either I kill Samantha, or she would set my house on fire with my family trapped inside."

Unable to hold his tongue any longer Sampson blurted, "Do you really expect us to buy this story, Mr. Joseph. A random woman who you never met tells you to kill Samantha or she is going to burn your family alive. How gullible do you think we are?"

"Damn it! It's the God damn truth!"

Agent Dabria shot a glance at Detective Sampson. "Please continue," she said.

Adam took another gulp of warm water, the last one in the cup. "She told me I had a choice to make. Save Samantha or save my family. She warned me if I tried to point the gun at her, she would kill me, then Samantha, and then set fire to my house. I stared at the clock as it ticked backward. She said if the clock finished its countdown, she would execute my family by fire." The vacant horror crept back over his face and into his eyes.

"I looked at Samantha... I looked at her as she cried, her eyes pleading with me not to kill her. But my girls, Courtney, Chasity and my baby, Megan. I could not – I would not let them die. Not that way. Not because of something I had done. Not because I had been unfaithful to their mother, my wife. I again looked at Samantha." Now the tears were streaming from his closed eyes. "I looked at her and I looked back at the timer. It was now under one minute. I would not let my girls die. So, I raised the gun, asked the Lord for forgiveness and I pulled the trigger."

The silence in the interrogation room was deafening. Detective Sampson looked as if he wanted to say something; however, he withheld all comments. Adam Joseph looked like a beaten man. A man who relived the worst decision he made in his life. Donatella broke the silence, "And then what happened?" she asked feeling there was more to tell.

"That woman retrieved the gun from me and told me to

drive straight home. She told me not to contact the police and not to make any stops. If I did either one, she would make good on her promise to execute my family, but this time, she would make sure I was part of the equation. So, I did what I was told. I left the building, rushed to my car and eventually I arrived back at my house."

"Thank you, Mr. Joseph. Detective, do you mind if we speak a moment in private, say back in your office?"

Unsure of anything else he could say, Detective Sampson nodded his head and this time he was the first to stand.

Once they were back in Sampson's office with the door closed Donatella began to speak. "The woman in the picture," she lay the phone down for Sampson to observe, "Is Terri Buckley. She is cold, calculated and extremely dangerous. I have no doubt she watched Adam and Samantha until she was ready to make her move. Is there anything else I should know about this case Detective Sampson?"

Sampson pondered his response and if he wanted to share anything with this agent. True to her word she was able to extract information from the suspect in mere minutes, something they had not been able to do in hours of interrogations. He wasn't sure why, but he felt he could trust this woman. Turning toward his computer he entered his username and password and waited for the login sequence to complete. Once it did, he pulled up the case in search of one picture he had not shared with the suspect.

"Agent Dabria, there is one additional item that we did not share with the suspect. It was something we located at the crime scene that looked out of place and thus became a clue for our team." If Agent Dabria was interested, it didn't show, she sat perfectly still and waited for Sampson to continue.

"We found this card stuck inside the frame of a picture. It wasn't exactly hidden, but it also wasn't in plain sight." Detective

Sampson swiveled the monitor so that both he and Donatella could see the screen without either of them leaving their seats.

"This first side as you can see is blank. This is the side that was visible from the picture frame." Clicking his mouse and moving to the next picture, "This was on the back of the card."

Donatella stared wordlessly at the image illuminating from the screen. At the bottom of the card she saw the typed written words, "Five Days". In the middle of the card sat an embossed image of Auguste Rodin's *The Thinker* sculpture. Sampson could tell by the change in expression that Donatella was familiar with the sculpture as well.

"What do you think it means?"

Donatella sat pensively for several moments while staring at the image. The creaking sound of the old building along with the forced air blowing heat into the room were the only sounds that could be heard. When she finally spoke, she did so in her professorial voice.

"Detective Sampson, what we have before us are a plethora of clues. Please understand, Terri Buckley is a master of deception and nothing is ever as simple as it seems. When you look at the image on the screen you see three things. You see the image of *The Thinker*, you see the word 'Five' and you see the word 'Days'."

"In 1880 Auguste Rodin was commissioned to create a pair of bronze doors for a decorative art museum in Paris. As part of this work, Rodin constructed a series of clay figurines using Dante's Inferno as his inspiration. These figurines were to adorn the doors, and in most cases, they would be parts of the doors. Those doors, that structure, was called *The Gates of Hell* and sitting above the gates leading into Hell sat *The Thinker*. The museum itself never opened and *The Gates of Hell* sculpture was never finished; however, *The Thinker* was extracted from the work and became its own central standalone piece."

Detective Sampson hung on every word as Agent Dabria continued to speak.

"The words 'Five' and 'Days' given in this context are certainly a threat, more so, a promise from Terri. For the casual observer one would take this to mean in five days some event that she has planned will unfold. However, I'm convinced this is not the case. If you look closely at the words 'Five' and 'Days' you will notice they are separated by more than your normal one space between words. In fact, I'm willing to bet there are exactly five spaces between the words. Detective Sampson, this was no accident. This is yet another clue. Terri isn't saying there is an event that will take place in five days. What she wants you to see, what she wants me to know is that all hell will break loose on five separate days.'"

4

DECEMBER 11TH – 7:00 A.M

In a three-bedroom rented townhouse on the south side of Charlotte, Terri Buckley lay naked across the bed staring at the ceiling replaying the events from the night. Every element fell in place just as she expected it would. Although for a moment she really believed that fool Adam would choose that slut homewrecker over his family. That surely would have been an unexpected turn of events, but nothing she couldn't handle. The elimination of Samantha Taylor was key to the next phase of her plan. After the debacle and humiliation, she experienced from her last case, her employers at The Syndicate had not lost faith in her. Instead, they entrusted her with this new assignment, one that if done correctly would yield them plenty of capital for future investments. She would be given the resources she needed to execute her plan, and as a bonus she could incorporate additional torment to her former FBI partner, Donatella Dabria.

Terri had to admit that on some level she underestimated the abilities of Donatella when they faced off the last time. In her zeal to see that goody two-shoes bitch suffer before her death she now realized she left Donatella too many outs. This time she would not be so foolish. While Donatella's death would come soon enough, something The Syndicate stood firmly behind, suffering was the only goal for Terri at this stage in the game. Emotional and physical suffering. By the time Terri was done with her, she wanted Donatella to beg her for her own death – and then, only then she would be obliged to end her miserable existence.

Her nipples hardened with arousal thinking about how wonderful it would feel to finally rid the world of the Dabria line. When Donatella was 11, The Syndicate was responsible for the explosion that killed Donatella's parents. While Terri didn't know the motivation for her employers to wipe the earth clean of her parents, there were several reasons she wanted to see their daughter removed from this earth.

The last straw in her hatred for Donatella came when she informed their superiors at the FBI that she no longer wanted to have Terri as a partner. Donatella considered her a loose cannon and wasn't sure she could be trusted any longer. Buckley overheard Donatella telling this to Senior Special Agent John Brewer. Hearing her partner utter those words was a punch to the gut that sealed the hatred. However, the beginning came several months prior.

Smithville – 4 years prior

"NEW CASE, just in from Brewer. He wants us to get started on this right away," Buckley said handing the file over to Donatella. "Suspect is Aaron Smithville, wanted in connection to a drug smuggling ring, child trafficking, and dealing in illegal arms."

Donatella scanned the file as Terri droned away in the background. "He's evaded capture for several years and we received a tip that he's going to resurface within the next few days. This is our chance to catch him and put him away for good."

Leafing through the file Donatella spoke, "He really must have flown under the radar. This is the first time I have heard of Aaron Smithville. He has some rap sheet, did he have help to forge deeply underground?"

"Honestly I'm not sure. Everything we have on the suspect is in the file. I scanned through it enough to obtain the particulars and now I'm handing it over to you."

"You said Brewer gave this to you, why didn't he brief both of us?"

"Not sure partner, he looked like he had a lot on his mind. He gave me a cursory overview and told me to read the rest of the case. I thought it was out of character as well," she shrugged her shoulders, "but what was I to do?"

Donatella emulated the gesture, "Not much you can do but grab the file and bring home the result." Donatella was just about to look through the file again when Terri urged her.

"You can read that in the car. We better get going so we can observe the scene. Come on, grab your gear. I'm driving."

Buckley pulled her windbreaker from the back of her chair, extracted her firearm from her desk and began walking toward the door. Donatella sensing her eagerness, something she noted before, grabbed her gear, including the file, and trailed her partner out of the door.

December 11th – 7:30 a.m

THE ALARM CLOCK in Terri Buckley's 73-degrees heated bedroom chimed relentlessly. Prior to peeling her eyes from the ceiling, she reached over and smacked the off button silencing the alarm. Today would once again be a key day in her assignment – her plan. Her bare feet smacked the heated hardwood floor, a welcomed addition to this rented space as she proceeded to the closet. She flung aside one outfit after another until she found the attire that matched her mood for the day.

"Ah yes, this will do, this will do quite nicely." Not wanting to waste any time she lay her outfit across the bed and gave herself an appraising glance in the full-length mirror.

Terri stood 5 foot 7 inches with ebony black hair that was pulled neatly into a ponytail. Her elegant, smooth brown skin had a glow from the light cascading into the window from the morning sun. Her eyes, a light shade of brown, were both warm and menacing. When she smiled, her cheekbones blushed accentuating her soft, luscious doughy lips. Several times in her youth she had been mistaken as a runway model.

However, when she ran her eyes down her curvy toned body, she paused at the reflection of her legs in the mirror. Once her legs were as beautiful as the rest of her body but now she felt disgusted when she looked at them. She had surgery to repair her broken legs that left scars that were visible any time she wore a dress or shorts.

She furrowed her brows deciding the self-appraisal was complete and walked into the bathroom for her morning shower.

December 11th – 10:30 a.m

THE WIND HOWLED against the still morning jostling the branches on the leafless tree. The snow that fell the previous night began to melt against the emergence of the sun. With another gust, snow particles spun rapidly like a formidable tornado and crumbled the moment the Thompsons hustled past.

Jasmyn buried her head into her husband's shoulder in an attempt to protect herself from the wind as they walked from the car to the hospital entrance. As they did, a woman appeared from behind the sliding doors pushing a stroller covered with blankets to protect the baby from the elements. Jasmyn's heart warmed and she gave an involuntary grin thinking to herself in a few months that would be her new reality.

This was a reality that she embraced. She grew up as the only child and she wanted a litter of kids roaming their house. Marcellous too was an only child; however, he approached the topic of kids with a bit more caution. He was of the mindset that two kids would be plenty. Being outnumbered was something he didn't relish, but she figured she could convince him to have at least three... and then maybe even a fourth.

She could feel her blood thawing and circulating, fully providing feeling back to her exposed appendages. She wiggled her finger in an effort to assist the flow as the tingle slowly began to dissipate. Once the elevator gave the familiar double ding alerting them that they were at the top floor and that the elevator was making its descent once they exited, they stepped onto the floor belonging to the practice of Dr. Olivia Prince.

The fine hairs on the back of Jasmyn's neck began to stand as the aura in the waiting room emanated negative vibes. Marcellous stirred and she could tell he felt this as well. They approached the reception desk and to Jasmyn's surprise a new receptionist manned the desk.

"Good morning," the new girl spoke, "may I have your name?"

"Yes," the word stumbled from her throat. "Jasmyn Thompson here for an 11 o'clock appointment with Dr. Prince. If you don't mind me asking, where is Samantha?"

A grave solemn expression overcame the features of the receptionist. "Mrs. Thompson," she said in a barely audible whisper. "Samantha was murdered in her home last night."

Jasmyn's hand shot to her mouth in disbelief and the article from Sal Grandson played in Marcellous' mind upon hearing the name. "36-year-old Samantha Taylor was found murdered in her apartment at 631 Sapphire Ave. by an unidentified person."

"My God," was all she could say after hearing the news. "That poor woman." As Jasmyn peered around at the rest of the office staff, she could now see what she missed upon entering the floor. Two women stood over in the corner crying, arms embraced in a hug consoling one another. Another doctor, Dr. Theodore Smith, had red sullen eyes and looked as if he was just going through the motions. Jasmyn began to feel as if she needed to take a seat.

The receptionist spoke, "You look a little flush Mrs. Thompson, can I get you some water?"

"No, no thank you."

"Well if you need anything, anything at all you let me know. My name is Lucie T. Berkry"

"Thank you."

Marcellous, who had been silent throughout this exchange led his wife to a pair of chairs in front of the television showing old reruns of Matlock. Once they were settled in place Marcellous reached into his pocket, retrieved his cellphone and searched for Sal's article that he had read earlier that morning.

He read through the article again kicking himself for not recalling that Samantha was the receptionist at the doctor's office. Had he recalled who she was earlier, he could have prepared his wife. Instead she had to endure this shock just before heading into the ultrasound she had been looking forward to for weeks. Caught up in his own world he had not noticed the woman who sat next to his wife and was engaging her in a full-blown conversation.

"Dr. Prince has been amazing. She comes highly recommended and to date she has not disappointed. Is this your first baby?"

"Yes," replied the newcomer with a weary smile. "My husband, Troy, and I were pregnant once before; however, we lost the baby a week before the end of the first trimester." As she said this the sclera of her eye began to speckle red as liquid formed in the corners.

Genuinely she responded, "I'm so sorry to hear that and I'm sorry for your loss."

The tear that had been forming in the corner of the woman's eye streamed down her face. Jasmyn reached into her purse, extracted a couple of tissues and handed them to the woman. With a nod of thanks, the woman took the tissues in her trembling hand and dabbed the corners of her eyes.

"My name is Jasmyn by the way. Jasmyn Thompson. And this," she playfully elbowed her husband, "is my better half, Marcellous."

Not sure if he should shake the hand of this crying woman or simply give a head nod, he shot a hand in the air and gave her a wave.

"My name is Bethany Evans. It's a pleasure to meet you." She extended her hand, still trembling but not as much as before, toward Jasmyn and the two of them shook. Jasmyn cupped her left hand on top of Bethany's and gave a reassuring firm squeeze.

"Troy couldn't make it to the appointment today as they are in the middle of finals and this was the only appointment I could get. And now look at me, crying on the shoulder of a woman I just met."

"There is no need to apologize." Jasmyn said more quickly than she had intended. "It's no trouble at all. I'm always happy to help." She shot Bethany a warm reassuring smile and for her efforts, she received a smile in return.

Marcellous marveled at his wife. He knew she was taking the death of Samantha much harder than she was letting on, but when she saw a person in need, she forgot about all of her worries and tended to the other person. This is what made her such a great nurse, and if she ever decided, a great doctor.

"Jasmyn Thompson" the assistant bellowed from the partially opened door.

"Looks like that's us," Jasmyn uttered aloud. "Here is my cell-phone number. If you ever need to talk, feel free to give me a call."

"Thank you, I will."

The Thompsons stood from their seat, Jasmyn waved her hand at the assistant acknowledging her call and the three disappeared behind the closing lobby room door.

December 11th - 11:30 a.m

TERRI BUCKLEY SAT on a green bench bundled against the brisk air on this December morning. For two week she sat on this same bench at the same time observing, watching. The object of her desire had been the headquarters building located directly across the walkway. She watched every person that walked out the door. Some walked out alone each day while there were others who came out in groups.

However, Terri was increasingly interested in the people walking into the building versus the ones who walked out. To her delight and dismay she was surprised how lax the company had been with regards to corporate security. On a regular basis, she watched no less than three people holding doors for colleagues to enter, none of which displayed nor scanned a security badge.

Buckley, a master in social engineering, could utilize the lapse in security to her advantage. Each day at exactly 11:35 a.m., a group of three women and two men exited the main door and she knew today would be no different. She looked down at her watch, "11:34. It's time."

Buckley casually strolled across the walkway timing her stride. She needed to reach the door as the third person in the group would be passing through the exit. In her studies she realized the third person in a five-person group is in a perilous situation. Half of their party was outside while the other half was inside the building. With the frigid cold weather, they didn't want their lunchmates in the cold waiting any longer than necessary, so they were quick to allow a person going the opposite direction to passthrough as quickly as possible.

Ten paces to go. Predictable as always, the group reached the door and began filing out. Buckley picked up the pace promoting the thought she was rushing through the cold.

The rutty faced middle-aged woman she had begun to think of as Rose was the first one to walk through the door. Next through came the guy she thought of as Jimmy. On several occasions she noticed Jimmy watching the backside of Rose as he walked behind her. It was always a subtle view, but the slight tilt of his head was always a firm give away. She thought of him as Jimmy primarily because of the dated term for a sexual protection device - the Jimmy Hat.

Who would be the linchpin today, she thought as she bypassed Jimmy who was already trying to get a glimpse of Rose's ass underneath her waist cut peacoat.

Ah, Richard, the only African American in the group. From a distance he always appeared to be roughly six feet tall, but now as she prepared to pass him, she realized he was closer to 6 feet 2 inches.

As he prepared to push his way through the door, she quickly flashed him a smile. He pushed the door open, held the door with one arm extended, stood to one side, and motioned her through. Buckley spoke her thanks and continued to walk through the atrium and just like that, she was inside the offices of Global Insights Securities.

Again, in her casual walking manner, Terri crossed the atrium to the elevator banks. She pressed the up button and patiently waited the cars arrival. *A security company that fails miserably at their own corporate security, what a joke*. The elevator dinged once, and the doors opened.

Two men exited the elevator, "Who you got on the game this evening?"

"The Colts are looking good again, but I think I'm going with -"

The last words were cut off as the door closed and the elevator began its ascent to the fifth floor. A song from Taylor Swift played through the elevator speakers, Buckley tapped her foot in rhythm.

Her goal was to continue the illusion that she belonged in this building, another key element to social engineering.

The door opened onto the fifth floor and she made her way directly to the office on the northwest side of the building. She was able to secure a set of the company's floor map and she knew this was the office of Veronica King. It was immediately clear to Terri that the floor map wasn't set to any scale as the path from the elevator to the corner office was slightly longer than she expected.

Along her path she encountered a woman sitting at her desk, eating her lunch while watching an episode of "Designated

Survivor", and idly thought *how fitting*. She smiled at the woman who smiled back, and she continued her path to the corner.

Another woman struggled at her office door, hands full with her lunch and a file.

"Let me help you with that," Terri said opening the door and pushing it open.

"Thank you for your assistance," the woman said making her way into the office.

Terri nodded her head while picking up her speed. The office of Veronica King was a mere two offices away and she could feel her palms sweat with anticipation. When she arrived at the office, King faced the window, back to the door and she could be heard rehearsing her speech.

Terri walked in and closed the door that swung silently and latched shut with a barely audible click. She sat down in the plush leather visitors chair, and crossed her leg, waiting patiently.

"In closing, those are the changes that I recommend, and with your support, the growth of this company will no longer be a question."

"Well said," Terri spoke while clapping in a low, slow manner. Veronica King spun around, heart in her throat, pulsating her vocal cords preventing all speech. Her eyes grew wide with a lack of recognition and with a few gulps to push down the lump in her throat she managed to speak.

"Who are you and what are you doing in my office?" She noticed with alarm that her office door was now closed.

5

DECEMBER 11TH – 11:45 A.M

"Mrs. Veronica King. I have to say, it is a pleasure to finally meet you. I have read so much about you."

Veronica wasn't the type to scare easily, but the sight of this woman was causing her some serious anxiety. "I already asked you once. You had better tell me who you are and what you are doing in my office or I will call security." Absent-mindedly, she began to wonder how on earth this woman made it past security.

"Who I am, Mrs. King is not important. What I can do for you, and what you in turn can do for me is what's important at this moment."

"Enough!" Veronica said picking up the phone.

In a smooth yet threatening voice Buckley said, "Veronica, put it down."

Looking into the eyes of this stranger gave Veronica the notion that she should do as she was asked. She slowly placed the phone back into the cradle, "What is it that I can do for you Ms. –"

She waited on the woman to respond; however, the only

response she received was the woman pulling a tablet from her pocket.

"Veronica, do you know where your husband is at this moment?"

"Kyle! What have you done to Kyle?" Her legs came close to giving out from underneath her as she groped for her chair and sat down.

"Mrs. King, that is not how this works. I asked you a question and I expect an answer." Escalating the intensity in her voice, "Where is your husband?"

The change in tone was not lost on Veronica and she blurted, "He's at work!"

"Yes, that's what I thought you would say." She slid the tablet across the mahogany desk. "Please, go ahead and take a look."

With the tablet laying on the desk, she could make out images emanating from the screen. She picked up the tablet and there framed in the center in an extreme close up was her husband.

"Why do you have video of my husband?"

Buckley pulled her phone from her pocket, ignoring the question, and pressed the call button. After a few silent moments, the stranger spoke. "Go ahead and transition to the second view."

Veronica watched this stranger as she made the call with a mix of bewilderment. At that moment, she saw the image from the tablet change drastically drawing her attention. The display switched to a video of Kyle on an airplane holding hands with an attractive brunette, hair flowing past her shoulders. Veronica's eyes grew to the size of golf balls as she choked back a pained gasp.

"Your husband, who should be at work, is in fact on a plane headed to Nepal with his chummy co-worker Irena Petrov. A co-worker he has been sleeping with for the last three months. A co-worker that as of today he is officially leaving you for so that he can be with her."

Shock and disbelief registered on her face. "Not my Kyle," she said in a hurt, mousey voice.

"Mrs. King," the stranger continued, "It's time to discuss what I can do for you, and in turn what you can do for me. It's really simple, you have a presentation to the board of directors and the entire c-suite at the top of the hour."

Veronica nodded her head never taking her eyes from the screen.

"I need for you to kill them all."

Her head snapped up from the tablet, "You want me to do what!" she exclaimed.

"I want you to kill them – all of them. I will provide you with the method, you just need to execute the plan. If you refuse then I will trigger the bomb that has been loaded at the bottom of the plane killing your bastard of a husband and everyone on the plane."

A tennis ball sized knot began to twist in Veronica's stomach. Her mouth began to water uncontrollably along with the sour taste that proceeds the need to vomit. She eyed the woman and it was clear she was not kidding. She had every intention of blowing up the plane that her husband was on and all of the passengers.

She then began to think about her colleagues, the board, her boss. Her boss, a man she despised. But she enjoyed working with the rest of her colleagues and she liked the members of the board.

"Mrs. King, I would be remiss if I didn't inform you that you are on a time limit. If that plane should leave the ground and you have not done what I have asked, I will detonate the bomb."

The tennis ball sized knot had now grown into that of a bowling ball. She twisted the lid from the bottled water that she had planned to take to the meeting and took a long drink. The more she thought about it, innocent people were at risk in both scenarios, but she could not get past what she had seen on the video. If anyone deserved to die it was Kyle.

"I will not kill my co-workers. I will not have their blood on my hands. You go right ahead and blow that plane out of the air with that cheating bastard."

The stranger simply shook her head. "I had a feeling you would say that. Perhaps, I should give you two more crucial pieces of information. As it turns out, I know you plan to make a move for the CEO seat at the meeting today," she paused.

Veronica's eyebrows narrowed as she glared intently at the intruder.

"Somehow, CEO Stein has caught wind of this as well. He and the members of the board have been in a close good ole boys club for ages. They are all for you becoming the next CEO; however, they will not go against the wishes of Stein after he gave them this last night."

The intruder slid over a copy of an agreement to provide additional shares in the company for each year Stein stays at the helm as CEO. "Sure, it's highly illegal, but believe me, it has been done and frankly, this isn't the only time a deal like this has been struck."

Veronica skimmed the document as the bowling ball in her stomach had now grown to a weighted medicine ball. She could not believe what she was hearing – what she was reading. The board, her last chance to obtain what she rightfully deserved, was siding with Stein.

"One last thing," she said bringing the phone back to her mouth, "Please bring up the third angle."

Understanding the queue this time, Veronica immediately looked down at the tablet. Unlike last time when the new image seemed to appear immediately, this one seemed to be taking longer than the first. She could feel her breaths growing shallow and her chest tightening. Moments later the image redrew on the screen and a new video played.

"NOOOOOOO!!!"

Sitting on the other side of her husband, already buckled into her seatbelt sat her 3-year-old daughter, Gina.

The knot in her stomach gave way and she reached for the trash receptacle next to her desk and vomited nonstop for 20 seconds.

In a frankly cold voice, the visitor spoke, "If you do not agree to my request, not only will your cheating husband and his mistress become a casualty at 30,000 feet, your precious daughter, Gina, will suffer the same fate as the other innocent people on that flight."

The reality of her situation was finally, and unbelievably, dawning on Veronica. Her husband of five years was planning to leave the country with their daughter and his mistress. He was going to a country that didn't have an extradition treaty with the US and she would never see her daughter again.

"I know what you're thinking. They are already on the plane and your daughter is lost to you. Well, I'm willing to amend the parameters of our deal. Let's call it a negotiation. The plane your husband has boarded is scheduled to depart at 12:15 p.m. They are currently boarding the remaining passengers but that will only last for the next two minutes. At which time, the flight attendant will alert the passengers that the doors will be closing and this is the last chance for anyone that would like to exit the plane to do so. I can ensure that your husband is removed from the plane, along with his mistress, and your daughter. I can ensure your daughter exits from the gate. As for your husband and his mistress, let's just say they will never be heard from again. The flight manifest will show that he and his mistress continued on the flight and no one has to know that he disappeared."

Hope began to spread over her face as she began to contain her breathing.

"You will; however, need to execute your peers, and the board. In addition to that, you will become an official employee for my employer."

"Your employer! Who is your employer? Why are you doing this to me?

"You have 1 minute and 15 seconds to make your decision."

Veronica's head was spinning, and she could feel the nausea encroaching once again. She could not lose her daughter – she would not lose her daughter. The lives of her peers and that of the board did not compare to the life of her daughter. She didn't believe she could take a life, but she would for her daughter.

"I'll do it," she said full of resolve with her head held high. "I'll do it. Get my daughter off of that plane and do with my husband and that woman, whatever you like. You ensure my daughter is safe, and I will do as you have asked."

Buckley pulled the phone to her face once again, "We are a go." She pressed the end button on the phone and placed the phone into her pocket. She stood casually and walked behind Veronica as the image on the screen changed.

The perspective was that of a person standing, walking down the isle of the plane. It seemed as if the person had on a pair of glasses that transmitted the video directly to the tablet. The person stopped at the trio of seats containing her husband, his mistress, and their daughter. There was no sound emanating from the tablet but she could tell by Kyle's expression that he was not enjoying the conversation. Reluctantly, he and the woman stood up. He turned to their daughter and disengaged the seatbelt.

The three of them walked in front of the person wearing the

glasses toward the front of the plane. Upon exiting the plane, the view on the tablet turned back toward the door just in time to see it closing. Satisfied the door was closed and secure, the view turned back toward the walkway leading from the gate to the plane. At that point she saw her husband in protest with airport security, as their daughter was being walked away.

Veronica could feel the knot returning to her stomach as she saw her daughter being led away by an unknown person, separated from her father. The view on the tablet swung toward the door at the end of the walkway that sits across from the entrance to the plane.

The familiar yellow sign with red writing *Authorized Personnel Only* was visible momentarily before the door swung open. In a flash, two blurs passed in and out of view of the tablet. Veronica once again could feel the tightening in her chest as the image began to shift past the door, toward the ground outside.

Both hands shot to her mouth as she saw the figure of her husband and his mistress laying on the ground. Just as fast she saw a cart carrying luggage appear. Two individuals stepped from the cart, scooped up both bodies as if they were rag dolls, and tossed them onto the cart. They unfolded a previously unseen tarp, lay it over the bodies, and drove off.

Before the image on the tablet went dark, the person wearing the glasses watched after the departing cart. There were no other planes visible from that viewpoint and thus no one saw the bodies tumble to the ground.

"If you do not follow through on our agreement, your daughter will be carted away with your husband. Do you understand me?"

Veronica, unable to speak simply nodded her head.

"Good. Let's walk through what you need to do."

December 11th – 12:00 p.m

CEO Edward Stein sat at the head of the 16-person board room conference table. The table, said to be made in one piece from an oak tree handpicked by his grandfather, had to be lifted into the new headquarters by a crane during construction. Stein refused to have it cut into pieces to be reassembled in the board room and instead opted to pay for it to be placed into the board room during the framing of the building. This request caused the engineers and building crew some challenges but they were well compensated for their troubles.

As the others began to file into the room Stein turned around and admired the hand-painted portraits of his granddaddy and his father. Per tradition, once the CEO retired from the company, an artist was commissioned to create a portrait of the existing CEO sitting behind the table in the board room. Stein recalled with a sense of pride watching the artist take a blank canvas and transition it into a still replica of his father's living essence.

The shine in his firm, dark eyes. The creases that crossed his forehead as a result of his aging. The strong set of his jaw mixed with the hollow smile on his lips. He could still remember his father dressing the morning of the painting in his freshly tailored and cleaned solid black suit, white presidential button-down shirt, and his red power tie in the familiar Windsor knot. As he put the finishing knot in his tie, his father said to him, "Edward, one day you will sit in this seat, to have your likeness captured for eternity and to sit along me and your grandfather. When that day comes, I want you to look back on your career and feel comfortable saying you've made the world better off than when you took the reins today. Make us proud son."

Stein thought fondly back on that day and knew today would be a much different day. Today, in front of his direct reports and the board, Veronica King would make a play to push him out of his seat. However, today he would put her in her place and send her ass packing. He couldn't wait to see the look on her face when all members of the board, even those that backed her rise in the company, gave her a vote of no confidence and for her insubordination, would ask for her resignation. At that point, he would smile and watch as she left with her tail between her legs.

Everyone, seated in their normal positions, talked in hush tones around him. Looking down at his watch he noted it was six minutes after noon. He thought to himself that Veronica was never late. In fact, she was typically early for these meetings. Maybe she got cold feet and decided to tender her resignation silently instead of proceeding with this farfetched plan to overthrow him from power.

One minute later he realized this was not the case. Through the glass walls of the conference room located on the top floor of the GIS building he could see Veronica striding with purpose and determination. As she swung the door open their eyes locked. The cold, vacant, murderous look that covered her face sent chills down his spine.

December 11th – 12:00 p.m

WITNESSING the death of her husband, and now being told by this stranger that she needed to execute the members of her company's board, along with her peers, caused something to snap within Veronica King. However, for the sake of her daughter, she needed to hold it together and do what she considered to be unthinkable. She was being asked, make that forced, to commit mass murder. And to make matters worse, she got the sense from this woman that once this deed was complete, she still would not be free.

The woman, who she was told to call Bree, stated she would be asked to complete a few other tasks from her employer, The Syndicate. And when she was called upon, she simply needed to perform the duty she was asked to complete, and everything would be ok. If she refused, she would one day have the corpse of her daughter emailed back to her piece by piece. Today would be her first test of loyalty, today would go a long way in determining if she was with them or if she was against them.

Bree walked her through what she needed to do step by step. If she followed directions, she and her daughter would not be harmed. In the end, once everyone in the board room had expired, Veronica who was next in line, would take over as CEO, a position she had come to the office that day to fight for, and she could replace all of her colleagues with handpicked successors.

As Veronica rode the elevator to the top floor of the GIS headquarters building, a sense of numb calmness overcame her person. She no longer felt in control. She was operating on autopilot. An autopilot that was being controlled by the crazy woman that appeared in her office only 20 minutes prior.

When the doors of the elevator opened, she knew there would be no retreat. She clutched the bag affixed to her shoulder and began to stride toward the double doors to the board room. With her assured tardiness, all members of the board and her peers would already be seated in the room awaiting her arrival. The seat closest to the door, opposite to Edward Stein, always belonged to her.

She strode from the elevator determined. The only picture that was firmly implanted in her mind, was the image of her daughter being walked away by a faceless person just prior to her husband plunging to his death. As she reached for the handle of the door, she locked eyes with Edward Stein. For a brief moment he had the look of triumph in his eyes; however, as their eyes locked his look faded to concern.

She walked into the board room and the hushed conversations ended abruptly and all eyes were now focused on her. She sat her bag on the table and unlike the remainder of the room's occupants, Veronica King stood planted in place.

Her eyes roamed silently around the room connecting momentarily with each person. As she looked at Mike, the CIO, she thought about the two kids he had, a boy and a girl, ages 13 and 10. They both played sports and looked up to their father. She lingered on Tonya, the head of HR. She had three more years until retirement and was looking forward to spending time with her husband, Jake, who had retired earlier this year. Her eyes watered as she looked at Bev.

Bev was a member on the board who was the CEO of a non-profit organization who helped at-risk youth. Bev had been Veronica's biggest source of support and the only female member of the board. Finally, her eyes moved to the head of the table and landed on Edward Stein.

From the time she initially locked eyes with Stein until the moment she was now staring at him, the look on Stein's face had once again shifted. The look that originally conveyed concern, was now a look of horror. Everyone at the table followed the glare from Veronica and turned their heads back to CEO, Edward Stein.

Veronica pulled back the flap from the messenger bag that she had carried into the board room. She extracted the canister that she was given by the woman calling herself Bree and sat it down with a thud on the table. Without a moment's hesitation, she pressed the button on the canister, retrieved the bag and walked back out of the door she had entered. Upon exiting the room, she affixed two door stoppers underneath each of the glass doors moments before Mike rammed into the door. The glass that surrounded the conference room was designed to be shatterproof and in a few moments, it wouldn't matter.

A fine, green mist exploded from the canister and quickly began to disperse to the four corners of the room. For one additional moment, Veronica looked into the room catching an uncomprehending look of dismay from Bev as her eyes questioned, "Why?"

Veronica pressed the down button to the elevator which still lay in wait on the floor. She entered the elevator car and pressed the button marked with the letter "G" which denoted the exit and the garage level. From there she would walk to her car in her private parking spot and drive to her house where she was told her daughter would be waiting.

6

DECEMBER 11TH – 12:30 P.M

"Mr. and Mrs. Thompson, thank you for stopping in today. The baby is looking great. Continue to do what you are doing and minimize stress as much as possible. I want to keep an eye on your A1C levels. I see from the panel we did during your last visit that they are a little more elevated than I would like."

Dr. Prince could see the look of concern on both Marcellous and Jasmyn. Placing a delicate hand on top of Jasmyn's hand, "There is nothing to fear. Having a baby is hard work and your body goes through a multitude of changes, especially with the first one."

She shot a reassuring smile to Jasmyn and followed up with the same genuine smile in Marcellous' direction. The small gesture immediately put the couple at ease and brought a smile to their faces.

"Now, let's talk about the gender of your bundle of joy." The radiant smile on Jasmyn's face widened at the mention of her baby.

. . .

On their ride over to the hospital the couple continued to go back and forth on knowing the sex of the baby. This discussion went on until the moment Jasmyn laid back on the examination table awaiting the arrival of Dr. Prince. By the time the exam started they still had not decided. Even though Jasmyn was a nurse, she still had trouble making out the details on an ultrasound.

Marcellous, on the other hand, was completely oblivious to any of the details, but when the aide pointed out the heartbeat on the monitor, he swelled with pride and instantly looked for that continuous flutter on subsequent visits. Other than that, he might as well be reading a foreign language.

The moment of truth had come at last, "Are you guys ready to know what you're having?" Dr. Prince asked, anticipating a gleeful response. Instead, she received blank stares and uncertainty. Reading the situation for what it was, she hopped in.

"Well, it seems like you are on the fence."

She received nods.

"How about this. I have already determined the sex, but I do not need to tell you. I can seal the gender within an envelope and if you decide at some point prior to the birth to know the sex, all you need to do is open the envelope."

Both parents looked at each other, hope spread across their faces.

"I've heard of countless couples doing a gender reveal party with family and close friends. You can take the envelope to your local baker, have them bake a cake and the color of the cake will reveal the sex of the baby."

The light illuminated for both Jasmyn and Marcellous at the same time.

"Why didn't we think of that? It's a brilliant idea." In that moment the couple made a decision, a decision to delay the decision even further.

. . .

"THIS ENVELOPE CONTAINS the sex of the baby as we discussed. The reveal is totally in your hands. I look forward to hearing how you go about the reveal. I've had some really creative ones."

Dr. Prince began walking the couple back toward the reception desk.

"Lucie will be able to schedule your next appointment," the devastation traveled through her voice.

Before she realized it, Jasmyn was speaking, "I'm so sorry to hear about what happened to Samantha. It is absolutely terrible."

"Thank you. She was a loved and valued member of our staff. Everyone is taking her death with sadness and disbelief. We all plan to attend her funeral to pay our final respects."

Turning the corner Dr. Prince noticed Joy sitting at the receptionist desk.

"Where is the new girl, Lucie?"

"She stepped away for lunch and is running a few minutes late returning. She gave me a call to let me know she was running five minutes behind."

Dr. Prince sighed with disapproval, "Good help is impossible to find. That is one thing I never had to worry about with Samantha, she was never late, and always put our patients first. I guess I shouldn't be too hard on the girl. She walked into a tough situation on such short notice. I should be grateful that we were able to find someone with only one call last night. Joy can you –"

Lucie came walking through the door in a rush, "I'm so sorry Dr. Prince. I was held up in traffic while making my way back."

She quickly removed her coat, tossing it on the back of her chair that was vacated by Joy once she entered the room.

"Please schedule a three-week follow-up appointment for

Mrs. Thompson."

"Yes, Dr. Prince. I'll take care of it."

Dr. Prince shook hands with the couple and headed back to attend to her next patient, Mrs. Evans.

December 11th – 3:30 p.m

DETECTIVE CARL SAMPSON rode the elevator to the fifth floor of the Global Insights Security building. According to Vanessa, his trusty dispatch operator, there had been a mass murder of the top executives and members of the Global Insights board. Vanessa received a frantic call from Sasha Wright, the executive admin for Edward Stein.

Sampson was eager to speak with this witness as she was the first person on the scene of the crime and thus could give the best account of how everything looked when she arrived. It was key that he obtain as much information from her while it was still fresh in her mind as she may have seen things that would be crucial to the investigation.

Upon reaching the fifth floor, he could see that the office had been cleared of all working personnel, except that of Sasha Wright. He saw a female officer sitting with Mrs. Wright as the two carried on in conversation. Walking toward her desk he mused how deadly quiet such a large room was in the middle of the day.

"I'll take it from here Officer Lewis," Sampson stated as he approached the two women.

"Good afternoon, Mrs. Wright. My name is Detective Sampson with the Charlotte Metro Police Department. First, let me say I'm sorry for your loss and sorry that you were the one who had to find your boss and the rest of his team."

"Thank you," she responded demurely.

"I know this will be difficult to do, but it would go a long way in helping me find the people responsible for the deaths in the board room today if you could answer a few questions. Are you up to answering a few questions for me?"

She nodded her head in affirmation.

"It's my understanding that you were the first one to find the bodies in the board room. Is that correct?"

Again, she nodded her head.

"While you were upstairs, did you touch anything or did you see anything that was out of place, that didn't belong?"

In a firm, yet hollow voice she responded, "No I didn't touch anything or see anything that didn't belong. I honestly cannot recall if there was anything out of place. Once I realized what I was looking at, I stumbled my way back to the elevator, came down to my office and phoned the police."

"That's good, Mrs. Wright. You did right by not touching anything and giving us a call immediately. Do you mind walking me through the events that led up to you calling the station?"

She tentatively started the tale, her eyes reddening as she spoke.

"Mr. Stein had not returned from the board meeting that started at noon. The meeting was expected to last roughly two hours. He had a subsequent meeting at 2:30 with Thomas Butterton, CEO of Atoms Hardware. They specialize in the manufacturing of miniature data storage. At 2:25 I called Mr. Stein's cellphone but I did not receive an answer. It was unlike him to be late for any meeting, so I tried him again five minutes later. Receiving no answer for the second time, I stuck my head into the conference room to advise Mr. Butterton that Mr. Stein was running late. I asked him if he needed anything to drink – he declined, and so I went back to my desk."

"I grew increasingly concerned and decided I would take the

elevator up to the board room. The ride seemed to take longer than it normally did. I don't know if it was my anxiousness to ensure he didn't miss his meeting or if it was my subconscious telling me danger was ahead."

"When the elevator door swung open, I could sense the room was still occupied, but it wasn't until I drew closer that I realized the horror that lay in front of me. Half of the occupants were strewn across the board room floor. The other half seemed to be frozen in place in their chairs, unwilling or unable to move. I could tell from where I stood that none of them were breathing. I screamed at the top of my lungs, paralyzed in place for a minute, maybe more. When my conscious brain took over, I screamed again."

"Witnessing the grotesque features that spread across their faces made my stomach turn countless times until I felt I would vomit."

Throughout the retelling of her story, Sampson didn't utter a word, simply listened to everything she had to say.

"At that moment, I decided I needed to make my way down to my office to call for help and that's exactly what I did."

The emotion that had built behind her vacant eyes finally gave way as a stream of tears bubbled over the edges and flowed down her cheeks. Sampson, a man who grew up in the inner city, was accustomed to violence but on this day he too lamented that this was too much violence. Mrs. Wright whisked away the tears with a well-worn, folded tissue.

"Thank you for your time during this unforgivable ordeal. Officer Lewis will see to it that you are accompanied home if you are not up to driving."

Behind the silent sob, Sasha gave her acknowledgement. Detective Sampson stood from his seat, walked back to the elevator and ascended to the top floor. When the doors opened Sampson was surprised to see Special Agent Donatella Dabria standing patiently just beyond the elevator entrance with her hands steepled in front of her – eyes closed.

"Detective Sampson," she said in her honeyed voice, eyes still closed. "I've been awaiting your arrival."

"How is it that you already know about this crime and furthermore, how did you gain access to the crime scene?"

Opening her eyes and walking toward the board room, "Detective Sampson, I have not entered the crime scene. I've patiently waited on the periphery for your timely arrival. The crime scene is behind those two doors." She pointed her finger toward the board room as Sampson took a few hurried long strides to catch up. "I have every reason to believe Terri Buckley is behind this heinous act."

"What makes you so sure?"

"As we investigate the scene, I'm sure it will become obvious."

Reaching the exterior of the board room, two men in hazmat suits greeted Agent Dabria and Detective Sampson. "Before you can gain entry into this room, we suggest you put these on," the man said handing them each a full hazmat suit.

Donatella raised an eyebrow at this request and gave the man a quizzical look.

"It seems all harmful agents have been expelled from the room; however, I would feel better if you, at minimum, placed the mask on."

Donatella took the proffered garments and began pulling the suit over her attire while Sampson did the same. Once they were fully dressed, Agent Dabria motioned toward the door with her arm extended to Sampson, "After you."

A smile creased his face from beneath the mask while thinking, *how chivalrous of you.* He pulled the door open and prepared to walk into the carnage that lay before him.

The body of one man and one woman fell across the

threshold of the door once it was swung outward. The man's eyes were bulging and pupils floating in the inner corner of his eyes. His lips were twisted as if he had been assaulted with a baseball bat and his head turned to the right well beyond 90 degrees.

The woman, dried blood streaks that leaked from her ears and her nose, had one eye open and one eye closed. The eye that was visible had gone completely red, no pupil in sight, as if the blood had floated around in her cranium until her heart quit pumping.

Surveying the room didn't yield any better results. Each member of the board, and each member of the senior management team had undergone a fate more cruel than imagination could offer. At the edge of the table, closest to the door, sat a single canister – waiting to be addressed.

Sampson began to speak, "Do you think –"

"Yes, I do. I suggest we handle this with care."

They appraisingly stared at the canister before approaching it. The thought coursing through the room, *Is there another surprise waiting?*

The canister, solid black, roughly the size of your everyday pressurized container of shaving cream, sat ominously staring at them. It contained no marking from what she could see and it was clear that this did not belong in the boardroom. Donatella picked up the canister – seemed empty. Realizing upon closer inspection that the canister didn't have any marking on the outside, she flipped it over to look at the bottom. There, engraved on the concaved metal surface at the bottom, lay a sign. Donatella turned the container so that Detective Sampson could fully see the image that was on the bottom. The image that would help to convince him. The image of The Thinker.

No words passed from his constricting vocal cords through his parting lips. The changes in his expression said all it needed to say. Donatella motioned for the two of them to step outside the room.

Once outside, he tried to break the silence but words still seemed unable to escape him. Throughout his career, the most terrible scene he had worked was a gang turf war shooting where he witnessed kids as young as 14 years old cut in half by assault rifles. However, this – this was much worse.

Agent Dabria, sensing his consternation spoke, "Sampson, we are dealing with a sick individual. One that will continue her murderous ways until she is caught. She obviously has an endgame in mind, and to stop her, we need to determine where she is leading us."

"But what on earth is her motive?"

Donatella sighed, "Her employer, The Syndicate, is likely behind the initial course of her actions. Terri has been given an assignment, and how she chooses to execute her assignment is totally up to her. The sensational way in which she is executing this plan is to taunt me."

A troubled look of confusion lay over Sampson's brows.

"Buckley was my partner with the FBI for a period of time. Our careers in the Bureau took a proportionally inversed path. While my status began to soar, her status began to nosedive. What became of her career she firmly places on my shoulders, never willing to take accountability for the actions that landed her where she is."

"Our partnership dissolved as a result of her actions on the Smithville case a few years ago. What she did, what she was planning to do, I could not and would not condone. I went to our superior and advised him that she could not be trusted, and in reality, she should have been fired. I told him I would not work with her as my partner any longer. The decision was then made that I would work solo from that day forward."

"Terri saw this as another slight toward her and the beginning of the end of her career. She orchestrated events a few months ago to end my life and the lives of those I care about. I was able to beat her at her own sadistic game. The last time I saw her, I thought she had died. It wasn't until days later when her body had not been found that I knew she survived."

"While I'm sure The Syndicate has a reason for some of the actions she has taken, the over-the-top killing is meant for me. She is baiting me into a showdown. One I have not yet figured out, but one she clearly feels will give her the upper hand."

"So, you see detective, there are two cases that need to be solved."

"Two?" Sampson asked.

"The first, what is The Syndicate after? Buckley hasn't gone rogue. There is something here, in this building, that they wanted and I'm sure before the people in that room died, Terri Buckley obtained that item."

"Second, what dark trap is she laying for me? Terri is skilled enough to execute any plan without the theatrics. She wants me to know it's her and that she is coming for me."

"Speaking of which, how is it that you continue to know about these killing before any information is shared with the public?"

Donatella ignored the question and continued, "Whatever the endgame, if we don't begin to make progress, the body count will continue to rise."

Detective Sampson took a moment to absorb what he heard and knew that the Special Agent was correct. From everything he had learned about this killer, she was relentless, calculated, and she was only getting started.

"Special Agent Dabria, I don't like what she is doing in my city, and I feel with this latest episode, the balance of power is shifting from the CMPD over to the FBI. If that is the case, I would like to stay on and assist as much as I can. I want to see this woman go down for the damage she has caused."

"Detective, I appreciate the offer, but I work best alone."

"Bullshit! Sure, you have been successful up to this point but if Terri Buckley is as formidable as you say she is, you need someone that can watch your back."

"Detective, you need to understand, Terri Buckley does not play fair and in her mind, everyone is fair game. I do not need to worry about anyone else getting hurt in the process."

"Damn it, Agent Dabria! Part of my job is danger."

"Not like this. You haven't dealt with someone as singularly focused on my destruction. She will stop at nothing to see me go down. She will go through anyone to see me go down." Agent Dabria thought back to the moment her goddaughter had been secured to a chair with C4 affixed to the bottom waiting to blow her, the building, and Donatella off the face of the earth.

"Again, you are making my point for me, if she is that dangerous, you will need help. You will need assistance. You cannot go at this alone."

"I have all the assistance I need Detective. I –"

"With or without you, I'm going to continue my investigation. So, either we work together, or we work separately, but I'm not giving up on this case."

SA Dabria knew that Sampson would not give in. "Fine. But I need you to understand, tracking Terri Buckley is not akin to tracking a normal suspect. She is a master of hiding in plain sight."

Smithville – 4 years prior

THE NONDESCRIPT FBI sedan stalked around I-485 in the early afternoon on this sunny day. After being alerted to the location of a wanted felon, Aaron Smithville, Agents Buckley and Dabria obtained the gear needed to apprehend their suspect. While Buckley drove, Donatella continued to review the file. There was something about this suspect that was not settling well with her. She hoped reviewing the file would provide the clarity she needed; however, the feeling still lingered and grew stronger.

"How do you want to approach Smithville?" Donatella inquired pulling her eyes from the page.

"I think we need to be prepared to encounter a contingent of hostile actors. For our Rules of Engagement, ROE, I suggest we prepare to go lethal."

"Seems a little extreme considering we haven't obtained a lay of the land."

"Well Ms. Donatella since you seem to have everything figured out as always, what do you suggest?"

She ignored the latest yet constant jab from Buckley, "I suggest we observe the residence before we try to engage the suspect. It's in a residential neighborhood and we don't need any collateral damage."

Buckley rolled her eyes, something Donatella felt more than she saw, "He cannot slip through our fingers, not again."

"What do you mean again?"

"Never mind that. If you think the best course of action is to watch the building before we proceed, then that's what we will do."

Donatella could sense some unrest stirring within her partner, and it was making her feel uneasy. The two rode the next few miles in silence with different thoughts pulsating through their minds.

Although Buckley agreed to her partner's plan, she had no intention of keeping that word. She needed to find an opportune time to make her way into the building, with or without her partner. The more she thought about it, the more she believed going without her partner was the better option. But she would need an alibi after what transpired in the Alexander case. She would make the determination when the time was right on how she would proceed.

Dabria spent the time looking at the file again. She had been with the Bureau for a few years, but she did not recall hearing about Aaron Smithville. Indeed, there were other criminals who had a jacket similar to Smithville and she certainly did not know them all. However, there was something about this one that continued to stick out in an oddly familiar way.

After a few moments of reviewing the file, Donatella realized she was now absentmindedly flipping the pages. Her thoughts had gone elsewhere, *again*, she thought. Her subconscious told her she would need to watch Terri, and by the end of this day, her subconscious would prove to be correct.

December 11th – 5:30 p.m

DONATELLA PULLED her black Audi R8 Coupe, fully loaded with black rims, smoked grey window tint and red calibers, into her three-car garage. The four Michelin Pilot Sport Cup 2 R tires came to rest at their familiar spot in the dimly lit space. Countless thoughts raced through her mind as she made her way through the garage. Fifteen more people dead at the hands of Terri Buckley. Every time she felt she was gaining ground, she suddenly realized how far away she truly was.

She depressed the garage door button activating the garage. Her shoulder stung slightly when she rotated it to reach the button. During her last encounter with Terri, she had suffered two minor injuries, a shot in the left shoulder and another in her right leg. Both wounds had healed; however, from time to time she could still feel the effects from that battle.

She turned the handle of the door leading into the house, "Garage door open" the mechanical voice announced. A new update to the security system after the home intrusion she experienced months prior. As the insistent tone of the alarm system escalated in urgency, she entered in the six-digit code. Satisfied with her entry, the tones diminished, and thoughts of Buckley resurfaced.

She was escalating at an alarming rate even for her, she thought as she ambled through the kitchen. Donatella retrieved a bottle of smart water from the pantry as she made her way toward the foyer.

The foyer, the centerpiece within her Toll Brothers two-story chateau, had double helix staircases that wound toward the top floor. The polished marble flooring reflected the isolated table located by the front door. Donatella approached the table and gazed affectionately at the blue ocean breeze orchids that rested in the vase. Absentmindedly the enchantment of the flowers brought back fond memories of her mother.

"MAMA, what kind of flower do you have planted in our yard?"

"Well sweetheart," Mrs. Dabria stated while running her fingers through her daughter's silky long dark hair, "The flowers are not planted in our yard, they are planted in our flower bed. But to answer your question the flowers I have planted are called blue ocean breeze orchids. Why do you ask my dear?"

Biting her bottom lip and searching her mother with her hazelnut eyes, Donatella responded, "All of our neighbors have those red flowers –"

"Roses," her mother corrected.

"Right! All of our neighbors have roses planted in their yards, I mean flowerbeds, and we have these blue flowers, blue orchids. Why do we have to be different?"

With a natural smile that ran from ear to ear and lit up every room she walked into she responded, "My dear Donatella, in life we do not need to conform to what we see others doing or follow the trends that others have set forth. I think red roses are beautiful; however, it takes a special green thumb to grow a blue orchid. Your grandmother taught me the key to having the orchids bloom this color blue and I have never shared that secret with anyone else. When you get older my daughter, I will share the secret with you, and should you choose to grow your own blue orchids you'll be able to perfect this color as well."

Donatella looked inquisitively at her mother with another question hanging precariously from her tongue. A pregnant pause later she formed the courage to ask her next question. "Mama, do I have to turn my thumb green to grow them?"

Mrs. Dabria let out a boisterous laugh she could feel deep within her gut. Holding her stomach and composing herself she simply said, "No sweetheart, you will not have to turn your thumb green."

ALLOWING the memory to fade from her subconscious, she leaned forward and took a gentle whiff of the flowers. A month prior to the death of her parents, Donatella's mom shared with her the secret to help the orchids blossom blue. Donatella and her mother planted the buds the night before leaving for the trip. It wasn't until a few months later, when the orchids began to blossom, that Donatella even thought about the flowers again. The memories of the two of them planting the flowers and that being the last moment she spent with her mom came flooding back to her once again. She broke down in a stream of sobs and tears. Donatella vowed she would keep the tradition going and would always keep a vase of blue ocean breeze orchids present in her house. Donatella released her hold of the orchids, gave them a longing look and proceeded up the left side of the double helix staircase.

Once she reached the comfort and solitude of her bedroom, she sat on the edge of the bed and peeled off her Nisolo Heeled Chelsea Boots. She squared the shoes at the edge of the bed before repositioning herself in the middle of her bed where she sat cross legged with a firm straight back. She slowly closed the lids of her eyes and began to recount what started this feud, this hatred from Terri Buckley – The Smithville case.

Smithville – 4 years prior

THE SILENCE in the sedan was thick with anticipation and heavy with unanswered questions. The stiff breeze pounded on the exterior of the car rocking it slightly as if it was a bassinet. Donatella shifted her eyes to her partner who looked to be deep in thought. For the third time while leaving the FBI building, she wondered, *what are we doing here?*

Buckley turned her head, chin resting on her shoulder, eyes locked in a motionless bond with the hazelnut eyes of her partner. The two studied each other wordlessly until Buckley reached down to the center console, retrieved the binoculars and diverted her attention back to the window.

For this to be a high-powered operation, Donatella couldn't help but notice the obvious lack of security. There was a nagging feeling in the back of her head that something didn't add up. She continued looking at, glaring at her partner. She noticed how her muscles tensed and agitation radiated from every fiber of her being.

She prepared to break the silence when Buckley flung the door open, raced across the street toward the home of Aaron Smithville. Pushing the words back down her throat, she yanked her door open and sprinted after her partner. She was about to call out when she decided against it. Any such noise could bring attention to their approach and blow their cover. What cover they had left that is.

"What the hell is she thinking?" Donatella said out loud as she needed to utter some words for her ears to hear. She continued pumping her arms following Buckley around the back of the house. Although she considered herself to be relatively fast, Buckley was just a hair faster. In this particular instance she seemed to be moving faster than Donatella could remember.

By the time she turned the corner to the back of the house, Buckley was nowhere to be found. She stopped in her tracks and surveyed her surroundings. "Where did she go?" Foolishly, she did a 360-degree spin but soon logic hit. There is only one place she would have gone. She scrutinized Smithville's house. Upon closer inspection she recognized a door flush against the wall with a barely perceptible handle.

How in the hell did she know this was here she pondered, placing her hand through the opening and pulling the door open.

Once inside, she unholstered her Sig Sauer P226 pistol and stalked down the dark corridor. She tuned her ears to pick up any ambient noises; however, the corridor was as quiet as it was dark. It took her eyes a few moments to adjust and once they did she could see the faint outline of stairs ascending roughly 20 paces in front of her.

Agent Dabria pushed past her fear of the unknown and

quickly, but silently, climbed the stairs in an effort to ascertain the whereabouts of her now rogue partner. At the landing she was greeted with another door. Instinctively she knew Buckley had gone this way, yet the hairs at the nape of her neck stood signaling imminent danger.

She steadied her breathing, which surged with a rush of adrenaline, turned the handle of the door, and with a silent count of three, pushed the door open. Her gun snapped up, eye level, trained down the metal sights scanning for any adversarial movement. There was none. In fact, the hallway was empty. The hairs on her neck relaxed but her heart was still pounding.

The hallway, wide enough to accommodate two elephants standing side by side, nose to tail, was roughly 40 yards long. Although lights illuminated the corridor, visibility was still somewhat poor.

Donatella surveyed her surroundings and noticed that all of the doors were closed and eerily silent. *Where are all of the guards and where is Buckley*? She progressed down the hallway on the balls of her feet in an effort to reduce any noise she might make. She realized after taking a few steps forward that the awkward lighting worked to her advantage. There was only one door with light emanating from underneath it, the last one on the left.

Cautiously, but with haste she moved toward the door. She could feel her heart pounding against her rib cage as a multitude of thoughts processed through her mind. This case was given to them from their superior, for a suspect she had never heard of prior to today. The manner in which Buckley had been acting. Her running out of vehicle, presumably into this building after the two of them agreed to survey the surroundings before making any move. The –

"WHO THE HELL ARE YOU?"

The yell coming from the room at the end of the hallway forced Donatella to give up her stealthy approach. She took off in a sprint down the hallway, Sig Sauer poised in her right hand. Upon reaching the door she burst in gun raised, looking for any target.

What she saw gave her a moment of pause. Buckley stood, both arms extended, right hand on the grip of her pistol, left hand cradling the bottom. Buckley's eyes didn't move when Donatella burst into the room, but what Donatella saw behind those eyes is something she would never forget. The tinge of hurt mixed with the full fury of rage, and every intent of murder.

Agent Dabria quickly surveyed the room for occupants. Eyes still locked behind the sights of her weapon she looked to the right of the room – no one. She looked behind Buckley – no one. Entering the room and walking to her left Donatella began to survey the left side of the room – no one. She continued to circle to the left so that she could obtain a better view of the room and so she could also keep an eye on the door she had just come through. If there were any adversaries in the building, she didn't want to have her back to them should they come lumbering down the hall ready to fire.

Laying on a sofa that was centered inside the room was the man she had seen in the file provided by Buckley, Aaron Smithville. His hair was disheveled, eyes semi-glazed over as if he had just awakened from sleep. He slowly began to sit up, hands raised and clarity forcing its way into his vision. He still had not noticed Donatella's entrance into the room as he was completely focused on the figure in front of him holding the gun.

Once he was in a fully seated position, he blinked twice, and Donatella swore she saw a look of disbelief in his eyes instead of fear. Recognition drew over his features.

"Becky? Becky Lurtire?"

Becky, Donatella thought. Who in the hell is Becky? Gun still trained on the doorway, she chanced a glance over at her partner. Buckley stood there, fixed in place like granite. The involuntary blink of one's eyes had not touched her face and her gun had not once wavered.

"What the hell are you doing in my house?"

In a flat, emotionless, calmly sadistic voice "I'm going to kill you."

"You're going to what?" Aaron replied with a grunt of laughter.

"I'm going to apply pressure with my index finger to the trigger of this gun, and I'm going to blow your fucking head off, you sick bastard!"

"Terri!" Donatella exclaimed finally finding her voice. "You cannot do that!"

The other two occupants in the room turned toward the sound of her voice, noticing her in the room for the first time.

"Who in the hell are you? Are you here to kill me too?" he asked with a sardonic grin.

"Terri, you cannot shoot this man! Holster your weapon. Please, Terri! Holster your weapon."

"Becky, Terri, whatever your name is, I suggest you listen to the woman. Besides, you don't have the guts to shoot me so do what she said and holster your weapon!"

Donatella noticed the slight shift in her partner's finger as she started applying pressure to the trigger. *She really was going to shoot him!* In that split second, and without understanding why, Donatella turned her gun toward Buckley.

"Terri, this man is unarmed, you have broken into his house, and you are threatening to kill him in cold blood. You know I cannot let you do that. Please, put your gun away."

"You don't understand what this man has done! You don't understand who he is!"

"Why don't you put your gun away and we can talk about what he has done and who he is."

Although Donatella spoke the words, she had a clear sense that Buckley had not heard any of them.

"When I was just 18 years old, a freshman at college, I met Aaron. He was the star point guard on the basketball team. At the time he was a junior who had ambitions of going to the NBA. Being a student of the university, we received discounts for season tickets to all sporting events and I attended each of the basketball games. There was a time I wanted to play basketball, but by the time I was a sophomore in high school it was clear I wasn't cut out for it. Nonetheless, I still liked going to as many games as I could. To be honest I didn't know much about the team, nor much about Aaron. I simply enjoyed the game and wanted to support the university team.

One day as I walked across campus leaving from my math lecture, there were a group of boys, men, coming from the opposite direction. I smiled and spoke, and they returned the gesture; however, one of the boys came hustling back.

"Excuse me. Excuse me, Miss."

I realized the voice was talking to me, so I turned around.

"I've seen you before, haven't I?"

"I don't think so."

"Yes, I have! I would never forget such a beautiful face." He placed his forefinger across the bottom of his chin and squinted his eyes. "I know where I've seen you!" You sit in the student section directly behind the basket at the basketball games. Anytime I'm at the free throw line I look to see if you are still there. I don't think you have missed any games!"

He introduced himself as Aaron and flashed that perfect smile. He asked if he could have my number and who was I to refuse.

The star basketball player asking me for my number. Me, a freshman, being asked for my number by a guy who could have any woman on the campus. I gave him my number and to this day, I wish I never had!"

A tear that had been forming in the corner of her eye, pushed over her eyelid and rolled down her cheek leaving a trail of salty wetness that ended at her chin. Donatella could still see the pressure being applied to the trigger, but no additional pressure had been added. Terri continued to focus her intent glare on Aaron.

"A week later he called and asked if he could stop by my dorm room later that night. I agreed and told him my dorm and room number. When he knocked on the door, my heart skipped a few beats, but I managed to compose myself. I opened the door and there he stood again with his perfect smile. I let him in and noticed something that at the time I hadn't paid much attention to – a red bow tied to the handle of the door.

As I shut the door and turned around, he had started to play a CD he put into my boombox. Naively, I asked him what he wanted to do. Did he want to just listen to some music or watch a little television. He responded, "You know why I'm here," and walked over toward me, put his arm around my waist and pulled me closer to him.

I could taste the Crest coming off of his breath as he kissed me and put his tongue into my mouth. I pulled away, at least I attempted to pull away, and told him this is not what I wanted. He pulled me to him with more force, this time placing his other hand on my bottom while simultaneously putting his tongue back in my mouth. I tried to push him away –"

"You lying bitch!" he snarled breaking the monologue.

Buckley increased the pressure on the grip of her Sig Sauer as her knuckles that were already bulging pushed tighter against her skin thus losing more of the elasticity.

"This sorry piece of shit raped me, in my own room. In my own bed. To a soundtrack he brought specifically for the occasion. When he was done, he ejected the CD, opened the door and removed the red bow that was tied to the handle of my door. I later realized the red bow was a universal sign within the dorm that sexual activity was taking place in the room. It was meant for the roommate so they knew what could be happening behind the door and for them to enter at their own risk.

Little did he know; my roommate had gone home for the weekend. I lay in my bed motionless and crying for the next three hours. The silence in the room was maddening against the wails of my tears pouring into my pillows."

"I never told anyone. Not one person"

"That's because you are a lying bitch! That never happened!"

"I felt karma had caught up to Mr. Aaron Smithville as he shattered both knees and fractured his spine in a car accident a couple of days later. Although he was not paralyzed, he would never play basketball again and there went his dream of going to the NBA.

For years I thought this would be enough; however, about a year ago I was serious with a guy for the first time since this happened. When we prepared to make love, I froze, I screamed, and all of the memories and the pain came flooding back at once. I made him leave and cried into my pillows again for hours.

I could not live this way, and I would not live this way. Him losing his career was not enough for me. I needed," another tear rolled down her cheek. "I needed for him to lose his life. Then and only then could I move on."

"Terri," Donatella said taking a step toward her partner. "We can arrest him, right here, right now, and make him pay for his crimes. If you kill him, you are throwing your life away. And you know I cannot let you kill him."

"Donatella," she said turning those brown eyes that were filled with murderous intent. "If I don't kill him, I'm throwing my life away. You should understand that!"

There was a part of Donatella that understood where she was coming from, Donatella had every intention of killing the people responsible for killing her parents. Although she had never told this to anyone, she could tell that Terri sensed this about her. However, Aaron had not killed anyone. What he did he should be brought to trial for and be sentenced accordingly.

Terri slowly turned her head back to Aaron Smithville and for the first time since Donatella burst through the door, she saw Terri blink her eyes. It was a slow exaggerated blink, one that made Donatella think she had made up her mind – she was going to pull the trigger.

"Daddy," a voice came from the doorway into the room.

Donatella, Buckley, and Aaron simultaneously turned toward the noise. There, in the entrance, stood a little girl roughly 5 years old holding a pink teddy bear with a white shirt that said, "I love you beary much".

Training kicked in and Donatella had swung her gun toward the sound while applying pressure to her own trigger. Heart pounding and adrenaline pumping she nearly pulled the trigger, but somewhere in her subconscious she recognized the voice as that of a child and she paused.

Wiping her eyes and trying to bring her world into focus the little girl asked, "Daddy, who are these people and why is everyone making so much noise?" Without realizing it, the little girl, half asleep, continued making her way toward Aaron until she was sitting next to him on the sofa. She curled her feet up on the sofa and lay her head in the lap of her father.

Buckley tracked the toddler's progression from the threshold of the door until she reached her father sitting on the couch – all the time eyes unblinking.

"Terri, you have to put the gun away. There is a child, an innocent child that doesn't need to be involved in the middle of this."

Buckley, arms still fully extended, didn't waver. The pressure she had exerted on the smooth finish of the trigger hadn't lessened. The rage in her eyes still burned.

"Do you remember the Alexander case?" Buckley asked in the flat voice that originated from thousands of miles away. "Do you remember Ashley Lewis? The 13-year-old girl that was raped, strangled, and then buried in a shallow grave. Do you remember when we apprehended the suspect? Do you remember the trial? Do you remember the not guilty verdict handed down by the jury of his peers? DO YOU REMEMBER HIS SMILE AS HE WALKED OUT!?

I will not trust the system that failed 13-year-old Ashley Lewis. I will not trust the system that allowed the man who did what he did to her to walk free. I will not trust the system that left the mother and father of that poor little girl sobbing in the courtroom after the verdict was rendered.

I still hear their sobs. When I think back to what happened to me and I cry into my pillows, I hear their sobs. Their sobs are my sobs and my burden.

I will not trust the system to exact the necessary justice for this – this monster. I'm here, at this moment, right now, and I will exact justice for me, for Ashley, and for anyone else the system has failed!"

The tear that left its trail on Terri Buckley's cheek had completely dried and no new tears were forming. The intent to kill this man had etched itself over every ounce of her face.

"Terri – the little girl. You can't"

"I can – and I will!"

A single shot was fired.

7

The report of the gunshot reverberated around the enclosed space as the little girl that had curled up on the sofa to sit with her daddy began to scream. Donatella quickly holstered her gun and pulled out her phone.

"I have a 10-3 and a 10-24. Agent has been shot and needs medical assistance." She rushed over to the sofa where Aaron Smithville sat stunned at the developments. "Mr. Smithville, I'm going to need you to stand up. You are still going to be placed under arrest."

His daughter clinging to him and still screaming, he did as he was told. "It's going to be alright, sweetheart," he said. As he stood and Donatella placed the flex cuffs around his wrist, he looked down at Terri Buckley, who now lay on the ground clutching her right shoulder. "Serves you right you lying bitch!"

"Sit down and shut your mouth!" Donatella spewed as she pushed him back in his spot on the sofa. His daughter once again clung to him and began to pull herself under control.

Donatella walked over to her partner and took a knee. Terri Buckley had not said a word since Donatella had pulled the trigger.

"Terri, I'm sorry. I couldn't let you kill that man, especially in front of his daughter." Terri simply looked at her with cold, brown eyes. The murderous intent had been removed and had been supplanted with hatred.

DONATELLA WAS JOLTED back into reality by the vibrations from her phone. She opened her eyes and peered down at the screen, *BJ*.

Bryce Jacobs who goes by "BJ" was a child genius. At the age of 15 he scored a perfect score on the ACT, 36 out of 36, followed up the next week with a perfect score on the SAT, 1600 out of 1600. BJ spent most of his academic youth in fruitless fights with his instructors as he felt he knew more than they could offer. Finally, at the age of 15, with perfect scores on both the ACT and the SAT, he petitioned to be accepted into MIT though he had not received his high school diploma. He won his petition, enrolled that same fall and within two years he graduated summa cum laude and sat at the top of his class.

At 18, he had graduated from the top technology school in the country and concluded his fight with the academic system. However, he hadn't planned for what was next. Bored out of his mind, he decided he would write an algorithm that would predict the outcome of the lottery. Many people had used mathematical formulas before to predict where the winning scratch off tickets would land, but no one had truly succeeded in predicting the lottery numbers.

BJ focused his initial efforts in his hometown of Chicago, Illinois. The winning numbers obtained by normal and legal means could be pulled from the lottery's website. However, the data only went back one year. He knew he would need more data for his statistical analysis, so he broke into the lottery database and was able to retrieve 25 years of lottery data. Within three months he was able to correctly predict the Pick 3 95% of the time, the Pick 4 80% of the time, and the Lotto 55% of the time.

He popped up on the FBI radar when he accessed the lottery databases in four other states: Ohio, Virginia, Tennessee, and North Carolina. Agent Dabria was put in charge of the case and she worked meticulously to collar this criminal. However, he would not face any jail time. Although he had accessed databases illegally across multiple states, he did not profit from his efforts. He had not played the lottery and he had not capitalized on the algorithm that he created. He was put on five years of probation at the request of Agent Dabria and the two stayed in constant contact over the years.

Every so often Agent Dabria would reach out to BJ when she needed something done that she felt toed the ethical line, figured no one else could do, or simply because she also didn't like to follow the rules.

"Yes BJ?" she answered while pulling the phone to her ear.

"It's B – wait, you called me BJ. Is everything alright? You hardly ever –"

"Bryce, it's been a long day and it's getting late, what do you need?"

"Well at least you are straight to the point, as always. Anyway, I heard about the fiasco at the headquarters of Global Insights Security. The more I heard, the more I began to question. See, Agent Dabria, the news reported that all 15 board and senior management members had been killed in the attack."

"Yes BJ, that is something that I already know."

"Hold on a minute. There may have been 15 people killed in the attack; however, there should have been 16."

With this, Donatella shifted to the edge of her bed and stood up. In situations like this, BJ was notorious for having some video proof and she wanted time for her laptop to power up so she would be ready.

"I found this to be curious to say the least. If there is a board meeting taking place, why was there a board member missing? So, I did a little research on my own. I temporarily tapped into the video feeds for Global Insights Security. I promise I didn't steal anything, I was simply a voyeur today.

I started by watching the video footage in the lobby of the building. Everything moved along as expected up to 11 a.m."

"What happened at 11 a.m.?" Donatella responded, urging BJ to quicken the story.

"At 11 a.m. the video footage went dark so I tapped into the video footage of the other cameras too. Each of them had gone dark as well. At exactly 11 a.m. I read about a technology that GIS was working on that recorded in 4-hour segments. Although they live stream the footage to an offsite storage facility, they always keep the 4-hour segment running onsite.

And before you ask, yes, I found out where the offsite storage facility is located. Yes, I snooped around in there as well. And yes, it too is completely blank. It became clear that someone wanted to keep what happened in this building a secret."

"Thanks BJ, but I'm not sure how this helps. We already know the murders took place during this window of time."

"Well if you would stay patient just a little longer, you'll understand."

"BJ," Donatella said in a tired voice. "I need for you to get to the point."

"Ok, ok, ok. I just sent you a video file from the garage underneath the GIS building. In particular I sent you the segment for the executive reserved parking area. Starting at 7 a.m., when the new video recording segment started, you see a number of executives pull into their reserved spots. By 8:30 a.m., every executive spot is accounted for. Fast forward past the 4-hour block we missed from 11 a.m. – 3 p.m. and you see –"

"An executive's car has been moved. Who's spot –"

Before the words could come out of her mouth, the camera zoomed into plate denoting, "Parking Reserved for V. King"

"The V. King this spot is reserved for is Mrs. Veronica King, COO," BJ stated, "I can confirm that at 7:15 a.m., she parked her car in that spot and walked into the building. However, by the time this massacre had ended, she was nowhere to be found.

I've sent you her address, phone number, and a quick write up on her as I know you will want to pay her a visit."

"BJ," she said with all sincerity, "You have done fantastic work. Thank you!"

And with that she disconnected the call.

Headline: ***Massacre at Global Insights Security***
www.TheSalReport.com
By: Sal Grandson

Today in the headquarters of Global Insights Security, GIS, an unknown substance was released in the board room wiping out the executive team. At this time, we do not know the motive for this senseless crime or if it was a terrorist act. The CEO and chairman of the board, Edward Stein, was among those who lost their life in the building this day. Stein, a respected member of the community, took over the company from his father.

Since he took over at the helm, the company has become one of the most well-respected security firms within the country.

Police and crime scene investigators have been milling in and out of the building since their arrival on the scene. Sources within the CMPD have confirmed that they do not have any suspects at this time. They continue to question employees that were in the building today as well as reviewing video footage in the hopes to find that one thread that will point them in the right direction.

Should any additional information become available, I'll have it right here on The Sal Report.

December 12th – 4:30 a.m

VERONICA KING AWOKE SUDDENLY from the nightmare that plagued her every time she closed her eyes. She recalled her husband, the no-good, cheating bastard, and his mistress tumbling to their death on the tarmac; however, in each version of her dream her daughter was being clutched in the arms of her father. Then the scene shifted to the glass board room. She could see her peers gasping for air while clawing feverishly at their throats to allow fresh air into their lungs.

For the third time this night the nightmare manifested into her, soaking through her pajamas with perspiration. Looking at the clock that now read 4:30 a.m. meant there was no reason for her to pretend that sleep was going to happen. Her daughter, Gina, lay snuggled next to her, oblivious to the horrors her mother had unleashed the previous day. Thinking about it made her want to retch. In fact, she had done so several times, ridding herself of all the food she had consumed that day. Now she just experienced dry heaves which made her throat raw and voice scratchy.

She pulled the covers back, also damp from her perspiration, and ambled out of the bed. She didn't know what this day would bring but one thing was for certain, she didn't want to deal with anyone given the state she was in and the things she had done.

She slipped on her robe to give her some warmth as she made her way to the kitchen. She would have a cup of coffee, take a hot, long shower and then climb back in bed. Today was Friday and she would keep Gina out of school. She couldn't bear the thought of leaving her unattended for one minute. She would not let her out of her sight. Not for anything!

As she turned the corner to enter the kitchen, she flipped on the light.

"Good morning, Veronica," a voice said as the lights began to illuminate the room.

Veronica King nearly peed her silk pajamas as the voice echoed across the room. It was a voice she would never forget and she would find out later that she had indeed peed herself.

"How - how did you get into my house?" she asked looking around frantically for any other intruders. *My daughter,* she thought now filled with fear.

As if she had read her mind Terri Buckley, who Veronica knew as Bree, said, "No worries, it's just me here. It's your first day on the job and you have a lot to do."

Although she should of felt a sense of relief, she didn't. This woman who sat across from her forced her to destroy the lives of people she called friends and that sick feeling started to creep over her again.

"Please have a seat, we have many things to discuss this morning."

In her mind she wanted to put up a fight and tell this woman to get the hell out of her house. She wanted to put her hands around her neck and squeeze the light out of her eyes. But she knew better. This woman had already proved to be well connected and any wrong move she made would put her daughter in danger – mortal danger.

She pulled her left foot, which felt like lead, from the ground and propelled herself forward toward the proffered seat. Once seated she could see three orb-shaped items sitting in a semi-circle in the middle of her island that were not there the night before. She also noticed a slender 12-inch metal tube located precariously next to the orb in the middle. The metal tube had a blinking red light about three-fourths of the way from the base of the object. Veronica prepared herself to ask a question but before she could a vertical light burst from each of the orbs. The lights stopped level with the top of the metal tube. The light formed the shape of an upside-down pyramid and was roughly 8 inches across. She stared in wonderment at the scene that had been laid out in front of her.

Veronica looked up at her visitor, Bree, who sat with a stoic expression on her face and then back down at the orbs. As she did, an image began to appear within the middle orb. This was followed by the one on the right and finally the one on the left. A silhouette was encased within the light masking the faces. However, she could tell enough from the silhouette to know that the person on the left was a slender man with a close crew cut. The one on the right was a heavy-set woman who wore her hair in a bob and a necklace around her neck. The person in the middle was also a woman. Veronica discerned from her erect posture that she had some level of physical fitness. Her hair cascaded down to her shoulders, barely touching on each side.

Realization hit her. Even though she could not make out any of their features, she was sure they could make out every feature on her. She suddenly became self-conscious.

"Veronica King," the feminine voice spoke from the base of the middle orb, "We are happy you have become part of the team."

As if I had a choice, she thought.

"We have had our eye on you for some time and I must say

we are proud of all of the things you have been able to accomplish on your own. However," she said leaning forward, "Your talents were being wasted sitting behind that pompous, sexist, and racist pig, Edward Stein. You've been facing an uphill battle, one you were surely going to lose yesterday, so – we decided to, let us say, intervene."

Countless thoughts began to run through Veronica King's head. *How long had they been watching me? How did they know what I was planning to do yesterday? What else do these people know?* And most importantly, *who are these people?*

"Undoubtedly," the voice continued, "You would like to know more about us and who we are."

Shit, are they able to read my mind as well?

"For now, we will forgo official personal introductions. We are simply known as The Syndicate in many circles. An organization that operates in the shadows providing services to our clients who need to have a problem fixed. You can think of us as fixers. We are also an enterprise that dabbles in commercial trade, and that Mrs. King, is where you and your company come into play."

An uneasy feeling began to well in the pit of her stomach and she needed to take a couple of deep breaths to quell another bout of dry heaves.

The slender man on the left picked up the dialogue. King began to wonder if structurally he was the right-hand man of this woman.

"The Cleveland Museum of Art located in Cleveland, Ohio needs an overhaul to their security system. Suffice it to say, we aided them in this realization last week and they are now scrambling to replace their security system with a state-of-the-art security system. What hasn't been shared with the public yet is that they will be hosting an art exhibit of the previously unseen works of Jackson Pollock. This lost work was discovered hidden in a buried chest and they have been restoring the work for the last two months.

We found out about the restoration efforts from one of our contacts and began to put the wheels in motion to acquire the said artifacts."

The heavy-set woman with the bob hair on the right began to speak.

"While their security in this day and age was pretty useless, it still presented us with challenges of extracting the artwork without being detected. They plan to complete the restoration efforts sometime in April and the exhibit will be held in June. We, or should I say, our client, does not want this artwork to see the light of day. Our client would like for us to procure the artifacts, each of them, so that they can be sold on the underground market where a buyer is already lined up."

The woman in the middle picked up the tale.

"As you can see there are a number of moving pieces and a relatively short period of time to achieve what we need to without anyone noticing.

Your firm is well renowned as the best security firm in the country, if not the world. We need for you to offer your services to them."

Veronica who listened patiently to the series of monologues that ran around her kitchen island scuffed at this request. She was now back in business mode and responded, "They could never afford our service, and this is not something our board would go for."

As soon as the words left her mouth, she realized with horror what she said.

The woman in the middle sat forward once again, steepled her hands in front of her and simply said, "Mrs. King, this is not a request. This is an order. You will offer your services, free of charge in fact, to the Cleveland Museum of Art. Write it off as a charitable donation if you must, but this will be done.

As for your board of directors, I'm pretty sure they do not have any objections."

This statement hung in the room for what seemed like a full minute. Veronica could sense the non-existent bile creating a lump in her throat.

The woman continued, "You will hold a press conference today to speak out on the horrors that took place at your company and buoy the confidence that many have known you for as you have risen in the ranks of GIS.

You will also begin looking for new board members. Don't worry, we already have a list of candidates for you to bring on board. See that this is done.

Lastly, you will reach out to the board of the Cleveland Arts Museum and let them know that your company would like to donate a security system to them. I personally do not care what story you spin to make this happen, but you need to make it happen, and it needs to be done today. They are preparing to send out bids and we prefer to keep this under wraps. Our associate Ms. Buckley will be in touch should we need anything further."

All three images simultaneously disappeared and the blinking red light on the metal tube dimmed and then faded. Veronica sat there speechless until Terri broke the silence.

"There is one more time sensitive project that you will need to accomplish and I expect you to be just as proficient with this one as I'm sure you will be in completing the task that has just been asked of you."

For the next 20 minutes Terri walked her through the auxiliary plan that she had for Veronica to complete. Once she was done, she packed her gadgets in a brown messenger bag and walked toward the front door. Before she left, she turned and gave Veronica an appraising up and down glance followed by a wink and said, "Welcome to the team."

Once outside, Terri walked to her rented black Mercedes CLA, fired up the engine and drove north. Coming from the south, the black Audi R8 Coupe of Agent Donatella Dabria pulled up and took the spot that was freshly vacated by Terri Buckley.

8

DECEMBER 12TH – 5:30 A.M

Agent Donatella Dabria pulled up to the house of Veronica King. Throughout the course of the night and first thing this morning, she read all of the material that was sent to her by BJ. King was married, one daughter, and Chief Operating Officer for Global Insights Security. She obtained her BA from the University of North Carolina at Chapel Hill and her master's degree from The Ohio State University. She later returned to North Carolina where she obtained her Juris Doctorate degree from UNC School of Law.

She came into GIS and earned everything that had come her way. From all accounts, she was a rising star and someone Donatella could respect. However, at this moment she had more questions than answers as it related to Mrs. King. By all accounts she was in the building prior to the incident but miraculously missing from the board meeting when the attack took place. As Donatella approached the door, she was determined that King would have some answers.

She considered the early call just before ringing the doorbell. Nonetheless she rang the doorbell and proceeded to wait. To her surprise Veronica opened the door with speed as if she was expecting someone. For a moment Donatella felt she exhibited a look of confusion as she was expecting someone else.

"May I help you?"

"I apologize for the early visit. My name is Special Agent Donatella Dabria with the Federal Bureau of Investigation. Do you have a few minutes for us to talk?"

She thought back to the conversation she just had with the woman calling herself Bree.

"IT'S ONLY a matter of time before you will be paid a visit from someone from the FBI. If I had to guess, it'll be from Special Agent Dabria. She's sharp and will likely know more about you than you would think is possible. Do not underestimate her!

She's going to want to know where you were and how you were able to survive when all of your peers did not. Keep your answers short and to the point. We have provided enough of a trail that your answers will hold up as long as you stick to the script. Do not deviate under any circumstance. She will pick up on the slightest hesitation or notable deception."

Veronica thought idly, *this is all a deception.*

"Lastly, and for some incentive, your daughter's life depends on you convincing her of what we have discussed. You do that and everything will be just fine. You don't and –"

Veronica knew exactly what this woman meant without it being spelled out for her. She would need to keep her composure, perhaps put on the best performance of her life.

"SURE, COME ON IN," she said opening the door fully. She led Special Agent Dabria down the hallway to the kitchen. "I was just about to put on some coffee. Can I interest you in some?"

"No thank you, and again, I apologize for coming at such an

early hour. With everything that has transpired, I know you and your husband must be out of your minds with grief."

Veronica remembered the advice – warning from her prior visitor and decided she better tread lightly.

"It certainly is a trying time for us all and all of the families who were affected by this barbaric travesty."

"Yes, a travesty," Agent Dabria responded in her warm, southern voice. "I must say, Mrs. King, I'm surprised that you were not present for the board meeting. I understand there were some key developments that pertained to your future with the firm."

This was a statement Veronica had not expected and she hoped the agent didn't pick up on her shock. *How did so many people know about this? Well maybe it wasn't a lot of people who had known. Just the two women she was dealing with at the moment.*

"I was in the office earlier that morning; however, my daughter came down ill at school and I had to go and pick her up."

"I see. I would think with such important developments taking place at work, your husband could have picked your daughter up from school."

Feeling a little indignant, she responded, "Special Agent Dabria, I take it you do not have children. If you did, you would know that nothing stands between a mother and the health of her child!"

"Forgive me," she said again in that smooth honey, southern voice, "By no means did I mean to offend. You are right, I do not have any kids, but I have a goddaughter and I would do anything to ensure her safety."

Veronica took this statement well and nodded her approval.

"Nonetheless, I would have thought with such a big day, your husband, Kyle, could have ensured your daughter's safety," she said this last part raising her eyebrow.

Veronica gave a tired laugh. "Ms. Dabria, would I be wrong in my assumption that you are not married as well? If you were, you would know that in many situations both the husband and the wife work. This is our situation as well. My husband, Kyle," the words felt like bile in the back of her throat, "Had to take a business trip yesterday morning. So, you see, it was left to me to ensure our daughter was, as you put it, safe."

She had to admit, she didn't like the choice of words the agent had used. Was she hinting that she knew her, and her daughter, were not safe? Possibly. During her conversation with the woman calling herself Bree – which she was sure was a lie – she had the vague sense that the two of them had a run in before. If this was the case, could she trust this agent? Could the agent keep her and her daughter safe? Could she tell her about the atrocity that she was forced to take part in for which she felt deeply ashamed? Could she – no she couldn't. The woman from the orb with the shoulder length hair had impressed upon her that she could not. She could not trust anyone when it came to keeping her daughter safe. No one but The Syndicate.

"Look, I hate to cut this short, but I have a lot of things to get done this morning. I feel horrible about everything that happened to my friends and colleagues yesterday. I am grateful in a sick way, that my daughter came down ill yesterday. If not for that, my daughter like many other children, would be waking to the realization that their mother or father would not be coming home again. As the only officer left in the company, it's up to me to answer the questions and alleviate fear."

"I understand," Agent Dabria said while standing. "If there is anything you need or if you recall anything else that will be of use, don't hesitate to give me a call." Veronica took the business card from the extended hand and with that Agent Dabria headed for the door. As she did so she thought, *I understand you truly feel horrible about what happened to your friends and colleagues. I also understand you are lying to me!*

December 12th – 10:30 a.m

SAL GRANDSON PRIDED himself on his network of informants and people in high places. During his time with the *New York Daily*, Sal managed to have a network so extensive that he had tips coming to him all hours of the day. So much so that he needed to pick and choose which leads to follow. However, since he arrived in Charlotte his network was growing slowly. Sal reminded himself that it wasn't the quantity of informants, but the quality. He also mused that quantity never hurt as well.

Nonetheless, today his stooge in the police department gave him an inside tip that the lone survivor of the massacre at the GIS headquarters was planning to make a public statement. The content of her press conference had not been divulged but Sal knew a story when it was staring him in the face. His journalist mind still wanted to know how she managed to survive while all of her peers had not. He was sure it was a simple explanation but he sensed there was more to it than that.

When he pulled up to the building, the scene was surreal. Police officers paced the perimeter looking for anyone they considered suspicious. They had what looked like assault rifles laying across their chests. Sal knew next to nothing about guns and that was ok with him. He also noticed a couple of bomb-sniffing dogs pacing peacefully next to their human handlers. A podium was being erected in front of the GIS building roughly 30 yards from the main entrance. Sal idly thought they would not be holding this press conference outside in New York; however, in Charlotte, the weather on this winter day had warmed up considerably and was hovering at a pleasant 57 degrees.

Sal continued his drive around the building looking for somewhere to park. At the moment, there were a couple of news affiliates setting up their camera equipment. A couple walking alongside the building rubbernecking to determine the reason for the commotion.

After moments of searching Sal found the perfect spot and parked his well-used yet still functional 2002 Honda Accord. The mileage continued to stretch skyward yet she still purred like a kitten.

"Once the remainder of the media outlets caught wind of a press conference being given by the lone member of the board, they will descend on this building like kids to a Christmas tree on Christmas morning," Sal spoke aloud while winding himself out of the car.

"Now that you're here Sal, old buddy, what's your plan? Maybe I'll just pull in for a front row seat. Nah, that won't do. There has to be something more. Think damn it, think."

Sal looked around the grounds for some inspiration to hit, or maybe a sign from the good Lord. Again, he noticed some stage-hands preparing the elevated podium. The police milling around with a keen eye for anything suspicious. A couple a squirrels running full speed chasing one another. And then – yes that was his ticket. He hadn't noticed it before because of the couple walking by that grabbed his attention, but there it was, right there in front of him.

Sal casually strolled down the street, pondering if he locked his car door, and keeping a keen eye toward his destination. "Slow and easy as if you are just another passerby," he said to himself. In 10 more paces he would be level with the edge of the GIS building and at least invisible to the majority of the police officers that were around. As he continued his straight path, one of the dogs turned its head and began to look – no glare at Sal. He wasn't sure if the dog could sense his nervousness and thus making him a suspect. Or could the dog just be taking interest in everyone walking around? Nonetheless Sal's breath was caught in his chest and it took his supreme will not to simply turn around and go back to his car.

The last two paces had Sal feeling like he was walking in mud but nonetheless, he was securely tucked against the side of the building. Once again, he focused on the object, his way in.

Parked at the loading dock was a service truck with the words Jerry's Rug Cleaning and Restoration painted on the side. From his vantage point, Sal figured they were taking rugs into the building and not bringing them out. When inclement weather hit, companies placed rugs over the marble to ensure guest security while walking across the floor. With a building this size it's bound to be a large number of rugs that need to be delivered. Sal noticed the two men riding in the cabin of the truck exit and each take a handful of rugs into the building. He also noticed that they left the door to the van open in an effort to expedite their process.

Sal continued to casually traipse toward the van scanning left and right to ensure no one was paying him any attention. All was clear. He approached the double doors at the back of the truck and took a quick look inside. Inside the truck he saw approximately 15 more rugs to be delivered into the building. Each set of rugs were affixed with a label denoting which floor they were to be delivered to. Sal looked around the van and settled on a set slated for the fifth floor.

Prior to hefting the rugs from their resting place, Sal took another look around. To his amazement, hanging against an interior wall of the truck rested a Jerry's Rug Cleaning and Restoration jacket. Sal pulled the jacket from the hanger pulling his arm through one sleeve and then the other. He grimaced realizing the jacket sleeves were too short. Pulling the bottom ends of the jacket together, he prepared to zip the jacket.

"Here goes nothing."

With a steady zip, the jacket closed; however, Sal felt if he took one too many deep breaths, the jacket would not hold.

"Better get moving."

Sal hefted a few rugs slated for the fifth floor and shuffled quickly toward the entrance. The last thing he needed was for the delivery men to appear at the loading dock while he made his approach.

Turning the corner and nearing the entrance Sal realized that the door the two delivery men entered was now closed. Next to the door sat a sign *Ring for deliveries.*

"Shit!"

Sal plastered his best smile to his face, depressed the bell, and waited.

"Yea," came a voice from the speaker box.

"Rug delivery for the fifth floor." Sal had noticed the camera hanging over the door and ensured the company name and logo could be seen on his jacket.

"I thought there were only two of you guys."

"Typically, that is the case; however, this is my first week and I'm sort of training. I'll have my own rotation starting next Monday." Sal could feel his insides doing flips. At that moment he wished he had opted for the cereal Jane had instead of the eggs and bacon he decided on earlier in the day.

"Yea, training for a new job can be the pits. I remember training for this job. I felt like I was being babysat for much too long." The magnetic lock disengaged "Come on in."

Sal let out a long stream of air he hadn't realized he was holding as he pulled the door open.

Once inside a young male around 25, a shade under 5 and a

half feet tall with freckles and red hair exited the delivery office off to the right side of the door.

"The elevator is right this way," the freckled face lad stated as he began walking deeper into the building. "Good luck on your training and maybe I'll see you around." He pressed the up button next to the service elevator.

"Thanks, I wouldn't mind being on this route full time. We make some interesting stops," he lied.

The elevator doors slid open noiselessly and Sal stepped inside. The young man hit the button for the fifth floor, nodded at Sal, "Have a good day sir." And walked back toward his office.

As the elevator cage began to lift toward floor five, Sal unzipped his borrowed jacket and began to breathe normally again. Now that he was inside the building, he pondered what he would do next? *Was it too bold to seek out the office of the lone survivor?* Sal had been bold before, sometime to his detriment, but he'd come this far he might as well see where it leads.

The elevator stopped moving and once again the doors slid open. Sal stepped from the elevator and quickly surveyed his surroundings. As he expected, no one was in sight. He placed the rugs next to the elevator, sitting the jacket on top. He began walking toward the center of the fifth floor when he heard a faint sound – almost like a whimper. He stopped dead in his tracks and held his breath. There it was again; he was sure of it. Someone was crying on this floor and the sound was traveling to his ears. He wasn't 100 percent sure where the sound originated, but he was sure it came from around the corner.

Sal cautiously stalked the edge of the wall, stooping below eye level so he could not be seen and chanced a glance around the corner. In an office diagonal from his location he could spy a woman dabbing at her eyes with a handkerchief and silently crying to herself.

She gave every impression that she was both consoling

herself and strengthening herself at the same time. She took a couple of deep inhalations, looked into the mirror that she held in her hand, and began silently sobbing once again. This chain continued two more times and was only broken by the sound of the main elevator cascading a *ding* across the empty floor.

The woman who was on the tail end of her latest sob, dabbed her eyes once again, took a deep breath and put the compact mirror away. She ran her hands through her hair, once, twice, and dabbed her leaking eyes one more time.

"Mrs. King," a voice said approaching the office from the elevator. "We are ready to get you downstairs and complete final preparations for your speech."

"Thank you," she responded with a voice much stronger than Sal would have thought she could muster.

So, this was the lone executive survivor. No wonder she is such a mess. And to think she now has to go and put on a brave face for the cameras. Terrible!

Sal watched as Veronica King stood from behind her desk, shuffled some papers on her desk, and walked out of the office – following the voice that had come to retrieve her. Once Sal heard the main elevator doors shut, he counted to 10 before making his way to the now vacant office.

Entering the office of Mrs. Veronica King, Sal began looking around without touching anything. On her mellette L-shaped executive desk there were a few files, awaiting attention, butted perfectly against the top right corner of the desk. Pictures of her family – her husband and herself in one picture, a picture of a baby in a second picture, and a picture of all three with Veronica cradling the baby with tender loving care. Stationary that read from the desk of Veronica King sitting next to an expensive looking pen and pencil set – both within arm's reach of her seated position. To her right, on the other half of the L-shaped desk, sat twin 26-inch wide screen monitors, a docking station for an Apple laptop, and a nondescript office phone.

Sal took another quick look over the desk, "Not much here at all." He stood in the center of the office and did a 360-degree rotation willing his eye to catch something of interest. Sal prepared himself to move on, realizing this gamble had not panned out. And if he was honest with himself, he knew this was a long shot.

Sal prepared to leave the office when he had another thought. He pulled out the high-back executive chair and sat down. To his left he found what he was looking for, the wastebasket. Nine times out of ten you can find some valuable items within someone's wastebasket. He pulled the cylinder from underneath the desk, "Pay dirt!"

Inside the trash receptacle he spotted stationary that had been torn into several pieces. While reaching his hand in to retrieve the paper he heard voices.

"He said he was part of the team and just going through training," came the voice of the freckled kid.

"We are the only two that are working this job," came from a voice he didn't recognize. "As you can see, the rugs are still sitting right here along with the jacket."

Alarms started sounding within Sal's mind. *Those damn noiseless elevator doors gave me no warning. And aren't their supposed to be chimes alerting to the direction the elevator is going once it hits your floor.*

"Call security," he heard a third voice speak closing the distance between them and his location.

Sal thrust his hand into the wastebasket and pulled out the shredded papers stuffing them in his pocket. A couple fluttered to the ground underneath the desk. Sal stood realizing he didn't have enough time to secure the fallen pieces and began making his way toward the door.

"There he is!" he heard bellow from the freckled face young man who had a walkie talkie plastered to his cheek.

Sal walked out of the office, turned to his right, and took off in a dead sprint.

"Hey you, STOP!" Sal heard the words trailing as he took off for the stairwell. He could hear the footsteps of all three men followed by, "He's headed for the north stairwell."

Sal burst through the closed doors wasting little time. Once he hit the stairwell, he began descending the flight leading from the fifth floor to the fourth floor. He heard a door open beneath his location, but it sounded as if it was a set of basement doors. He could hear the faint report of the walkie talkie and he knew he would not make it to the first floor before they did. Once he hit the fourth-floor landing, he continued descending to the third floor where he pulled on the door while simultaneously turning the handle. As he stepped through the doorway, he heard the door open above him. At this point, Sal took off in an all-out sprint, slowing briefly to press a button at the elevator bank. Sal hoped this slight diversion would give him the time he needed. He continued his path toward the back half of the floor aiming for the service elevator.

As he prepared to turn the corner, he heard two things happen at the same time. The *double ding* of the elevator announcing its arrival and denoting its intention to go down.

The second thing he heard was the door for the stairwell open, followed by gasping and hurried voices. "He took the elevator down to the first floor," he heard one voice state between pants. Sal turned the corner, now out of sight of his pursuers and depressed the down button. The service elevator arrived within six seconds and the noiseless doors opened once again. Sal pressed the button marked with a G and in another six seconds he arrived at his destination and headed to the delivery dock. He quickly made his way through the hallway and back to the comforts of the cool December breeze.

Sal turned the corner past the delivery truck quickening his pace back toward his car. At the edge of the building he was once again spotted by the dog that he encountered earlier. Sal looked at the dog, the dog stared at Sal. Sal then looked at the dog handler and realized he was listening intently to some radio chatter. The pair began to make their way toward the front entrance with the dog reluctantly following along.

December 12th – 11:00 a.m

VERONICA KING STOOD JUST inside the Global Insights Security building awaiting her moment on the podium. The sick feeling deep within the pit of her stomach was turning more rancid and for a moment she didn't think she could do this. However, she realized with absolute certainty, if she didn't, they would kill her daughter and likely spare her life for her own suffering. She was being forced to play out their game and to what end, for some God damn artwork?

So many people have already lost their lives because of this desire to gain money and prestige. The horrid look in Bev's eyes as she placed the stoppers underneath the door was something she would never forget.

However, she would also never forget the look on the face of Stein. From the moment their eyes locked as she walked into the board room, he could sense something was wrong. In that moment she felt power, unyielding power. A power that radiated through her core and manifested a glow to her skin.

As she and Stein stared each other down she could feel his resolve waver and he was the first to break eye contact in that moment. The moment she was about to sacrifice the life of everyone in that room to save her daughter. The moment she was about to ascend to the top seat in his granddaddy's company. The moment she would be the one to call the shots. In that moment she felt no remorse. For that racist, sexist, son of a bitch was about to meet his maker at the hands of a strong, intelligent, unforgiving woman.

He knew at that moment that he had lost. Just how much he had lost he didn't realize until the mist began to fill the room. Until the first person collapsed and he started to feel the effects of whatever spewed from the canister. He lost, and she had won.

Sitting in her office, Veronica was a mix of emotions. She felt horrible about what she had done. She felt horrible for the sons, daughters, husbands, and wives who had lost someone yesterday.

But - Veronica King felt free. She felt power. She was free because that cheating husband of hers and that hussy trollop met their end, and she only had to give the word. In that sense she had power. But she also now had the power to run Global Insights Security the way she wanted. There was no more good ole boys club. She made the decisions and deep, just below that sick feeling in her gut, she liked this power. What's done is now done and it was time she made the best out of a bad situation.

Veronica had been in business long enough to know that the tides do change and the wind does shift. The Syndicate had her in a compromising position and as the old saying goes, if you can't beat them...

"Mrs. King," the voice said breaking her train of thought. "We are ready for you."

The two walked toward the entrance of GIS headquarters where two police officers were holding the door open for her. As she stepped to the podium, all eyes and cameras trained on her, ready to hang on every word she had to say, she had a thought.

Are they really ready for me? Are they really ready for the new Veronica King? In a moment of reflection, yesterday's events and the conversation in her kitchen earlier this morning had taught her a valuable lesson. It's not good enough to be the best at what you do. Sometimes you have to be flat out ruthless.

"Thank you everyone for your time here today. Before I begin, let us first have a moment of silence for everyone who was tragically taken from us in that heinous, cowardly attack yesterday..."

PART II

Orchestration

9

FEBRUARY 4TH – 11:15 A.M

Patti Jones traversed the dank, semi-dark corridor toward the double doors at the end of the hallway. Her soundless heels padded the floor with each step as she loosened the medical gloves from her long frail fingers. Her colorless hand pressed against the cold stainless steel, and as she did, she recalled what brought her to this place in life.

From the age of seven Patricia "Patti" Jones knew she would be a doctor. She started her doctoral career performing complex operations on her Barbie dolls. It started simple with stitches and creating a splint to set a broken bone. Then she graduated to delivering a baby and then on to heart surgery. Of course, this was all fictitious; however, for Patti it was real.

Patti's parents hardly spent any time with her, and since she was an only child her make believe world was her reality. It was there that she felt connected to the happenings in the real world, though everything she was experiencing was not real. When she played doctor, she always had her trusty imaginary assistant, Claude, with her to ensure the surgeries and deliveries went as expected. The need and the draw to be a surgeon was all Patti could think about day in and day out.

At the age of 12 she began reading any book she could get her hands on that dealt with being a practicing surgeon. She read case studies during the day and technical books before bed. When the books were not enough, she would search online for videos that focused on her career aspirations. The more books she read and the more videos she watched, the more she fell in love with becoming a surgeon.

Once enrolled at the state university, Patti breezed through the perfunctory undergraduate classes that are meant to make students well-rounded and prepare them to enter med school. This; however, is where things took an unexpected turn for Patti.

On a warm summer day in June, Patti and her medical laboratory partner were tasked with dissecting a human corpse. All of her adolescent hobbies and college training had brought her to this point. Eager to delve into the process, Patti requested that she go first and her partner had no objection to that.

Patti walked calmly over to the stainless-steel medical tray and began to reach for the scalpel. As she did, something happened to Patti that she would have never imagined – her hand began to shake. She looked down at her right hand in disbelief, willing it and begging it to stop. But the shaking continued in earnest. To make matters worse, she began to feel as if she was short of breath. For whatever reason, her body was failing her at this crucial point in her life.

Her partner, realizing what was happening, tapped Patti on the shoulder and said she would go first. Dumbfounded, Patti couldn't find any words to move from her mind through her vocal cords. The best she could do was take a couple of steps backward while her partner picked up the scalpel and began the dissection. By the time class had concluded, every pair in the room had performed admirably on the task, even Patti and her partner. However, her partner had done all the work while she stood by hands still shaking and breath still shallow.

That evening she went back to her apartment trying to determine what happened to her. In conducting her online research, she determined she was likely suffering from a panic attack. She found it hard to believe but she couldn't deny she exhibited some of the symptoms. She concluded in her mind that this was a one-time occurrence and that she would persevere the next time.

However, the next time, and each time after that she felt that same sense of dread as her symptoms began to manifest once again. Patti, a girl who achieved everything she wanted in life up to this point, was devastated. She wasn't sure where she should turn or what she should do. She tried talking it through with her parents but both of them were completely useless, something she felt all the time while growing up.

She sought refuge in her academic advisor, Charlie Maxwell, and what he told her was devastating.

"Patti, academically you are one of the most gifted students to come into our med school. But these," he searched to find the right words, "Attacks you keep having are greatly inhibiting your chance to proceed through med school as a surgeon. Have you strongly given consideration into a different avenue in medicine that you could take?"

She hadn't. Being a surgeon was all she thought about since she was seven years old. There was no Plan B and certainly no Plan C.

After spending several weeks contemplating her next move, she decided she would transfer into the nursing program. She couldn't bear the thought of going through medical school with all the classmates that witnessed her fail so miserably. She needed to move into a program where she could start over. Transferring to the nursing program was a blow to her ego but she knew deep in her heart that she was not going to succeed in medical school.

Nursing school for Patti went pretty much how all of her normal schooling went – she breezed through without any complications. She finished at the top of her class and by all accounts everyone saw her as an absolute success.

This placated Patti for a while but there was still that burning desire deep through her core to pursue her dream. She began to wonder with the passage of time, would her anxiety, her panic attacks, subside to the point that she could achieve her dream? Not likely, she continued to tell herself but that fire still burned.

Upon graduation, Patti secured a nursing position at Good Samaritan Hospital in Dayton, Ohio. The work was pleasant enough and she made several friends – family on her shifts. Although she was the youngest nurse on the staff, the other nurses treated her as an equal and none of them became territorial. The city, from what she understood, was once a thriving, prosperous city, was now a shell of itself.

Many of the Fortune 500 headquarters that resided in the city during the '80s and '90s had shuttered their doors and moved their headquarters to another state. Communities that had children playing in the streets until the streetlights illuminated the sidewalks were now dilapidated ghost towns that were rife with crime and prostitution. The citizens residing within the city limits seemed to age at double the rate than those who lived outside the city limits.

Yet given this, Patti, a career overachiever, was satisfied with calling this place home – because Patti had a secret. A dark, lucrative secret.

Patti walked through the stainless-steel door into a bright white operating room. Within this room stood several nurses in full green scrubs, faces partially obscured by the matching mask. In the middle of the room lay a woman on a birthing table, arms spread perpendicular to her body. The abdomen and upper half of the woman was visible to Patti as she walked through the operating room door. The remainder of the woman's body was obscured with a makeshift contraption similar to a curtain. Patti gave the woman a reassuring smile as she passed by preparing for what was next to come.

By this time Patti had brought a dozen children into this world by cesarean delivery and she had no reason to believe this one would be any different. Her team was both practiced and proficient in the choreographed dance about to take place. Patti adjusted her mask into place and was ready to begin.

The woman was still conscious but had been given a nerve block prior to being wheeled into the operating room and could not feel anything that was happening to her body. All she knew was the time was drawing ever closer for her to meet her baby boy. She didn't have anyone in the delivery room with her as she had come to the hospital alone. The baby's father ran out on her when he was told she was pregnant and her family, a strictly catholic group, had disowned her for bringing a baby into this world without being married.

She was introduced to Patti during one of her well visits at the hospital because she had been a nervous wreck. Patti turned on the charm and within minutes she comforted the woman by helping her understand the changes her body would go through during the pregnancy. She also helped her understand how she should deal with the emotional highs and lows that she would experience.

As the months flew by this woman began to rely more and more on Patti and her sage wisdom. Patti had been there during the ultrasounds to ensure that the baby was growing as expected. The woman had called on Patti several times at 1 and 2 o'clock in the morning when she was fighting through bouts of morning sickness and in some cases just because she couldn't sleep. Patti reassured her that she didn't mind and that the woman could call her anytime she needed. The woman had grown to trust and rely on Patti and this trust and reliance was key for what Patti had in store.

Earlier that day, the woman called on Patti because she felt strange, as if she was having contractions. Patti, who by that point had promised she would take her to the hospital when it was time to deliver the baby, said she would be right over. Within minutes she arrived at the woman's house and drove her directly to the hospital. Instead of going to the entrance meant for labor and delivery, Patti drove her into an entrance underneath the hospital. Although the woman thought this strange, she had absolute trust in Patti.

When they arrived, there was a nurse waiting with a wheelchair. Patti maneuvered the car haphazardly next to the waiting woman and unlocked the door. Two other nurses materialized from the dark recesses of the building to aid the woman into the wheelchair and in a flurry, she was whisked into the waiting doors and into an open elevator.

Now, as the woman watched the makeshift curtain shaking from left to right and then right to left, she knew the moment was drawing closer and her excitement grew. She couldn't wait to hold her son in her hands. A life she created, a life she would do anything to protect. Although the baby's father wanted nothing to do with him and her family had disowned her, her son would know nothing but love. Unconditional, everlasting love.

Just then she heard a whimper, a cry. Her son's first sounds. She knew instinctively what was to come next from all the labor and delivery videos that she watched in the middle of the night when she could not sleep. They would need to go and suction the mucus from the baby and give him a quick clean and then he would be all hers.

She turned her head so she could see the action as best she

could and she heard another whimper, another cry. The other nurses in the room had their backs to her and their collective bodies were partially obscuring her view. She could faintly make out the table that they were going to suction the mucus from her son and for a brief moment – just for one moment she saw her son. In that moment she could see his fine, dark hair plastered to his scalp. His little nose, it looked so tiny, and his perfect little lips. And then she could see no more.

She waited with great anticipation for what seemed like 30 minutes. Distantly she heard a door open, to which she paid no mind because the bodies were parting and her baby was surely making his way to her. However, when the last body had parted she saw Patti standing there in front of her empty handed.

She wildly looked around for the nurse who was holding her baby – bringing him to her, but no other person came forth. She looked into the face of Patti and she saw both concern and triumph washed over her features.

"Susan," she said in her familiar soothing voice. "I'm sorry to tell you but your son – he was stillborn. He didn't make it."

Susan finding her voice yelled a faint whisper, "What do you mean my son was stillborn? I heard him. I saw him. He cried on at least two, if not three, occasions." Susan could feel the panic rising in her.

"I assure you he made no sounds as he took no breaths."

Susan struggled to wrap her mind around the words that were assaulting her ears. She knew without a shadow of a doubt that her baby had been born. She knew she heard his cry. She looked at Patti with an intensity she had never felt before.

"Bring me my baby! Bring him here."

"Susan we cannot do that. In a situation in which the baby is stillborn, we immediately have him or her checked to see what may have caused this abnormality."

Feeling stronger her whispered yell came with more ferocity,

"Bring me my baby now!" She wanted to get up and go find her baby, but the nerve block made it impossible to move her lower body.

"I'm sorry, Susan," Patti said before turning and walking toward the door. Behind her she could hear the continued pleas from Susan until she walked through the stainless-steel door and it had closed behind her.

Outside of the operating room she walked up to the figure waiting for her in the hallway. The figure, a slender woman in her mid-40s, stood patiently in her black knee-length pencil dress.

"Did the transfer go as planned?" Patti asked in a flat voice.

"Yes," responded the woman in a high nasally voice. The Dumont's are the proud recipients of a healthy baby boy and the agreed upon sum has been transferred into your account."

"Thank you, Beth," came the reply.

"And what should we do about Susan?" the woman asked looking back at the door.

"No need to make it complicated. She has an IV in place, give her enough morphine to permanently end her pains. Have Raul and Ricky dispose of the body," she said without an ounce of the compassion she had shown to the woman waiting on the other side of the door.

"See to it that this is done quickly and that the room is sterilized. I have a feeling Amy Johnson will be ready to pop any day now."

February 4th – 11:15 a.m

DETECTIVE CARL SAMPSON stewed while he idly spun in his office chair with his face aimed toward the ceiling. Over a month had passed and he had not apprehended the person responsible for the death of Samantha Taylor and, worse, the massacre at GIS headquarters. Every lead he reviewed led to a spiderweb of misinformation. He had to admit that the trail, as sensational as it was, had now gone cold. His only solace came from the knowledge that the FBI woman, Donatella Dabria, had not solved the case as well.

On several occasions he wondered if she purposefully withheld information from him to solve the case herself. Several times he picked up his desk phone and began dialing the number to her cell phone. Each time he stopped with his finger poised above the last digit and hung up the phone. It was better to believe the FBI agent didn't have any additional information than to believe she was holding out on him.

There was also a part of detective Sampson that longed to hear that southern smooth voice emanating from the beautiful woman. At times her eyes felt as if they were piercing his soul and other times, he felt enchanted by their gaze. Nonetheless calling her was out of the question, at least for now. He had been searching for a clue, any clue, he could bring to the investigation before making the call, yet he was still coming up empty.

"Earth to Sampson," a voice chided breaking him from deep contemplation. He rotated his chair another 90 degrees so he could face the person who had entered his office.

"Yes, Officer Johnson," Sampson responded, eyes fixed on the visitor.

"Um sir, we are placing a lunch order from Crispy Banh Mi so I'm checking to see if you wanted anything."

"No, thank you. I packed my lunch today and I have a ton of work to catch up on. You guys enjoy."

"Ok sir, enjoy your lunch sir." Johnson walked away, swiftly stirring the papers on Sampson's desk leaving them askew.

Sampson, a self-proclaimed perfectionist, began arranging the papers back in a tidy stack at the corner of his desk.

As he focused on adjusting the papers, he felt a presence looming at the door. Preparing to ask Officer Johnson if he had something more on his mind, he looked up to see the elegant Agent Dabria in her black two-piece suit. Tongue leaden in his mouth he was only able to produce an incoherent sound.

"Good day, Detective Sampson," came the smooth harmonic voice from the FBI agent.

Clearing his throat, "Good morning, Agent Dabria. Please come on in and have a seat," he said standing to his feet.

"You're too kind," she responded tilting her head forward with a subtle nod. "I don't much care for police departments. Do you have any plans for lunch?"

"No. Absolutely not," he stammered a little too quickly.

"Good. I know a spot not far from here that we can acquire something light. Do you mind accompanying me for a quick bite? I'd love to compare notes on the progress to bring Terri Buckley to justice."

Sampson thought to himself, *I haven't made any progress*, yet instead he said, "Sure, let me grab my jacket."

Picking up his jacket from the back of the chair and moving toward the door, he placed his right arm into the jacket sleeve swinging it behind his back to insert his left arm into the other sleeve. In doing so the papers at the edge of his desk were transported with the gust of wind to the middle of the desk. Sampson eyeballed the papers and decided they could wait.

"After you," he said motioning with his right hand for Donatella to exit the office. She obliged again with the same subtle nod and he followed her pulling the door closed behind him.

They walked silently through the hallway, Donatella in the lead followed by Sampson. Sampson could sense averted eyes following their synchronized paces toward the elevator. He could feel a bead of sweat forming on his brow as he inwardly pleaded for the elevator to be there waiting on their arrival. He also noticed Officer Johnson from the corner of his eye unable to conceal his stare as well as the others. His mouth momentarily hinged open before he could will his jaw muscles to pull his mouth shut.

At the elevator, Donatella reached her smooth, silky brown left hand toward the buttons and depressed the one pointing down. He noticed from habits of his single life that she didn't sport a ring on her ring finger. This would be information he would file away for a later date. Mercifully the elevator was on their floor and the doors parted with the double ding he was all too familiar with.

The pair rode the elevator down to the ground level in silence. Once the door opened Agent Dabria broke the silence.

"We can head over to Brent's Coffee Shop – I'll drive." Without a moment's hesitation she pushed through the doors of the headquarters making her way to the parking lot. Detective Sampson realized with some amazement that he had to quicken his pace to keep up with her long silky strides. Although every step looked as if she was gliding across the pavement, the distance she covered was remarkable.

Turning the corner and not paying attention, Detective Sampson ran into a woman coming the opposite direction.

"Oh, I'm sorry Ms.," he said holding her up so she didn't fall to the ground.

The woman gave the detective a sideway look and continued on her journey – he did the same. Drawing his attention back to Agent Dabria who was a few paces from a sparkling black Audi R8, he was once again amazed. *She drives that* he thought in astonishment. He casually walked over to the passenger side, opened the door, and slid into the black leather seat with red trim. Everything about the interior of the vehicle yelled sleek and seeing Donatella grip the steering wheel with familiarity, he knew she could handle the car and its power.

Within five minutes of leaving headquarters they pulled up to Brent's on Trade St. Walking through the front door Sampson could smell the unmistakable aroma of coffee and the delightful surprise of fresh baked goods. He took a detective's survey of the establishment to realize Brent's had more to offer than he initially expected. Communal seating that was meant for comfort and relaxing rather than function. Several bays with electrical outlets and USB attachments. A subtle track played effortlessly from the speakers giving additional warmth to the atmosphere. Groups of varying sizes sat around consuming their purchases, chatting away without a care in the world.

There were still two patrons in front of Sampson and Dabria and at this moment he turned his attention to the menu. They carried an assortment of coffees from espresso to latte, including their home-brewed house blend. His nose had not been deceived as he eyeballed the dessert menu. Shortbread, pecan rolls, and muffins were prominent on the menu that proclaimed, "Baked Fresh Daily".

Their selection of sandwiches, soups, and salads anchored the menu. From locally sourced meats, veggies and cheeses to their homemade breads, spreads, and sauces. Taking in the entire atmosphere Sampson felt this would not be his last time at this establishment. As he prepared to commend Donatella on her selection of eateries, they were next in line. A girl in her mid to late 20s with pink hair smiled ear-to-ear as they approached the counter. Sampson figured this was part of her job until –

"Special Agent Donatella! Oh my God it's so good to see you again. Anything hot and juicy I can help you with today?"

"Good afternoon, Margaret," Donatella spoke, a smile caressing her face. "This is Detective Carl Sampson," she motioned to the figure standing next to her. "We're just here for a bite to eat today."

The woman shot out her hand toward Sampson. He raised his hand to meet hers and she pumped it feverishly. "It's so good to meet you Mr. Sampson, I mean Detective Sampson. My name is Margaret and I'm at your service."

Sampson returned the smile, it was almost contagious at this point, and responded, "It's nice to meet you, Margaret."

She squeezed his hand one more time before asking, "What can I get you two today, it's on the house."

Both Agent Dabria and Detective Sampson gave their order and in turn were given the number 37 to sit on their table. They found a place to sit at one of the more functional settings, a table with two chairs, next to the window.

"Detective Sampson," came the smooth voice from Donatella, "I grow ever more concerned with our lack of progress in tracking down our prey. Terri is not one to sit idly by which makes me grow ever more concerned to what she is plotting."

Sampson had been pondering something for the last couple of weeks, yet had not spoken the words out loud, until now. "Are you positive this is the work of Terri Buckley? I mean it's been a few weeks and we have not made any progress and there hasn't been any other activity. Maybe the clue from the first murder scene, that of Samantha Taylor, was read incorrectly. I'm –"

The words snapped off in his esophagus as the hazelnut eyes sliced through the remainder of his train of thought.

"Detective, I have known Terri Buckley for many years. I was her partner for many years. I have witnessed firsthand what she is capable of when her mind is made up. I know how she thinks and I know that she will stop at nothing to achieve her end goal – whatever that goal happens to be in this situation. So, make no mistake, Terri Buckley is the person behind the Samantha

Taylor murder and what happened to those poor individuals at Global Insights Security – of that I have no doubt."

Sampson, somewhat skeptical, decided it was in his best interest to keep quiet on the matter. Instead he changed course.

"I'm still curious about the lone survivor and current CEO of GIS, Veronica King. Something doesn't sit right with me and her disappearance during the massacre."

Dabria nodded her head and before she could speak the pink-haired girl personally brought their food to the table.

"Is there anything else I can get for you guys? Any help I can lend?" she asked with a glimmer in her eyes.

During the last case Donatella worked, Margaret along with the stock boy, Lave, were able to identify Terri Buckley and thus help Donatella solve the case. Margaret, always eager to assist, looked for every opportunity to help even if no help was warranted.

"That'll be all," came the response from Donatella.

Smile fading slightly and a hint of dejection, Margaret dropped off a few extra napkins that she held in her hand and walked back toward the counter.

"Indeed, her story seems to have holes, but each one can be explained away. All but the fact that her husband has not come back from the business trip. I called in a few favors and he was confirmed as a passenger on the flight. I'm waiting to hear back from another contact to see if anyone has come across Mr. King since his arrival."

"Is there anything that would give you a reason to believe he isn't where he said he'd be?"

"When I spoke with Mrs. King, I'm 100 percent sure she was lying to me; however, I haven't determined the source of her lie. A couple of days ago I began to focus on the husband. See detective, Terri is a woman who likes leverage and if Veronica King is alive, and Terri is behind the attack, I'm sure she had some leverage – a sense of influence, on Veronica. I want to know what that was and how she could be using Mrs. King."

"For arguments sake, let's say you're right. What could possibly be her endgame? Veronica is now the CEO of GIS, a move many in the industry speculated was going to happen fairly soon. She started a foundation in honor of those who were slain. She set up an educational trust for the children or grand-children of her colleagues who were killed. She announced her company would aid the Cleveland Art Museum with a new security system after hearing that they were hacked. In essence, Veronica King is going on running the company as one would expect."

"Yes... nothing seems amiss, and yet something certainly must be."

Sampson, resisting the urge to roll his eyes, felt his phone vibrate in his pocket. He reached inside to stave off the vibration when he realized something strange. Inside his pocket, next to his phone was a folded sheet of paper. Sampson did not keep paper in his pockets, thus this foreign intrusion was jarring.

He pulled it from his pocket with an expression of confusion plastered across his face. This brought a raised eyebrow from Donatella. He unfolded the note, read the contents silently, and then in a surprise, handed the note to Donatella.

Curious, she plucked the note from Sampson, turned it around so the contents faced her and read:

Detective Sampson. I see you have taken a keen interest in the case along with Special Agent Donatella Dabria. I'd be careful not to stay too close to her, as those that are close end up being hurt. Not to mention, she is still destined to die, and so are those she cares about. If I were you, I'd leave while you have the chance.

As Donatella read, Sampson racked his brain trying to figure out where the note had come from.

Donatella folded the note, "Where did you get this?"

"It was in my pocket. I'm not sure –" at that moment it dawned on him.

"When we were leaving the headquarters, a woman bumped into me turning the corner headed to the parking lot. Do you think –"

"Yes," Donatella said without a hint of surprise. "Terri Buckley slipped you that note. And that can only mean one thing – she is prepared to strike once again."

Sampson looked into her face and in that instant, he knew Donatella was right. He also knew they were probably too late to stop whatever this psycho had planned next.

10

FEBRUARY 4TH – 8:15 P.M

Penny Hampton drove around the outer loop of I-485 in a hurried patience eager to arrive home. Valentine's Day was only 10 days away and this was one of her favorite "Hallmark Card" days. Neil, her husband of 21 years, felt she went over the top at times but he secretly loved the attention.

The two started dating when they were freshmen in college and after her standard one month trial run, she knew Neil was the one. She knew he was the one she could pour her love into and that he would be grateful and appreciative. Their first Valentine's Day together she started off somewhat small to see how he would respond. The response was exactly what she was looking for. The shock and appreciation written over his face was all she needed.

Since that day some 24 years ago, she continued to up the ante. She never wanted to go so far that she didn't feel she could top herself the next year, but she surely didn't want to put out a dud as compared to the previous year. To that end, Penny started planning the next Valentine's Day on the 15th of February each year. She didn't mind putting forth the effort because even though Neil knew something would be coming, he didn't have that air of expectation – and to Penny, this made the planning that much more enjoyable.

Penny slowed down and moved over into the fast lane as a tow truck driver was working on the berm rescuing a stranded traveler. Once she passed the scene, she moved back over to the right-hand lane and picked up her speed yet again.

Today, Penny received the notification that the final piece of her masterplan had arrived giving her a few days to now pull it all together. Neil, per usual, beat her home tonight; however, she had one of the neighbors sign for the package and she would pick it up before she went into the house.

The remainder of the drive home went by in a blur as Penny devised plans and contingency plans on how she would unveil the surprise for Neil. Penny pulled into the driveway and waited while the garage door to their three-car garage continued to creep open. She figured she would pull into the garage and then walk next door and retrieve her package from Beatrice. Penny had already given her the heads up that she would be stopping by so her quick jaunt next door should not create suspicion in Neil if he heard the garage door open. She would simply pull into the garage, run next door, press the doorbell for the already waiting Beatrice, obtain the package and rush back to her garage. *Easy peasy*, she thought.

Penny pulled into the garage and killed the ignition to her late model Ford Escape. As Penny began to exit the car, she noticed the garage door had begun to close, and to her horror, she felt the presence of someone else in her garage.

February 4th – 8:15 p.m

Terri Buckley drove her rented Mercedes CLA into the Bevel subdivision on the south side of Charlotte. This was a new-build community working midway through their second phase of the development. She had driven through the subdivision several times during the daytime hours familiarizing herself with the traffic patterns and the community layout. During her reconnaissance, she found two properties that would serve her needs – both in different states of development. *Tonight*, she thought, *I'll take the one furthest away from the target.*

She continued her drive toward her destination and mapped out the choreographed sequence in her head once again. Satisfied that she had not missed a step, she pulled the car over and stepped out.

This community was a family friendly community and for the most part all families had grade school aged children. The plus side to this is at this time of night, most families are settling in preparing for school and work tomorrow. Therefore, Terri had the advantage of walking through the neighborhood unseen. She still walked casually in case someone happened upon her, but she knew that was a remote possibility.

Reaching her destination, Terri stepped into the shadows between the two adjacent structures, steadied her breathing, and waited. Her target, Mrs. Penny Hampton, should be arriving home any moment. Terri watched the woman for the last couple of weeks, working out her routines. Without fail, her shift ended at 7 p.m., she wrapped up any outstanding paperwork, and left reliably within an 8-minute window between 7:41 p.m. and 7:49 p.m. If her commute didn't encounter any traffic alterations, she arrived safely at her dwellings between 8:20 p.m. and 8:26 p.m. She observed Mrs. Penny could have a little bit of a leadfoot at times but nothing that would garner attention from a patrol officer on radar duty.

Distantly, she heard a door open. It sounded a couple of

houses away. She focused her attention searching for any additional sounds. After a few seconds the door closed again. Terri listened for another minute before deciding it was nothing to worry about. A moment later, she heard a vehicle on approach and then, the sound of the garage door opening. The car idled in the driveway as the garage door opened slowly emitting screeching sounds the whole time.

She heard the Ford Escape move into the garage and with a practiced motion, she stood, walked around the corner and prepared to enter the garage. Before she did, she lifted the cover to the keypad that control the garage from the outside and entered in the six-digit admin code that had not been changed. As the garage began to close, Terri slipped unnoticed under the door.

By the time Terri stood erect she could see the woman had begun to exit the vehicle – a reality she fully expected. The woman didn't spend much time in her car once she pulled into the garage. Tracing the route she had mapped she moved silently and quickly staying out of sight of the woman.

"Neil. Is that you?" Penny asked as she closed the SUV door.

Terri nuzzled in closely behind the woman who was still looking at the entrance to the house from the garage. She inserted the needle into the side of her neck and depressed the plunger. Again, a practiced move she had performed on countless occasions.

The woman fell limp into Terri's left arm, already out on her feet. She didn't know how much time she had but she knew it was not infinite. She pulled the woman by her shoulders toward the service door on the side of the garage. Once she was in place, she pulled a remote detonator from her pocket, pulled back the cover, and pressed the button. A mile down the road, a distribution transformer received an unexpected surge in electricity causing that transformer to blow. The Bevel subdivision, along with several other adjacent subdivisions, were cast into complete darkness.

Terri opened the service door, pulled Penny through and laid her on the ground. She reached back into the garage, turned the lock and pulled the door closed. She hefted the woman into the wheel barrel the Hampton's left on the side of the house and with all the speed she could muster, wheeled the woman to her waiting car. She popped the trunk on her approach and quickly transported the woman from the wheel barrel to the trunk. A moment of decision – did she take the wheel barrel back to the house or did she leave it and hop in the car.

If she took the wheel barrel back to the house, nothing would seem out of place and the speed in which they could start to narrow down clues would be extended. If she left the wheel barrel, there was a high probability someone would notice the wheel barrel even, in the darkness, and questions would surface. She decided the risk of going back to the house was too great, so she hopped into the driver's seat and headed for the vacant house at the end of a cul-de-sac toward the back of the subdivision.

11

FEBRUARY 5TH – 10:20 A.M

Jasmyn Thompson sat motionless in her car staring off into the far distance. She pulled into the parking lot of the practice and took one of the four spots that read, "For Expecting Mothers or those with small children". She could get used to this pampering, but she couldn't get use to the anxiety that she felt.

Five months into her pregnancy and she had consumed as much knowledge as possible about being a new mom. Yet she still felt there was more she needed to learn. She learned the two-finger method of burping a newborn right after they ate. She learned that swaddling a baby as snug as possible was comforting to a baby, though as an adult she couldn't imagine being wrapped like that.

She heard from different mothers how different each baby can be. One woman mentioned her baby slept through the night at six weeks old, while another stated how her baby had colic and she didn't get a full night's rest until he was nearly two. Another woman talked about how the doctor was worried the baby wasn't gaining the proper weight between well visits and how nervous that had made her.

She had a 30-minute conversation with a woman in the grocery store who stood outside her car bawling. When Jasmyn stepped over to see if she could help the woman, the woman brightened up and put on a happy face. She had noticed Jasmyn was pregnant and stated this was the first time she had went anywhere without her newborn. Her house was only around the corner and she left their daughter with her husband. She knew her daughter was in good hands with him; however, she couldn't help the feeling of dread that had overcome her for leaving her daughter alone. She should have brought her to the store with her. Her husband convinced her to take a day away and all she had done was come over to the grocery store and cried.

While Jasmyn didn't know the feeling, she felt a maternal connection to the woman. By the end of the conversation, the woman was talking about all of the positive things that came from having her baby girl. She was able to talk about how much she loved her and how having her was the light she needed in her life. When they prepared to part, the woman gave Jasmyn a sincere embrace. Jasmyn could feel the transfer of power she had given to the woman to carry on with her day and that made her feel good.

However, as Jasmyn sat in this car, recalling all of the positive interactions she had, she was now worried. She began to worry if she was going to be as strong as many of the women that she had talked to over the past few months. She worried what she would do if their son, or daughter, became sick in the middle of the night and there was no doctor around to assist. More than anything, she worried that she would not be a good mother.

There would be a life totally dependent on her and Marcellous for all of their needs. The fear had begun to grip her, and she couldn't explain why. She and Marcellous had a love that could endure anything – but was that enough? Was that enough when it came to raising a child? She wasn't sure and that caused her anxiety.

Still sitting in her car at Dr. Prince's office, she continued to stare out of the window. Should she tell her doctor how she was feeling? Was this a normal feeling? The thought of telling Dr. Prince and then finding out it was not normal would devastate her. She didn't think she could handle it and that added to her anxiety.

A knock on the driver's side window startled her causing an involuntary jump. She turned and noticed the woman from the waiting room the last time she visited Dr. Prince. She rolled down the window.

"I'm soooo sorry. I didn't mean to startle you," came the voice from the woman. "We met a few months ago in Dr. Prince's office. I'm Bethany Evans."

"Yes, I remember you. How can I help you?"

"I noticed you sitting in the car and I wanted to make sure you were ok. I just left my appointment. Are you here for one as well?"

The sad reality was, Jasmyn didn't have an appointment. She hadn't worked out a plan other than just appearing at the office. The woman looked over Jasmyn again and interjected.

"How do you feel about going to get a coffee – well maybe some tea in our case?"

"I'd like that very much," Jasmyn said grasping firmly on the olive branch.

"Are you familiar with Brent's Coffee Shop? I hear they have some killer pastries and I sure could go for one."

"Yes," came her voice with more strength behind it.

"Good. Why don't we meet over there and that'll give us a chance to catch up."

"Sure, I'll see you there in about 10 minutes."

She watched as the woman, Bethany, made her way toward her car. Jasmyn once again fired up her engine and drove off.

FIFTEEN MINUTES LATER, they sat in the oversized chairs at Brent's Coffee Shop with their teas and pastries. Bethany took a large bite from her cheese Danish and in exaltation stated, "This is exactly what I needed" as she fell into the chairs comforting embrace.

Jasmyn rattled the ice in her cup before extracting the last drink of tea through her straw. "Ahh!" She exclaimed, finishing the drink and placing the cup back on the table. "Thanks for suggesting we come here. It has been a welcome distraction."

"No problem. I make way for a treat once a month and there was no need to sit alone and enjoy this delectable, culinary creation," she said this placing the last piece in her mouth and chewing with reckless abandon. A curl touched the edge of her lips bringing her face into a full-on smile, "Who am I kidding? I had one of these last week too."

The women burst into laughter causing the other patrons to look around for the joke they had missed.

Bethany didn't want to ask Jasmyn if anything was wrong because she figured she knew. "I remember when Troy and I were pregnant the first time, I was scared out of my mind. I felt I was just trying to figure out life and we were preparing to bring another life into this world. We didn't live by any family members, still don't, so I worried constantly about how we would make it."

She could see Jasmyn nodding, so she carried on.

"I think as first-time parents, we jump to the worst possible outcome and feel that will be me. Then I ran into this old, sage woman and she said, 'As a parent, you are going to make mistakes, the question is, do you give up when you make one?

Any parent who tells you they were perfect is lying through their teeth and should be struck down by lightning.'"

Again, the women shared a laugh but a little more tamed than the last.

"And you know what, the old woman was right. I thought back to my childhood and realized my parents weren't perfect. They did the best they could to raise me and at the end of the day, that's our job as parents. I guess what I'm trying to say is, if you ever begin to doubt your skills as a parent think back to the words of the old woman. Continue to fight the fight and do the best you can."

Jasmyn, whose eyes were now filling with tears, walked over to Bethany and gave her a huge hug "Thank you," came her trembling voice, "Thank you." As Jasmyn made her way back to her seat, she wiped away the tears. Clearing her throat, she asked, "Have you and Troy settled on a place to live? We still have an opening in our community and I know you guys will fit right in with the neighborhood."

"Nope not yet, why don't you tell me more about it. I'd like to be settled into our new home before the baby arrives."

February 5th – 12:45 p.m

SAL GRANDSON SAT in his favorite kitchen chair staring at the blank word-processing document. He sat there, prepared to write an article for his website, The Sal Report, but he felt sapped of creativity. Instead of placing his fingers to the keyboard and spinning a masterpiece, he pressed his fingers to his temples fighting off a headache.

He believed two factors were affecting his current mood. The first factor was there hadn't been any interesting news lately. He had reached out to his police contacts and they didn't have anything for him. One of their detectives was following up on a missing woman from the Bevel subdivision on the south side but he didn't hear anything of interest in that story. His contacts on the street hadn't heard anything either. The only news they had were a couple of store break-ins after a brief power outage. Nothing high-end was stolen as the outage only lasted an hour. Nonetheless, some cops had a day full of paperwork in front of them.

The second factor affecting Sal's mood was that his routine was shot. Ever since Jane moved in with him, he slowly felt himself losing control of his environment. It started with her putting a few pictures on the wall. Sal liked the blank wall because he always thought of it as a blank canvas for creative thought. Jane on the other hand agreed it was a blank canvas, one that had potential and she was the one to showcase that potential.

The pictures were one thing, but then she bought this oversized roman numeral clock. The clock design was aesthetically pleasing; however, the constant tick of the second hand was driving Sal mad. He enjoyed ambient noise when he wrote because when it was too quiet his mind would wonder. But he didn't like a noise that was consistent and evenly paced. His mind started to focus on the rhythm and that became a major distraction. He told Jane and her response was, "It's like white noise. After a few weeks you won't notice it anymore."

She was wrong. He did notice and he couldn't do anything but notice. The tic – tic – tic was ever present and, on several occasions, he thought about smashing the clock. However, he knew that would not end well. Still, the clock wasn't his biggest problem. His biggest issue came from his workout routine – or lack thereof.

Sal woke up every morning at 4:00 a.m. for his five-mile run.

However, his morning run had been sabotaged by Jane wrapping her body around him making it nearly impossible to disentangle without waking her. He tried, on several occasions, but each time he managed to extract himself, she woke up. She gave him those perfect, pouty lips and would ask him to come back to bed to keep her warm, and each time, he did as she requested. He could have denied her request but Jane believed in an eye for an eye and she would certainly deny his request later.

This morning, just like yesterday, and the day before Sal missed his five-mile run. He could literally feel himself out of sorts and he would need to do something about it – and soon. Two nights ago, Jane made a passing comment about updating more of the décor. She said this while they sat at his kitchen table eating dinner. He could tell by the look in her face that the décor she was referring to was the dinette set.

This is where he was going to put his foot down. This is where he would make his stand. Sal loved this set, this chair. He had written many of his best articles sitting at this table, in this chair and she couldn't – she wouldn't simply take that away from him... too. There weren't many hills Sal was willing to die on, but she would have to remove this dinette set over his cold, stiff, dead –

"Everything ok Sal?"

"Uh!?"

"You have an intense, ready to do war look plastered over your face," Jane said adding sugar into her coffee. Sal didn't realize she had entered the room.

"Yea, yea. Everything is ok. Just thinking about my next article."

"Oh yea, something good and juicy? Can I get a sneak peek?"

"No. I'm still at the beginning stages. Nothing worth sharing yet."

Jane gave him a sarcastic smirk and said, "Ok. Keep your

secret. Remember, I'm not writing anymore. We are on the same side. Anyway, I'm about to head out. I have a few errands I need to run. I think I'll run past the furniture store and look for a new dinette. I think it's time we replace this one."

Sal could feel the blood rushing to his cheeks. Ready to stand his ground – ready to hash this one out, Jane continued, "By the way, I found this paper in your coat pocket. I figured while I was out, I could take it to the cleaners. The paper, or should I say shreds of paper didn't look like much, but I figured I would ask before I tossed them."

She reached her hand out, handing Sal a handful of torn up paper. It dawned on Sal that it was the paper from the office of Veronica King. He had almost forgotten about it. He took the paper from Jane saying, "Thanks", before thinking back to that day.

RETURNING to his car after avoiding both the GIS security team and the K-9 unit patrolling the building, Sal's heart pound audibly through his chest.

"Still cutting it too close," he chided. He retrieved the scraps of paper extracted from the trashcan of Veronica King. He placed the pieces on the seat next to him and stared at the contents.

Sal maneuvered the pieces of this shredded puzzle around; however, it quickly dawned on him that there were pieces missing.

He reached back in his pocket – empty. He realized the vital pieces to complete the puzzle lay within the wastebasket.

"Do I chance another break-in to retrieve the missing pieces when she starts the conference?" he asked himself out loud.

No, he thought to himself. *I'm not as young as I once was, and they are likely already on high alert.* At that moment he decided he would take the scraps back to his home and unscramble the mystery there.

However, when he arrived home, Jane had been measuring the dimensions of the eating area and broached the subject of replacing the dinette.

Her words brought him out of his trance, "Don't mention it." She leaned over and kissed him fully on the lips. He could smell her perfume and he could taste her nude lips. "I'll be back in a few hours."

And with a whirl and a stride to the door, she was out of the apartment.

"You're not taking my dinette," he said out loud to Jane's departed aroma.

Sal looked down to the scraps of paper in his hand. He moved his laptop to the side and lay the scraps down one by one. As he did, he quickly recalled that there were some pieces missing and he thought back to sitting in Veronica's office chair. There were a couple of pieces left in the trashcan that he was not able to retrieve. He would make do with what he had.

Aligning the paper as best he could, he only made out letters on the two lines of text. The top line read "Br" followed by "ley". The second line read "Wh" followed by "he?". He chuckled inwardly. He had some letters, and that was basically it. He figured he would play around with it for a while since writing was obviously a no-go at this hour. He looked up one last time toward the door, "You're not taking my dinette!"

12

FEBRUARY 5TH – 3:15 P.M

Patti Jones walked out of the operating room with a distressed demeanor accentuating her face. Her brows stitched together as if she was in deep contemplation. Beth, who had only seen this look on Patti once before, knew without the necessity of words that something had gone wrong.

Beth first encountered Patti when they both joined the nursing staff at Good Sam. At the time, Patti didn't say much and went about executing the job she was tasked to undertake. However, during each of their interactions Beth knew under that calm facade that Patti was a brilliant woman. It all stemmed from the manner in which she carried herself into her deliberate mannerisms.

Over the course of six months Beth and Patti grew closer. Beth wouldn't characterize what they had as a friendship, but the two certainly had a mutual respect for one another. For Beth, she saw Patti as a wealth of knowledge. A knowledge that span the entire spectrum of medicine and operational procedures. There were many times that Beth pondered why Patti had not become a surgeon but decided she would leave that question unasked.

For Patti, she saw Beth as a more than capable nurse. Someone who knew her job and the job of all those in the room. She was flexible and Patti enjoyed the conversations the two had during their time together. She saw Beth as someone she could trust, and trust was something that didn't come easy for Patti.

As Patti began walking toward her, Beth thought back to the first time she had seen the expression Patti currently wore on her face.

It was during a routine delivery in which a couple had agreed to be a surrogate for a friend of the wife. Throughout the pregnancy everything was going fine. The baby's vitals and measurements were always on point. The couple was excited to be going through this adventure, and the mother-to-be was grateful for the family agreeing to aide in her desire to have a child. However, as the time drew near for the baby to be born a change had overcome the dynamic of this trio.

It would come out later in the court proceedings that the mother-to-be overheard the surrogates talking about having a family of their own one day soon. She mistook this to mean they planned on keeping the baby she had dreamed about for so long and was now only a few weeks away.

Patti and Beth were working in the delivery room that faithful day. The surrogate was proceeding through the birthing process as well as could be expected. Her husband was in the room coaching her along and doing a wonderful job keeping her calm and focused. These two were meant to perform this duty and they were performing it well. Beth could still hear the last words the doctor spoke.

"I can see the head, let me rotate slightly to allow the shoulders through."

At that moment a commotion broke out. The mother-to-be walked into the delivery room. A placid look had overcome her face as if she was wearing a mask. She walked up behind the doctor, scalpel in hand, and plunged it into his neck once, twice. The doctor instinctively reached for his neck, losing contact with the baby. Patti saw this; however, she was too slow to react. The baby's shoulders now free plunged headfirst toward the ground.

Patti rushed to the baby who was still connected to the mother via the umbilical cord. She found the sterilized scissors, cut the cord, and rushed the baby over to the waiting cart. She searched for the pulse but she didn't feel anything. The baby had not cried once and seemed lifeless.

The mother-to-be, continuing her murderous systematic killing spree, took out the surrogate's husband next followed by the surrogate herself. Beth, in an instance of clarity, looked over at Patti who was doing everything to revive the baby. She saw her stop with a grave look on her face. It was in that moment, surrounded by death circling around them, Beth knew the baby was not alive. When Patti raised her head, her brows were stitched together intent on her next course of action.

The mother-to-be searched out her next victim now that the surrogate couple had been dispatched, she set her eyes on Beth. She methodically made her approach, shoulders heaving from the exertion of death she left in her wake. Beth, who had been frozen in place, knew this would be the end; however, before the woman could attack, she fell face first into the ground at Beth's feet. In her back, between the shoulder blades were the sterile scissors Patti used to cut the umbilical cord.

Patti broke her recollection, "Amy and the baby didn't make it. Can you break the news to the Dells? Let them know we will start the acquisition process as soon as possible."

"And if they ask for a refund of their deposit?"

"Kindly remind them that we have a no refund policy. We will find them a suitable replacement. Should they balk, remind them of everything that is at stake. That should cool their jets for a while."

Beth nodded her head.

"In the meantime, I'm headed to my office and would appreciate not being disturbed. Once things are settled with the Dells, please ensure the operating room receives a thorough cleaning."

"I'll see that it's taken care of within the hour."

Patti began to walk down the hall, footfalls silent in the corridor. She couldn't believe she lost the baby. He was only the second baby she had lost and this feeling stung. She needed to go into her office, clear her head, and pick herself up for tomorrow.

She pushed open the partially closed door to her office, stepped in and swung the door behind her as she walked toward her desk. With practiced precision the door slid closed barely registering a click once completely closed.

"Patti Jones," came the hushed voice from within the office. "You're back much earlier than I expected. Did something go wrong with your – extraction?"

She froze, back still turned to the voice deciding what she should do. Not one to scare easily, Patti sat down in her chair and turned to face the stranger.

"You seem to have me at a disadvantage," she said giving the visitor a quick once-over. "You know my name, but I don't know who I have the pleasure of speaking with."

"Names are unimportant at this moment, but if you need to call a name for any reason during this conversation you can call me, Amy."

Patti's skin suddenly felt damp, her mind racing. For the stranger, she kept the same stoic external demeanor; however, inside she wondered if she had been caught. Scenario after scenario raced through her mind on what she should do next, yet nothing yielded a satisfactory outcome.

"Ok Amy, how can I help you today?"

"Before we get to what you can do to help me, let me start off with a story. Do you mind?" the woman asked crossing her feet on the top of Patti's desk.

"Sure, go right ahead."

"In the early 1900s a woman by the name of Georgia Tann began a practice that in today's society would have her arrested before any transaction would have been completed. You see, Ms. Tann operated the Tennessee Children's Home Society. Are you familiar with this Home Society, Ms. Jones?"

Patti shook her head.

"The Tennessee Children's Home Society was an adoption agency that was founded by Ms. Tann. She operated this agency in Memphis, Tennessee for a number of years. During her years of operation, she matched hundreds, thousands, of babies with perspective parents."

Patti could feel the damp feeling spreading across her body.

"There was something peculiar about Ms. Tann's clientele – they were all rich. Well rich in the standards of the early 1900s. Though some of her more, shall we say, famous clients would still be rich by today's standards. But that wasn't the only thing peculiar about Ms. Tann and her adoption agency. The babies, infants, and toddlers that she provided for adoption all came from poor, underprivileged families."

Patti shifted uncomfortably in her chair.

"Now I know what you are thinking. Sounds like a win for everyone involved. The adopted child would grow up in a more stable environment, the adopting family had a child they wanted and would care for, and the family giving up the child for adoption knew the baby, infant, toddler, was in a much better place."

"But," she said waving her index finger while shaking her head, "That isn't exactly how the story goes. You see Patti, I can call you Patti, right? The poor, underprivileged families had not agreed to put their child up for adoption. In fact, in many cases the child was stolen from the family. Some under the guise that they were working for the Department of Social Services and that they had received calls about a child being in danger.

There were times when the child was taken from in front of the house while they played, and worst of all," she said turning her gaze toward Patti and staring her straight in the eyes, "There were times when the baby was taken at the time of birth."

She let this declaration hang in the air before continuing.

"Of course, the parents of the kidnapped children went to the local authorities but because of their class, their status in life, they were not given the time of day and no one would challenge Ms. Georgia Tann. She went on in this matter for decades, trafficking thousands of kids through her adoption agency."

"Fascinating story, but I don't see your point," Patti said in an effort to gain some control in this encounter.

"The point, Patti," she said with a bit more menace in her tone. "My organization has been watching you for a number of years. And I must say, you are an upgraded version of Georgia Tann. None of your parents live to see the sun again once they enter your operating room. I must say you have perfected the art of the perfect crime. Not to mention your clientele is much more luxurious than anything Ms. Tann could have ever had. But alas, we have reached the point in the story in which I lay out what you can do for me."

Patti quickly realized this woman knew more about her operation than she would have thought possible. She had always been so careful – so meticulous. Within the span of moments, this woman was threatening her operation – her freedom.

"I have a project that I'm working on in which I need someone with your skillset. While this may be a one-time task,

I'm willing to offer you much more in return for your cooperation. Please understand, I'm not going to make you agree to my terms; however," she placed a sealed folder on the desk.

"I'd prefer for the contents of this folder, which is a summary of our discussion here today, never see the light of day." She slid the folder over to Patti. "Feel free to open it, but I assure you there isn't anything in there that you do not have first-hand knowledge of."

Patti looked down at the folder and then she glared back at the woman sitting across from her in the visitor's chair. Once again, scenario after scenario raced through her mind. And once again, she didn't see an out. Realizing a checkmate when she saw it, she simply asked.

"What – do you need – from me?"

February 5th – 6:00 p.m

JASMYN WATCHED from her gourmet kitchen as Marcellous and Donatella spoke in an animated fashion. Marcellous' normal laid-back demeanor, can be enticed to step out of its comfort zone when discussing a topic he's passionate about - and whatever they were discussing had him riled up. His hands are always a dead giveaway. The more he tries to argue his point of view, the higher his hands go above his torso.

From her vantage point she couldn't discern the topic of discussion, but she figured she better go and save Donatella. Then again, knowing the FBI woman, it might be Marcellous who needed the saving.

She walked back into the family room, the smell of cinnamon potpourri tickling her nose. She raised her Yeti to her lips and took a sip of water, "So tell us," she said interrupting. "Any new cases you can share with us?"

Donatella pondered how much she would share with the couple and decided she would only hold back the details of the case.

"Terri Buckley has reemerged from the shadows and is playing a reprehensible game. She has already murdered a civilian, and we're pretty sure she is responsible for what happened at Global Insights."

Jasmyn, fighting back a surge of morning sickness, chimed in, "It's unbelievable the lengths she will go through in the name of revenge."

Donatella flashed back to the Smithville case as Jasmyn continued.

"There is way too much crime and murder in this world, heck even in our city." Just a couple of weeks ago Samantha, the receptionist at my OB's office, was murdered in her own apartment.

Donatella shot Jasmyn a quizzical look.

Taken back by the intensity of the glare, Jasmyn asked, "Did I say something wrong?"

"By chance was the receptionist full name Samantha Taylor?"

"Yea! How did you –"

"Terri was the one responsible for that murder. While she wasn't the one who pulled the trigger, she is the one that orchestrated the events that led to her demise."

"Oh my God," Jasmyn said hand raising to cover her mouth.

Donatella didn't believe in coincidences and made a mental note to contact BJ and check the connection between Samantha and Terri. She chided herself for not thinking of it sooner.

"Terri is unstable, laser focused, and brilliant. Every step of the way she has been in front of this investigation. While there is a part of me that believes her endgame is set on my destruction, this feels different."

"In what way?" asked Marcellous.

"The killing of Samantha and the massacre at GIS have nothing to do with me. I think something else is driving her actions this time. I don't see how these pieces fit together and her plan is not clear yet."

Donatella thought back to The Thinker and how that puzzle pieces didn't seem to fit either. Yet she was leaving signs of it as her calling card. A feeling of unease began to swell within Donatella. A feeling she didn't like, a feeling that worried her.

She looked over at the Thompsons, and her godchild that Jasmyn was carrying. It had only been a few months since Terri tried to harm Donatella by going after another one of her godchildren. While she felt it was unlikely Terri was targeting Jasmyn, she wasn't willing to take any chances.

"Jasmyn – Marcellous. Take extra precautions and stay aware of everyone and everything around you."

A flushed look came over Jasmyn's face and Marcellous looked as if he wanted to speak but he held his tongue.

"I don't think Buckley is after you, but it never hurts to show some extra vigilance. The couple looked at each other and then back at Agent Dabria. In unison they nodded and for now the matter was settled.

"In other news," Jasmyn said looking to lighten the mood, "I ran into Bethany Evans again at Dr. Prince's office."

"Who?" Marcellous asked genuinely confused.

"Bethany. She was in the waiting room the day we found out about Samantha. At the time it was her first visit with Dr. Prince."

"Yea, I remember her. Sorry, I was drawing a blank."

"Well she and her husband are still looking for a place to

live. I told her that the Grant's old house is still up for sale. I gave her the name of the realtor and she said they would follow up."

Donatella listened to this exchange, "Bethany Evans. Had you known her before meeting her at Dr. Prince's office?"

"No. I met her for the first time in the waiting room."

"I see. What did you think of her husband?"

"Well, I haven't met her husband, Troy. He couldn't make the first appointment and he wasn't there today."

Donatella didn't like this development. With Terri running around, she felt increasingly uncomfortable with newcomers inserting themselves into Jasmyn's life.

"I'd love to meet her someday especially if we are going to be neighbors. We should have them over to dinner when they come to see the Grant's old house."

"I'll set something up," Jasmyn said with the smile widening across her face.

In response, Donatella thought, Bethany Evans is one more person BJ will need to do an extensive background check on. She didn't know the woman and thus she didn't trust the woman.

13

FEBRUARY 5TH – 9:00 P.M

Veronica King stood like a sentry outside of her daughter's bedroom door. Gina, who had turned three years old late last year, had transitioned into her toddler bed on her third birthday. Veronica and Kyle never had a problem with Gina sleeping through the night and her transition to the toddler bed made sense. Shortly after her second birthday she was fully potty-trained and the toddler bed gave her another sense of freedom.

As she stood in the archway, she prayed her daughter was having pleasant dreams, because the only dream Veronica had was the last vision of her colleagues as she walked away from the boardroom. Although she had come to terms with the decision she had to make, the only decision she could make to save her daughter, the look on their faces would be with her for some time to come.

She had upheld her end of the bargain she made with that psychopath, Bree Buckley. She reached out to the board of the Cleveland Museum of Art offering the services of her company to perform a complete security overhaul. They were skeptical of the offer, as they should have been, but Veronica had always been a master negotiator. By the end of the call they had a verbal agreement for which Veronica had their legal team draw up the official contract terms. The installation had gone smoothly.

Motion sensor cameras covered every square inch of the museum. 24/7 video surveillance live streamed to an offsite location to prevent tampering. Badged access controls were installed in any sensitive areas in the museum including entry into the building after hours. The badges themselves were tagged and could be tracked anywhere in the building. Pressure sensitive devices had been affixed to any display the museum wanted to add an extra layer of security to. This would deter anyone from handling the artwork.

All gates in the museum had been replaced and several others were added as Veronica's team pointed out multiple vulnerable spots. The gates were tied to the security system and if any alarm was set off, the gates would close automatically. There was also an override that would allow for each gate to be controlled individually.

At this point, they were about 80 percent of the way through the installation and her project manager gave assurances that the installation would be completed by the deadline.

Satisfied with the progress being made, Veronica turned her attention to filling the empty seats on the board. After her initial intrusion into Veronica's home, the woman calling herself Bree had paid the host one more visit. During this second visit, her guest walked her through her next assignment. Veronica, unclear as to the goal of the request, set those wheels into motion as well.

The first request was to update the firmware on all of the security systems still operating on version 4.245 of the Onyx system. This system was mainly used by high-end restaurants, hospitals, and convention centers. Nonetheless, she worked with her IT department to push out the latest update. This was completed in a matter of days, all systems showing the upgrade had downloaded and installed successfully.

The second request had to do with the members of the board. Bree had already given Veronica three names for consideration. She also made it clear that the only consideration Veronica needed to make was when they would be taking their seats on the board. She followed up this request, if you could call it that, by informing Veronica she needed to keep two seats open. She started to fight this request and realized it would be futile. She would keep the seats open and that was the end of the story. She hadn't received a timetable for when the seats would be filled or who would be filling the seats.

She watched as her daughter turned from her left side onto her right side. From this angle it was clear how much she looked like her father, Kyle. She still could not believe the son of a bitch was preparing to leave the country and take their daughter with him. Gina hadn't asked about her father in the last couple of days and she hoped over time she would forget he ever existed. She blew her daughter a kiss goodnight and took her leave.

Veronica unfastened her ASOS DESIGN skinny full metal waist belt that hugged her midsection providing depth to her hips. She reached around her back with her right hand and unzipped the black fitted skirt letting it fall to the ground. As she began to undo the buttons to her blouse, her cell phone began to vibrate.

The display read *number unknown* while the clock on the phone read 9:15 p.m.

"Veronica King," she spoke into the handset.

"Mrs. King, or is it Ms. King now? I can never tell," came the voice from the other end.

Her spine went rigid hearing the voice of Buckley. "Yes, what can I do for you?" she responded in a semi-robotic voice.

"No need to be so formal, come on down to the kitchen. We have some business to discuss."

She's in my house? Her throat went dry.

"I don't have all night," came the voice, prompting her into movement. She finished unbuttoning her blouse and quickly tossed the garment on the bed. She grabbed her robe, idly recalling it was the one Kyle bought her for Christmas the previous year. She wrapped the robe around her frame and tightened it with the belt before heading downstairs.

When she turned the corner, Bree Buckley was sitting at the island drinking water from a bottle while watching Veronica cross the room. She both felt and saw the intruder give her the up and down once-over with a smirk curling at the corner of her mouth. Swallowing the water, she placed the bottle on the island. "You know, I've always liked that robe. It goes well with your eyes."

Veronica froze in place *how long has this woman been watching me?* She suddenly felt self-conscious pulling her robe tighter. In doing so the fabric hugged her breast and she felt her visitor's eyes shift. She quickly released her hold and sat on the opposite side of the island.

Buckley caught the hint; however, she pressed forward. "In this envelope you'll find your next board member for consideration. I'll ask that you wait until she is announced for her new position."

"What position? Who is this woman?"

Ignoring the questions, Buckley continued, "I'll be in touch about your final board seat. In the meantime, be sure the security at the museum is completed per spec and on time. You don't want to disappoint your new employers."

She stood up and began walking toward the front door. *How the hell did she get into the house in the first place?* Looking over her shoulder Buckley said, "Your hair looks better down, wear it like that next time." She then opened the door and walked out.

Once again Veronica was left sitting in the kitchen, at the island, speechless and motionless. She stood, picked up the folder, and walked back upstairs to her bedroom.

February 5th– 9:00 p.m

In the two-story chateau at 300 Calgary Way, Donatella sat in the study with both eyes closed. She took measured deep breaths in an effort to clear her mind – to focus her mind. Since the massacre at GIS Buckley had been relatively quiet. The question that continued to plague her mind, *what is Buckley up to?* To answer this question, she needed to understand Buckley's endgame. She decided she would start with the details that she knew.

The first murder victim, Samantha Young, worked as a receptionist at an OBs office. Not just any OB – Jasmyn's OB. This woman, Bethany Evans, just happens to be at the doctor's office the same day Jasmyn has an appointment and the day after Samantha had been killed. This Bethany is growing closer to Jasmyn and is prepared to move into the Driftwood Springs community. A community in which Jasmyn lives. When she spoke with BJ, she would have him run Bethany's background and design a method to covertly watch over Jasmyn.

The massacre at GIS had a number of open questions. Why was the board of a security company taken out? The obvious answer is to meddle in the affairs of some company utilizing their security services. She needed to check and see if a deal was postponed or all together cancelled because of the board being wiped out. Then there is Veronica King, the lone survivor of the GIS massacre.

Dabria was 100 percent sure the new CEO was lying to her and she could not figure out why and what she was lying about. Not to mention, her husband had not returned from his business trip. A trip he took on the day that the massacre took place. One could say that Veronica benefited from the death of the GIS board; however, by all accounts she was next in line to be the CEO so she had no reason to commit a crime, especially this heinous crime, against the board – her peers. Buckley made a point of letting her know she was the responsible party, but why? Was it done in a manner to throw her off?

And what is it with the calling card of The Thinker not to mention the note "Five Days". If she was correct, Buckley had five separate events planned. So far there had been two events. The thought crossed her mind, there were two events that Buckley wanted her to know about. However, could there have been some other events she didn't want to make obvious? When she connected with BJ, she would need him to look into any other crimes that seemed out of place.

Donatella opened her eyes to the ringing of her phone, *Detective Sampson.*

"Yes, Detective?" she said in her southern drawl.

"Agent Dabria," came the voice in a matter of fact tone. "I'm sending you an address that may be of interest to our case. I just received a call and I'm headed to the scene."

"Can you provide any details?"

"Let's discuss it at the scene." The line went dead and Donatella stared at the phone. *Did he just hang up on me?*

TWENTY-FIVE MINUTES later Agent Dabria pulled up to a brick two-story home with a walkout basement on Sickle Dr. in the subdivision of Bevel. Two police cruisers were situated in the front of the home parked head-to-head. The detective's car, belonging to Carl Sampson, was double parked next to the police cruisers, engine still ticking. Donatella nosed her R8 toward the tail of Sampson's vehicle and stepped out of the car. Two of the officers standing outside of the house eyed Donatella as she approached the house.

"She's with me," Sampson said stepping through the entrance. She noticed the haggard expression he wore on his face. "Let's take a drive." The two made their way to Sampson's car where he sat behind the wheel.

He fired up the car and pulled away from the curb. "Last night Mrs. Hampton arrived at home around 8:30pm; however, she never made it inside the house."

Donatella raised an eyebrow.

"I know how it sounds. Mr. Hampton heard the garage door open expecting his wife to walk through the door at any moment. However, shortly after hearing the garage door close, the subdivision, and several other locations around the area, lost electricity. At the time, he was upstairs in their room that sits above the garage. It took him a few moments to locate a flashlight before heading downstairs. When he did, he noticed his wife had not come in from the garage. He pulled the door open, noticed her Ford Escape sitting in its normal spot, but couldn't locate his wife."

Sampson slowed at the stop sign before making the right-hand turn continuing through the subdivision.

"Worried about his wife, he headed to the service entrance and that's where he began to notice something wasn't right. Although the bottom lock on the door was locked, the deadbolt was not locked. This struck him as odd as Penny made a big deal about their house being locked up tight and this included the service entrance. Therefore, he always made sure the locks, all of the locks were engaged – his wife did the same."

Donatella nodded her head signifying she was following.

"He unlocked the bottom lock, opened the door and stepped out onto the side of the house. Immediately he noticed the wheel barrel missing. Penny, meticulous about her flowers, worked in the flowerbed multiple times per week. Neil figured it was easier to keep the wheel barrel on the side of the house instead of in the shed. He used the flashlight to illuminate his surroundings. Heading toward the front of the house, the beam hit an object at the curb. As he closed in on the object, it became immediately clear that it was the wheel barrel, left haphazardly near the street.

While he stood in the street next to the wheel barrel, he heard a door swing open behind him. He snapped his head around expecting to see his wife; however, the sound came from his neighbor, Beatrice, opening her door."

Donatella, looking at the road ahead, saw a series of flashing lights further off in the distance.

"Beatrice went on to tell Mr. Hampton that Penny planned to stop by to retrieve a package before going into the house. However, she had not seen Penny all night. It was at this point Mr. Hampton gave our department a call.

At the time we didn't consider Mrs. Hampton as a missing person, primarily because it hadn't been 24 hours and there were no signs of foul play."

"However," he said turning on to the street with the flashing lights, "When a realtor called 911 screaming of a dead body, Mrs. Hampton immediately turned from a potential missing person to a murder victim."

Donatella took a moment to interject, "So I'm assuming her body has turned up?"

Sampson nodded his head toward the commotion, "Her

body was found just inside that home. The buyers were set to close on the house later in the week. I'm guessing that will not be the case now."

"And what makes you think this has anything to do with Terri Buckley? Sure, the method in which Mrs. Hampton was abducted was intricate. But that doesn't mean Buckley had anything to do with it."

Stepping out of the car and talking over the hood, "We began looking into the other element of the case, the power outage. Last night, the weather was clear and there is no reason the outage should have taken place. We checked with the power company. They cannot seem to explain the outage themselves but they do show a surge that caused the power to spike and blow. Repair crews didn't find any traces of tampering and the power company is baffled.

From everything you have told me about this woman, she is tier one when it comes to planning. A simple crook could not have tripped the power to the point that it was undetectable. Furthermore, Mrs. Hampton didn't have any enemies. Gangs are not prevalent in this area, so I highly doubt it was a gang initiation stunt."

Agent Dabria knew Sampson was correct. In fact, as he told the story she pretty much knew it had to be Buckley. She wanted to see what clues the detective had used to come to his conclusion. The pair entered the house after ducking under the crime scene tape.

"The body is upstairs in the owner's suite," he said headed toward the steps. They traversed the flight in silence until they reached the bedroom where the CSI team was still taking photos.

Mrs. Penny Hampton hung from the ceiling by her shoulders, feet affixed to the ground. A pulley system had been used to hoist her toward the ceiling. Her body looked to be stretched taut. The shear expression of anguish carried across her face.

Sampson called over the coroner, "Have you been able to determine the cause of death?"

"Not yet," came the timid voice of the coroner. First guess is she died from a heart attack. It looks as if she may have been tortured but it's way too soon to tell."

Donatella spoke, eyes fixated on the coroner, "Please make sure a full toxicology screen is run on this victim. Once you have done so, compare that report against that of any victim from the GIS case."

The intensity in her glare caused the coroner to shutter slightly, "Yes ma'am," he said quickly walking away.

"A toxicology report?" Sampson inquired.

"If you look at Mrs. Hampton's face, you'll recall the men and women left to their demise in the conference room had similar looks. Their looks were much more severe which tells me a similar substance was used on this poor woman. It seems the formula was altered compared to the one used at GIS. I'm willing to bet the stretching of the body is a ploy to make us think it was a heart attack brought on by torture. Terri is a lot of things, but prolonged torture is not on her list. In fact, she probably wanted to dispose of this victim as soon as possible."

"The question that we need to answer is why? Why would she purposely try to lead us down the wrong path? My gut says she didn't want us to know this victim ties back to her. If that is the case, then this victim holds a significant key that Terri doesn't want us to discover. What do we know about her?"

"Well, she's been married for over 20 years to the same man, Neil Hampton. They had two children, both grown living in different states. They have lived in this subdivision for the last five years. They were one of the first residents to buy a house here. She works as the Director of Nursing at Atrium Health, a position she has held for the last seven years. She graduated with a degree in nursing before going back two years later to obtain her master's. That's all we have on the prelim. I'm sure we will uncover more given some time."

"Once you have a full dossier, please share it with me right away. In the meantime, I find her position at the hospital peculiar. I'd like to speak with her superiors first thing in the morning."

"I'm certain that can be arranged. Agent Dabria," he said with a new fire in his eyes. "We need to find this psycho soon. I don't want to have any more blood on my hands."

"Let's see where Mrs. Hampton leads us," she said. She too prayed there would be no more blood, but more was coming, and she was certain she would be the one dealing out her fair share soon enough.

14

FEBRUARY 6TH – 9:00 A.M

The next morning Agent Dabria and Detective Sampson met with Harry Longstill. Longstill oversaw all operations within the hospital and Penny Hampton was one of his direct reports. News of her death came as a shock to him and would devastate the staff. Penny had been a valued member of the team for many years and the nurses under her charge respected and loved her.

Several times during the conversation Longstill removed his handkerchief to dab his eyes which continued to fill with tears. He thought back to when Penny was promoted to Director of Nursing. It was his first promotion during his tenure and one he was proud to perform. Penny had been a standout nurse and had the bedside manner of a saint. She had a calming influence on every patient she encountered and all the other nurses looked up to her.

When Longstill spoke to her about her promotion she was apprehensive at first. She enjoyed her position and her ability to touch so many lives. He was able to convince her that within her new role she would have the opportunity to touch even more lives and the care she already showed would help when tough conversations needed to take place with the families of patients in their care. By the end of the conversation, she felt better about the position and agreed that she would give it her level best.

They stood, shook hands and Longstill led her to the door. When he opened the door and she stepped out, all of the nurses stood outside giving her a round of applause. A cake sat in the middle of the group congratulating her on the promotion. Longstill recalled the look she gave him when she looked back blushing. He knew she would accept the position and every nurse on the staff stood firmly behind her.

She teared up as she left the office accepting hugs from each nurse in attendance – including Jasmyn Thompson.

IT WAS clear to Donatella and Sampson that Penny made her mark on Longstill and her staff. When asked if Mrs. Hampton had any known disputes or if anyone in particular stood out, Longstill could not think of anyone. He couldn't recount one instance in which she had a cross word with a patient or an employee.

She treated the patients with kid gloves most of the time but was firm when she needed to be. She set the expectations for her staff and was clear on what would be accepted and what would not be tolerated. She was fair with each of her nurses and that is all one could ask for.

Sampson and Dabria went through some additional perfunctory questions but they felt this was as much information as they would obtain. The pair thanked Longstill for his time, each shaking his hand and giving him a business card.

They asked if he remembered anything additional, that could be useful, that he give them a ring day or night.

"What's next?" inquired Sampson. "It feels like we are spinning our wheels and going nowhere fast."

"I've reached out to a trusted colleague and provided him with the details of the case. I hope he is able to delve into elements seeking a connection between all of these pieces. Terri is calculated in all of her decisions; we simply need to understand how the pieces fit together. If my contact provides me with any creditable data, I'll let you know."

She said this last part climbing behind the wheel of her R8.

"In the meantime, I have a visit to make to a certain Veronica King. Care to come along?"

This was the first time the FBI agent extended an offer to tag along as part of the investigation. Although they were working the case together, they in effect were working the case separately.

"Sure," he said making his way to the passenger seat. "To what pleasure are we visiting Mrs. King?"

"If you recall, Mrs. King stated she had to go home because her daughter was sick."

"Yes and this was corroborated by the principal at the school."

"Her husband's car was videotaped at the convenience store two blocks from the school. Fast forward 20 minutes, the same car can be seen leaving the direction of the school. While you cannot see the child in the car, it's clear something is in the backseat that wasn't there when he bypassed the convenience store the first time."

Sampson wondered how she was able to obtain this footage but decided he would keep the question to himself.

"Veronica's statement is her husband was gone for a business trip and could not pick up their daughter thus she had to leave work early. The thing is, her husband has not been heard of since that day."

"WHAT!" Sampson exclaimed. "We received confirmation from the airlines that he was on that flight. Their manifest shows him boarding the plane and the hotel shows him checking in."

"Yes; however, I had a colleague of mine do some additional digging. Although the manifest says he was on the flight, and the hotel shows he checked into the hotel, there isn't one person who can recall seeing him. Furthermore, I find it strange he would be gone this long."

Sampson could hardly believe what he was hearing. More than that, he needed to know who this secret colleague is that keeps providing information his team could not ascertain. From the sounds of it, the person in question didn't work for the FBI, and that made him even more intrigued.

"I'd like to look Mrs. King in the eyes when I ask her about her husband and when she's asked to explain his vehicle's proximity to the school the day of the GIS massacre."

February 6th – 9:00 a.m

SAL GRANDSON SAT at his kitchen table crumbling another sheet of paper and tossing it at the trashcan. Similar to his previous 27 crumbled sheets of paper, this one hit the side of the trashcan before falling harmlessly to the floor. He placed his head into his hands willing his brain to come up with an answer that made sense.

After his "break-in" at GIS he had forgotten about the shreds of paper he absconded with prior to escaping the building. Well, it wasn't a graceful exit. He was running from the long arm of the law. *And what was up with that dog?* Nonetheless, since Jane handed him the scraps of paper, he was like an old dog with a bone working tirelessly to solve the puzzle but making no progress.

Jane silently walked into the room witnessing the despair pulsating behind his clenched fingers. She had never seen him like this and in a way, it was comical. She could see his lips working wordlessly behind his fingers, eyes closed so tight that a vein began to materialize down the center of his head.

"Sal," she offered hesitantly, "What's wrong, honey?"

Sal, realizing for the first time that she entered the room, moved his hands from his head and stared at her with bloodshot eyes.

This is worse than I imagined, she thought. She pulled out one of the other dining room chairs, that she secretly despised, and sat next to him. "What's going on, Sal?"

His mouth motioned a few words before sound emanated from his throat, "...scraps of paper. It's those darn scraps of paper from GIS," he said finding his voice once again. "I have been sitting here trying to solve the puzzle to these scraps of paper. It could be nothing, but then again it could be something. The not knowing is driving me crazy."

"Scraps of paper – does this have to do with the scraps I found in your jacket the other day? And what does this have to do with GIS?"

"Yes, this has to do with the scraps of paper you gave me the other day, and... you're probably better off not knowing the answer to your last question."

She raised an eyebrow, "Really?"

"Really."

She shook her head knowing if he didn't want to tell her, he did something illegal to procure the information sitting on the kitchen table.

"Here, let me take a look," she said turning the paper around with the scraps affixed to it with scotch tape. On the paper she noticed the top line read "Br" followed by "ley". The second line read "Wh" followed by "he?".

"Hmm, not much detail to work from – "

"I know'," Sal said words rushing out in a tumble. "I've been burning brain cells trying to figure this out. The more I try to solve this intolerable riddle, the further away I become."

Jane cocked her head and said, "Well the second line looks like it's one of the 5 Ws: Who, What, When, Where, Why – and we can skip How as it doesn't start with a "Ho". She cocked her head to the other side.

"Who he?"

"What he?"

"When he?"

"Where he?"

"Why he?"

Sal took a moment to chime in, "I don't think they are two consecutive words. It wouldn't leave many options for the top line. Furthermore, the person who wrote this is well educated and I couldn't see them writing anything down like "What he?".

"That's fair," Jane conceded. "But I'm still convinced the first word is one of the remaining Ws. It most certainly is a question of some sort. Let's assume for a moment the word in the middle happens to be "is", that eliminates "When is he?". Unless we are dealing with some sort of cyborg, that eliminates "What is he?" as well. That leaves us with three possibilities.

"Who is he?"

"Where is he?"

"Why is he?"

Sal had to admit, her logic made sense and it was further than he had come. He smiled and said, "That is great work Jane and if you are right, that means the top portion is a name."

"Bingo!" she said. "I'll admit honey bear solving the name may still be impossible."

"Maybe not impossible," he said with a smile. I know a certain FBI agent who has a geek on her personal payroll that could probably help us figure this out."

He leaned over almost falling out of his chair and gave her a long, deep passionate kiss on the lips, "Thank you for throwing a lifeline to a drowning man."

"Anytime, babe," she said giving him a peck on the lips and stroking his hair. "By the way, did you look at the dinette options I left for you?"

February 6th – 11:00 a.m

DETECTIVE CARL SAMPSON and Agent Donatella Dabria entered the offices of Global Insights Security. Straight ahead sat the security desk being manned by a mid-40s guard with a receding hairline and a button up shirt that hung loosely from his shoulders. He handed the woman he was helping a visitor's badge and pointed her to the elevator.

"Hi, may I help you?" came a voice higher than you would have expected coming from his frame.

Agent Dabria flipped open her badge while Sampson did the same, "Special Agent Donatella Dabria and Detective Carl Sampson to see Veronica King."

He gave their badges a once over and turned toward his

computer monitor. He typed a few keys, louder than Dabria would have imagined necessary and plastered a frown on his face.

"I'm sorry, but I do not see an entry in our visitors manifest for either of you."

"That's because we do not have an appointment," came the retort from Sampson.

"Well, without an appointment I cannot let you up to see Mrs. King. She's a very busy woman and –"

Dabria was in no mood to banter back and forth with this guard. She felt it was due to Mercury Retrograde; however, that was still over a week away. In reality, she just didn't feel like small talk after seeing the body of Mrs. Hampton and the similarities between her body and that seen from the victims here at GIS.

"Our asking was a mere courtesy to allow you to perform the duty you have been tasked to complete. In reality Mr.," she looked with distain at his name badge, "Busch, me and my partner are going to walk over to the elevator and take it up to see Veronica King. Even if she is otherwise disposed, she will extract herself and see to it that we are not left waiting. You see, we are investigating the horrific scene that played out here some weeks prior and there isn't anything that will prevent us from completing that job."

She began walking toward the elevator bank and he opened his mouth to protest their movement. However, before the words could free themselves from his lips, he decided it was probably in his best interest not to interfere in official police business. He turned back to the entry log and entered their names to the list along with the time of their entry.

The elevator doors slid open on the fifth floor providing a glimpse into the working atmosphere. Unlike their first visit to the GIS offices, the floor was lively and gave off an air of confidence and optimism. The pair stepped onto the floor making a bee line to the office of Veronica King. Sampson found it curious she had not taken over the CEO's office – instead she decided to stay in the office where she made a name for herself.

They traversed down the hallway, Donatella in the lead, gliding as she always seemed to do. Sampson sensed a difference in the FBI agent. She seemed to have an edge different than she had displayed since he met her.

Less than 20 paces away from the office of CEO King, Veronica lifted her head sensing the determined movement headed her way. A "now what" look danced across her facial features as she stood politely to greet her visitors.

"Ah, Special Agent Dabria," she said extending her hand. "I'm surprised to see you here, without an appointment, nonetheless. And it looks like you have brought along a friend."

"Detective Carl Sampson," came the mellow tone taking the proffered hand after Donatella released her grip.

"Why don't you two come on in and have a seat. What is it I can do for the FBI and one of Charlotte's finest?"

Special Agent Dabria crossed her right leg over her left sitting back in the armed visitor's chair. "I'd like to go over the discussion we had at your home the day after the unfortunate events that unfolded here, in this very building."

"Sure, I'll do anything I can to assist."

"Before we get started, I must say, I'm curious as to why you didn't change offices. Surely being the CEO comes with a new office."

"Easy enough to answer, though I don't see the relevance. I like working closely with my staff. I always felt the CEO office was too far removed from the action, thus I decided to keep my former office. I have repurposed the office to a game room. It's a place where the staff can go and blow off a little steam or simply take a break after a grueling morning."

In truth, King hadn't moved into the office because every time she walked in there, she felt the spirits of her murdered colleagues. If she could have found a way to remove the office out of the building, she would have done so.

"I see. That's very noble of you," Dabria said nodding her head forward. "Mrs. King, where is your husband and his mistress Irena Petrov?"

Although she tried to mask her initial reaction, the shock registered before she was able to compose herself. Both King and Detective Sampson had not expected this question for totally different reasons.

Agent Dabria had not shared this information with him previously and he wondered for a brief moment if she made this up. However, after seeing the expression on the face of Veronica and knowing she had her ways of finding out information, he knew this was legit.

Veronica King was assured by her "new employers" that all tracks had been covered. How did this FBI woman know about the affair and how did she know the woman's name?

Agent Dabria sat there, calm, fingers tented patiently awaiting an answer. The silence in the room carried uncomfortably as the suspect, which Dabria began to think of her as, answered the question. She decided to let some of her true rage carry part of her answer so that it would seem legitimate.

"Honestly, I'm not sure. I found out the son of a bitch was having an affair with Ms. Petrov and told him I never wanted to see his cheating ass again. I guess he took that request seriously. A couple days after having a fight about his indiscretions, he took a flight and never returned. I had enough going on personally that him being away was the best thing for me."

"The day of the massacre, your husband picked your

daughter up from school. We caught his car on camera going to the school without your daughter and leaving the school with her snuggly tucked away in the back seat."

Dabria paused and simply looked at the woman across from her that began to shift in her seat ever so slightly. She hadn't asked a question, just a statement and now waited on Veronica to pick up the thread. Sampson could see the gears working in her head, calculating her response.

"I'm not sure what video you were watching, Agent Dabria, but I picked my daughter up from the school that day." She gave Donatella a cold glare, daring her to challenge her comment.

"Of course, that is what you told me previously. Must have slipped my mind. It's plausible a man matching your husband's description, driving the same car, would have a child at the same school."

"Indeed, it is," countered Veronica. "In fact, I would say it's likely. There are a lot of black Honda Civics cruising the streets of Charlotte by men in their early 40s."

Sampson could sense the tension building as each woman lobbed a volley back in the others court.

"Hell of a place to take a business trip. Nepal is one of those countries that has no extradition treaty with the United States. But I digress. Do you know the nature of your husband's visit there – for business?"

"No, I don't. He kept most of his business affairs to himself, as he obviously did with other affairs. Now if you will excuse me, I have a meeting with a woman who is poised to occupy one of our last two board seats."

"Absolutely, we don't want to get in the way of you running the company you have inherited." Though she didn't say the words, all three people in the room knew the implication. The company she inherited after the untimely death of the CEO and all other members of the board.

King stood, followed by Sampson and then Dabria.

"Thank you for taking time to stop by, and I do hope you are able to solve this case soon. However, I will have to ask that next time you make an appointment. I'm fairly busy these days and I wouldn't want to miss your visit. Detective Sampson," she said extending her hand yet again, "You must be the strong silent type."

She said this flashing him a smile which he politely smiled back.

"Agent Dabria, it was a pleasure meeting with you again," she reached out and shook the FBI agent's hand.

"Likewise. Oh, but I do have one more question. Are you and your daughter planning to take a trip soon?"

Veronica tried to find the trap in this question. She didn't see one.

"No, we are not taking any trips anytime soon."

"I see. I guess the issuance of her own passport must have been for a potential trip much later in the year."

Veronica extracted her hand from Agent Dabria's, kicking herself for not thinking about a passport.

"Well, you two have a wonderful rest of the day," she replied choosing to ignore the comment.

The women locked eyes for a moment and with a smooth motion, Donatella began to walk toward the door, exiting the office.

Back in the car, Sampson broke the silence, "Where did you get the information about the mistress and the passport? Why didn't you share this with me prior to going into the meeting? I don't necessarily mind a surprise, but wow, those were unexpected."

"The where is unimportant at this time. The key is the story they tell."

"Which is?"

"I'm going to drop you back off at your car. I have some additional errands I need to run. Thank you for coming along."

"I really didn't do much. Though it was good to get a front row seat."

"You did plenty, you were the strong silent guy."

15

FEBRUARY 20TH – 9:00 A.M

The on-scene correspondence from Channel 3 and Channel 9 were gathered with their camera crews in the atrium of Atrium Health. No traditional print journalists were here to cover the event; however, there were a number of online journalists. Sal Grandson, representing the latter, received a tip from one of his contacts that the company would be holding a conference. He suspected it had something to do with the murder of Penny Hampton.

The news of her death sent shockwaves through the community. Sal knew of the phenomenal job she did during her shift at the hospital; however, as news of her community involvement came to light, Sal found himself more intrigued with her story.

Twice a month on Saturdays she would volunteer at the local food bank in charge of the sorting, loading, and delivery of food that had been donated throughout the week. The other Saturdays of the month she volunteered at the local YMCA chapter that was in her neighborhood.

Once when she was asked about her work at the Y, she stated, "I basically grew up in their establishment. When I was young, I went there after school on a daily basis along with several of my friends. We managed our homework and extracurricular activities until our parents came to pick us up. For me it was like a home away from home. I see this as a way of me creating a safe environment for those boys and girls who need a place to go when they have nowhere else to turn."

By all accounts, Penny had touched so many lives. Lives that will be forever impacted by her generosity and saddened by her death.

Sal wondered why someone would do something so despicable to such a lovely woman. The world that Sal knew from his childhood was quickly disintegrating in front of his eyes. He made up his mind he would dedicate an article to the days of old before the end of the week, if for nothing else to feel better within himself.

He was tucked into his seat next to a young man with stud earrings racing up the cartilage of his ear. He had both nostrils pierced with a chain that ran from one side to the other. Sal could tell he was wearing contacts as his eyes were a shade of blue that nature never intended. He wore his hair spiked down the middle and shaved on the sides. He sat with his legs crossed, right over left, writing feverishly on his cellphone with his stylus.

On his other side sat a woman in grey sweatpants with white canvas Nikes with a black swoosh. She sported a white long sleeve t-shirt that read, "Will Write for Wine". She was balancing her Apple MacBook on her lap while holding her phone between her shoulder and her ear talking to George.

Sal found it hard to believe this was the future but at the same time he knew every generation felt the same way about all upcoming generations; however, in his case he knew he was right. This next generation, especially the journalists, had a lot to learn about the way of the world. Idly he thought with certainty that he could still write circles around each and every one of them.

Sal's attention was shifted to the podium as a man in his early to mid-60s walked toward the mic. He wore a severely tailored black suit that hugged his 5-foot-9-inch frame. He had a head full of black hair that was held firmly in place with the aid of synthetic chemicals. A white button shirt lay under the sport coat with a navy blue solid tie adorning his neck. From his vantage point he could see the man's eyes were slightly puffy as if he had been crying. He stepped to the mic and cleared his throat.

"Good morning and thank you all for being here today. For those that do not know me, my name is Harry Longstill. I'm the Director of Operations here at Atrium Health. As all of you are aware, two weeks ago we lost someone special to the Atrium family. Someone who made our patients feel like partners in their care and colleagues that felt like family in her home. A person who never had a cross word and would give the shirt off of her back if it meant making your day a better day.

We lost Penny Hampton to a vile and senseless crime that both her work family and home family are still reeling. She will forever be missed, and she will forever be loved."

Longstill took a moment to compose himself before continuing.

"With her passing, there was a hole that the Atrium family needed to fill. We are fortunate to have found the woman I'm going to bring to the stage. She has operated as the Director of Nursing at her previous employer, has impeccable recommendations, and has turned her nursing unit into one that has maintained the highest rating in her state. Please help me welcome to the podium, Ms. Patti Jones."

A round of applause made its way through the assembled

crowd as she made her way to the mic. Patti stood a shade over 5 feet 5 inches. She wore rectangular red frames that sat toward the edge of her nose. Her auburn hair stopped just above her shoulder and wrapped around the contours of her face. Her outfit was simple and straightforward, a black skirt that extended below the knees with a white blouse tucked in that swayed as she walked. Around her neck she wore a simple set of pearls but no earrings. She adjusted the mic down a few inches and looked over the crowd

"Thank you for the warm welcome. I know I have some large shoes to fill both within the hospital and within the community. From everything I have heard about Penny and from the display of love in the audience today, I know she was an irreplaceable woman. My goal is not to replace her but to carry forward the legacy she has built. My goal is to work with the nursing staff to ensure the service, friendship, and dedication our patients have been used to and will continue to be the staple in everything we do. Director Longstill," she said looking back at him, "The operational framework you have put in place has set us up for success. I look forward to joining the team and doing everything I can to make this a seamless experience for everyone. Thank you!"

Longstill and Jones shook hands while a couple of online journalists took pictures with their cellphones. Sal felt like the dinosaur in the room as he used his Cannon Rebel T6 to capture a few shots. Photo ops complete, the pair left the podium area and the crowd began to file out. As they did, Sal noticed Special Agent Dabria standing off to the side. He placed his camera back in his bag and made his way over toward the agent. As he did, he saw she was standing next to a guy whose stance and demeanor yelled, cop.

"Agent Dabria, fancy meeting you here. Are you working on the case involving Penny Hampton?"

She gave a faint, yet genuine smile at seeing the reporter.

During the conflict at Driftwood Springs, Sal played a vital role in helping to identify the person responsible for the kidnappings. He also found himself in the crosshairs of the mastermind and ended up being saved by the agent.

"Sal," she said in her cool southern voice, "It's good to see you again." The two shook hands before Donatella motioned toward Sampson. "This is Detective Carl Sampson with the CMPD. We have decided to share resources as we work to solve a couple of cases that seem to be linked."

Sal feeling the hairs on the back of his neck stand erect asked, "Are you saying the murder of Penny Hampton is tied into a case the two of you are working on? Wait – are you working the GIS case? The murder of the entire board including the CEO. Well, almost the entire board, everyone except the then COO and now CEO, Veronica King. Are you –"

"We are not at liberty to discuss the case," came the deep voice of Sampson.

Sal regarded the man, respectfully, but turned his full attention back to Agent Dabria. "I've been meaning to call you about that case. I have something I acquired from the facilities that I could use your help solving."

"Acquired from the facilities," repeated Sampson. "Are you saying you stole something from their building that you are not supposed to have?"

"I didn't steal anything; I just appropriated an item from Veronica's trashcan during one of my visits."

"Great!" Sampson said exasperated. "This just keeps getting better. We now have you for a B&E along with theft. I suggest you stop while you are ahead."

"What do you have Sal?" asked Donatella.

"I'm not sure exactly. Veronica tore the paper before tossing it in the trashcan. I dropped some pieces when I heard the security guards coming, hence the help I need from you. I managed to piece together most of it but there is still a piece I cannot crack. I'm willing to share the information and if it turns out to be useful, you cut me in on the full story of what's happening."

"You dropped some pieces when you heard the security guards coming," to this Sampson just shook his head pressing his palm against his temple staving off a headache.

Sal could tell the agent was curious, he needed to seal the deal.

"I have the paper at my apartment. Why don't you stop by later and take a look? If it's nothing, no harm, no foul. If it's something, you let me in on the story – deal?"

"We will stop by later, and if what you have is indeed valuable, we will share some additional information with you."

Sampson was about to open his mouth to protest, but Dabria stopped him with a raise of the hand.

"However, everything we give you cannot be printed until the cases are solved."

"Come on. How is that fair? I need something for my readers today."

"That's the deal. You can take it or leave it."

Sal knew the story would be a good one if it involved Agent Dabria.

"Ok, deal. I'll share what I have, and you'll share the details of the case. I'll hold off on releasing any information until the cases have been solved.

"Good. We will see you this evening."

Sal bid the agent and the detective a good day and walked away.

"Are you really going to share the details of the case with this reporter?"

"Indeed, I'll hold my end of the agreement. Should Sal have something that helps turn this case, I'm willing to share what we know."

"And what if he decides to print the story before the cases are solved?"

"Sal and I have some history. I trust he will hold the story until he has been given the greenlight to release it to the public."

"I hope you're right, and more than that, I hope he has something we can use!"

February 20th – 11:30 a.m

"THANK YOU, Dr. Prince, for everything you are doing to make this pregnancy as smooth as possible. I have to admit, there were a couple of times that I wanted to crawl up in the corner. Several times I asked myself, what have I gotten myself into, but I know I wouldn't trade it for the world."

"You've been a model patient, Mrs. Thompson. Every first-time mother experience doubt of some sort. You'll get there, the little one is right around the corner."

Dr. Prince gave Jasmyn a wide smile and a big hug. "You're doing great! I'd like to see you back next month."

Jasmyn returned the hug and felt fortunate to have found such a caring OB as Dr. Prince. They made their way to the checkout where the lobby was beginning to fill with patients.

"Lucie, please schedule Mrs. Thompson for a follow-up in four weeks. Jasmyn, remember to take it easy and everything will be just fine."

Jasmyn walked through the exit and around the corner to the receptionist. Lucie gave her the normal smile that played across her face. "Let's see – Dr. Prince has an opening on March 27th at 9:30. Will that work?"

"Sure, let me check my calendar." Jasmyn pulled out her smartphone and looked through her upcoming appointments and work schedule. "Yep, that'll work just fine. I don't need an appointment reminder, I'll go ahead and log the reminder in my phone."

"Great – I have you down for Friday, March 27th at 9:30 a.m. with Dr. Prince. Is there anything else I can do for you today?"

"No – well, yes. I hope you don't mind me asking. Lucie T. Berkry is an uncommon name. Do you mind if I ask where it came from?"

The receptionist smiled wanly focusing on Jasmyn. "Berkry is an old family name. My great-grandmother and great-grandfather grew up in Germany. They were not too fond of the direction the country was headed so they decided to escape to America. After their voyage, they settled originally in Maine. They didn't want to lose all of their heritage after they left everything behind, so my great-grandfather made the bold decision to keep his name. He thought he was going to receive a tremendous amount of scorn; however, the name never raised the ire of anyone he came across. We've kept the name in the family ever since."

"That's amazing," Jasmyn heard herself say without realizing it. "Well Lucie, I am certainly pleased I had a chance to meet you."

"No, Mrs. Thompson, the pleasure is all mine," she said with a smile that caused Jasmyn to pause. She wasn't sure what it was, but it was something in that tone and that look.

"Ok, well, I'll see you in a couple of weeks." She turned and made her way out of the office preparing for her drive back home where Marcellous was putting the final touches on lunch with the Evans.

It took Jasmyn longer than normal to arrive home because of an accident on I-77. There always seemed to be an accident somewhere on this highway which she couldn't understand. When she arrived, she noticed an unfamiliar vehicle parked on the curb in front of their house. Hurriedly, she pulled her car into the garage and killed the engine. Hearing the details of what happened to her Director of Nursing, Penny, she let the garage down before she exited the car. Though it was unlikely someone would be after her, the news of her death had everyone on edge.

When she walked into the house, she could smell the aroma of smoked beef brisket, spare ribs and baked beans simmering in the oven.

"Hey honey," Marcellous said greeting her with a kiss on the cheek. He was in his grilling element and had the full attire to match. He donned his white chef's coat and white chef's hat that he ordered online when they first were married. He had his grillmaster set atop the island with the long handle spatula and tongs missing from the set. She could see he had already whipped up his homemade barbeque sauce which he covered and sat off to the side.

"Sorry I'm late," she said slipping out of her jacket and hanging it in the coat closet. "There was an accident and Waze couldn't even find a better route than just powering through."

"Don't worry about it, babe. I'm happy you and Marcellous Jr. made it home safely."

"Oh – so it's Marcellous Jr. now? Just yesterday it was Tasha."

"Well – today it feels like it's a boy. So... Marcellous Jr. it is," he smiled placing his hand on her swollen belly. "Bethany and Troy are sitting in the family room. They arrived about 10 minutes ago."

"Lord, let me go in and say hello," she said as they made their way toward their guest.

"Bethany, Troy. I'm so sorry for running late. This traffic in Charlotte can be ridiculous."

The Evans stood to greet their hostess. Bethany leaned in giving both cheeks a kiss while Troy pulled in the other mother-to-be for a gentle hug.

"Troy, it's nice to finally meet you. Bethany has talked so much about you that I feel I know you already."

Troy stood a shade over six feet tall with dark brown hair and a slender but full face. He wore frameless rectangular clear frames that covered his dark brown eyes that matched his hair. He had an athletic build – a build that wasn't that of a professional athlete, but certainly that of a working man who took care of himself.

"You can't believe everything Bethany says," came the smooth professorial voice. "But most of it is true," he said with a wide smile.

Bethany gave him a slight elbow to the ribs and the group had a laugh.

The doorbell broke up the laughter and Marcellous stated that he would get the door. The other three took seats with Bethany and Troy sitting next to each other on the loveseat and Jasmyn sitting at the right arm of the sofa.

"You're just in time," came the voice of Marcellous as he entered into the room. Agent Dabria walked in carrying a gift bag in light pastel colors that said "Congrats on your baby". Behind her stood Detective Sampson carrying a bottle of wine with a bow affixed around its neck.

The three stood once again and exchanged pleasantries before retiring to their seats. Donatella sat next to Jasmyn while Detective Sampson walked into the kitchen to aid Marcellous in the final stages of lunch.

Donatella, still skeptical of the woman who had inserted herself into Jasmyn's life, asked, "Bethany and Troy – Jasmyn said you are interested in moving into the Grant's old home, how is that going?"

"Well," Bethany said with a Cheshire cat grin, "We were going to wait to share the news, but – we are scheduled to close on the house in two weeks."

"That's amazing," Jasmyn almost squealed with glee. "I'm so happy that we will be neighbors, you are going to love the neighborhood."

Yes, as am I, Donatella thought. *It'll help me to keep a closer eye on you.*

"You hear that Marcellous – we are going to have some new neighbors!"

"Welcome to the neighborhood," came the distant voice from the kitchen.

Not missing a beat, Donatella continued, "So, what do you guys do for a living?"

"Troy teaches creative writing at the university. I work as a consultant with a focus on project management."

"Interesting," Donatella said in her southern drawl. Jasmyn had heard that "interesting" before and glanced over at her.

"How long have you been in project management?"

"Well," Bethany said looking at Jasmyn and then back at Donatella. "I've worked as a PM for the past 11 years. I spent the first couple of years working for Yum Brands and then moved into consulting so I could work in different verticals. I've worked in everything from retail to financial to manufacturing. My current position is with a tech company."

Donatella raised her eyebrow, and Jasmyn noticed this movement. Before she could pepper Bethany with any other questions, Jasmyn interjected.

"Donatella works for the FBI and she cannot help but ask a lot of questions."

"Wow! A real live FBI agent. Any cases you are working on that we can know about?"

"No," she replied flatly, looking back over at Jasmyn who was giving her the "don't you start eyes." She realized she would not have any other questions answered, so she moved on.

"Jasmyn – I brought you a gift, please open it."

She smiled and gratefully took the package, "You didn't have to do this, but I will always accept a gift."

She pulled out the top tissue paper and pushed aside the rest. At the bottom of the bag was a jewelry box. She noticed the box didn't have any markings, but she had seen her fair share of jewelry boxes and was curious to know what was inside.

Jasmyn turned the case around and pulled open the lid. Her eyes lit up with excitement when she laid her eyes on the object inside.

"Donatella – this is too much," she said pulling the bracelet from the box. It was a Pandora bracelet with three charms each separated with a spacer. The first charm was of a mother, the second of a father, and the third of a baby.

"Go ahead and put it on, I'm sure it'll fit."

Jasmyn sat the box on the cushion next to her and fumbled a couple of times with the latch. She was finally able to catch the latch just right between her nails, lay the bracelet on her wrist and then her wrist to her leg. With a practiced motion she was able to secure the bracelet after only two tries. She shook her wrist a couple of times and the bracelet slid into place.

"It's beautiful," she said with a tear forming in her eye. "Thank you so much!" She stood up from her seat and walked over to give the special agent a hug.

"You're welcome. I hope that you will wear it all the time."

"I will," came the hurried reply. "I'll absolutely wear it all the time."

"Lunch is served," bellowed the voice from the kitchen. "Come and get it."

"You ain't got to tell me twice. One thing you don't do is get between a pregnant woman and her food. Come on, Bethany, let's go have some of this delicious food."

"Aye, aye, captain!"

The group made their way from the family room to the kitchen where Marcellous lay out a spread from both the grill and the oven.

"Babe, this looks great. Thank you for pulling this together."

"Yes, this looks amazing Marcellous. You'll have to give me the recipe for the baked beans," chimed in Detective Sampson.

"Family secrets people. Y'all ain't gonna have my grandma coming back from the afterlife to smite me for giving out her recipes. But I will give a toast. Everybody grab a glass."

The men all grabbed the necks of their beers and the women, including Donatella, raised a glass of water.

"To friends, old and new. To good health. And to bringing the little ones into this world safe and sound."

Everyone clinked their glasses, "Cheers!"

AGENT DABRIA and Detective Sampson pulled up to Sal Grandson's apartment. The exchange of words had been sparse since leaving the Thompson's house but Sampson could sense something underneath the surface. Donatella placed the car into park before speaking.

"I'm not so sure my suspicions about Bethany Evans are correct. Although her insertion into Jasmyn's life comes at an inopportune time, she seems to be on the up and up."

"She did seem to be nice, and certainly didn't seem to be a mastermind behind a nefarious plot. However," Sampson continued as they climbed the stairs to Sal's apartment, "I noticed something about her husband at the beginning of the conversation. It could have been my imagination, but I thought I saw him stiffen when Jasmyn mentioned you were an FBI agent. It could have been my imagination, and it could just be a normal response when in the presence of the FBI. I focused in on him the remainder of the evening and he seemed to be guarded."

Donatella looked over to Sampson thinking back to the remainder of the afternoon.

"I had my focus on Bethany, so I did not pay him much attention. However, now that you mention it, he didn't say much for the remainder of the afternoon. I wrote it off as part of his nature. I'm not certain he has anything to do with this case as it's Jasmyn's first time meeting him, but something to keep in mind for the future."

They knocked on the door and within 10 seconds Sal stood their beckoning them inside.

"Special Agent Dabria and Detective Sampson, I'd like you to meet Jane Markowitz."

Jane shook Sampson's hand and reached out to embrace Donatella.

"Thank you, thank you, thank you," she said squeezing with all her might. "Thank you for everything you did to ensure Sal came back home to me. I will forever be grateful to your heroics."

Sampson raised his eyebrows at this display of affection and wondered what it was that Donatella had exactly done. This was the second time that someone alluded to the fact that she had saved his life; however, he had yet to understand exactly how. He would need to inquire more about that at a later date.

Jane continued, "Can I offer either of you anything to drink? We have wine and beer chilled in the fridge, or water if you are officially on duty."

Both declined the offer and sat in the small living area. Once all four were situated in the room, the space felt suffocating. Almost as if they were all sitting in an MRI machine.

Sal, the last to enter the room, held a sheet of paper in his hand. "We still have a deal, right?" he inquired holding the paper as a bargaining chip.

"Indeed," came the smooth tone from Donatella. "A promise is a promise. If what you have propels the case forward, I will tell you about the cases and how they seem to be intertwined."

Sal handed over the document while sitting on the edge of his chair. Sampson looked over the shoulder of Donatella. At the top of the paper sat the taped together scraps of paper Sal took from the offices of GIS.

The top line read "Br" followed by "ley". The second line read "Wh" followed by "he?".

Underneath the scraps of paper in Sal's journalistic hand read the words, "Who is he?".

"That's about as far as we managed to get," Sal offered. We think the first line is a person's name but we could not figure out who "he" is.

Donatella took one last look at the document and slowly placed it on the table. Shocked, the entire group looked at her as her face had gone ashen.

"What is it?" Sal asked. "Do you know who he is?"

She looked at them each in turn starting with Sampson, then to Jane and finally Sal. The wheels in her brain were turning and each of them didn't like the look in her eyes.

"What is it?" Sampson followed up.

"There is no *he*," she said breaking the silence that had begun to build. "The last line isn't 'Who is he?'. The last line reads 'Who is she?'."

Sal and Jane both looked at each other stunned and tried to see how the agent had come to this conclusion. Staring at the paper yielded them no additional information. Sure, the "he" had been torn pretty close but they didn't see any other marking that could lead them to believe the word was "she" instead of "he".

Donatella continued, "Sal, Jane. You need to keep your distance from this matter. This isn't a mere game being played."

"Come on, Donatella. You cannot back out on me now. We had a deal and you made a promise. This seems to be some vital piece of information and you promised –"

Donatella interrupted Sal in mid-sentence, "The top line reads 'Bree Buckley'. It appears Terri is using an alias, that of my goddaughter she abducted a few months ago. Veronica King is looking into Bree, better known as Terri, Buckley which means that Terri has had some interaction with Mrs. King."

At the mention of Terri's name, Sampson noticed Sal go stiff, similar to what Troy had done at the mention of Donatella working for the FBI.

"Sal – a promise is a promise and I will tell you all about the cases. And with this information, more than previously thought, you will need to keep up your end of the bargain and not print a word of this until the cases are solved."

Sal nodded his head in agreement, though in the back of his mind he thought, *I agreed to not print anything, but I never said I would give up the investigation.*

"Good. I think I will take that wine after all and we will start with the death of Samantha Young."

PART III

Reckoning

16

MAY 20TH – 9:00 P.M

"Dr. Peterson, you're working awfully late this evening. Is everything ok?"

"Hey Bobby, everything is just fine," Dr. Peterson said with a sigh and a chagrined expression on his face. "The restoration specialist we hired for a special project finished much earlier than expected. I came by to scrutinize the final product. After several rounds of discussion, he finally agreed to fix an additional corner of the masterpiece."

"If anybody is going to keep them in line, I know you will," Bobby countered with a smile. "I'm anxious to hear more details about the secret show. Come on Dr. P. When will you spill the beans?"

The doctor gave Bobby a tired yet genuine smile. "Bobby, my man, I promise you'll be the first one I tell before the ink is even dry on the announcement."

"That's a deal, doc. Now you head on home and get some well-deserved rest and recharge those batteries over the weekend."

"Will do, Bobby, and you make sure no one meddles with my prized artifacts."

"With this state-of-the-art security system, we recently had installed, the cast from Ocean's Eleven couldn't find a way to break in here. Nonetheless, I think I'll start my rounds early and make sure everything is locked up tight. Have a good weekend, doc."

"You too, Bobby."

Bobby opened the door leading to the garage allowing Dr. Peterson to exit. Bobby liked Dr. Peterson and liked working at the museum in general. He had worked the security detail for the last six months after an early retirement from the police force. His family physician advised him the stress of the police force would be his undoing and the best way to ensure his longevity was to find a less stressful job.

When his wife, Kara, heard the news, he knew his time on the force had come to an end. Bobby Cliff loved being an officer and doing what he could to protect the citizens of Cleveland. He decided if he couldn't protect his people, he could protect his art.

A CLEVELAND, Ohio native, Bobby and his family attended all new art exhibits put on by the museum. His mother felt it was important for Bobby and his sister, Tiana, to be cultured. Early on he despised the trips to the museum; however, as he continued to grow, the exhibits began to grow on him.

He recalled going to the museum in the summer of 1977 to see The Milieu of Edvard Munch. He had not held out much for this showing; however, there was something different about this artist and how his work resonated with Bobby. The way the artist captured the raw human emotion with his brush strokes. His mother told him later that he was the artist who commissioned the famous painting, "The Scream".

Bobby went to the library the next day so he could find this painting and there it was on microfilm, a picture of the painting. Edvard Munch went on to describe how the painting represented an infinite scream of nature.

It was at that moment Bobby's interest in painting and art began to blossom. In a way, coming back to watch over the work of so many famous artists was like a homecoming for Bobby. He never truly felt like he was working because he spent so much time on the job learning about the artwork. Dr. Peterson, the head of the museum, had also taken a liking to Bobby.

He fed Bobby's desire to know as many facts about art as he could handle. He gave Bobby a heads up for all new exhibits coming and made sure both Bobby and Kara had tickets to the first showing. Admittedly so, Bobby was the first security personnel that had an interest in the art and showed a true desire to keep everything safe.

Bobby could still recall the day the secret artifacts arrived at the museum. Dr. Peterson, normally a cheerful but reserved guy, was bouncing off of the walls. All he told Bobby was this was a big deal and that the Cleveland Museum of Art would be the first museum in the country, make that the world, to show off this collection.

Peterson's excitement was contagious and before he knew it, Bobby was brimming with anticipation of this new exhibit, patiently awaiting his time to shine.

Bobby had been at the museum during the upgrades to the security system. This new system was some James Bond, Mission Impossible system that he didn't begin to understand how it fully operated. What he did know was, the system came highly recommended and virtually impenetrable. Some of the guys that still worked on the force had come up against another system created by this company Global Insights Security and they literally had to call the corporate office to have the system shutdown as they prepared for a raid. The techs had reviewed all scenarios but could not find a way to penetrate it without the help of the GIS team.

Once the warrants had been signed and all legal avenues had been crossed, then and only then did GIS deactivate the system allowing the raid to take place. It made Bobby feel better knowing such a stellar system was watching over the prized artifacts as closely as he was.

BOBBY CONTINUED to walk down the west wing of the 1916 building passing the Provenance restaurant making his way toward the down escalators. He hadn't visited the lower level in a couple of days but he wanted to make his way over to the Exhibition Gallery where the exhibit was under lock and key.

As he passed through the atrium, he drift into thoughts of his attire for the event. He kept a tux on hand for such occasions, but Kara had made the comment that it was getting a little snug around the midsection the last time he wore it. He did his best to discount the comment but he knew it was true. He had taken the tux jacket to the tailor before the last event and was told this was the last time they would be able to let out the jacket. The next time he would need to go up a size, maybe two.

With Dr. Peterson's excitement building day by day, he figured this was a good time to purchase a new one.

He hopped on the escalator swinging his flashlight like a security guard in those B-rated movies. The only difference between them and him was, Bobby also carried a gun. Being a former cop, he had a license to carry and he never left his house without his piece.

Midway down the smooth descent of the escalator, Bobby heard a metallic clang originate from down below. It gave him a moment of pause as Dr. Peterson was typically the last person to leave the museum.

May 20th – 9:00 p.m

"AND YOU'RE sure we're clear?" came the husky voice of Marc Blackstone speaking into the mic on his lapel. Blackstone, a career criminal, had been hired by The Syndicate a few years back due to his ability to infiltrate buildings unseen. He normally worked alone; however, because of the delicate nature of this assignment he was asked to bring along a partner. Typically, he would put up a fight, but not tonight.

His partner, a 5 foot 7 or 8 inches, he could never tell, black clad, fully curved, drop dead gorgeous woman, was his partner for the evening. He noted the intensity in her constantly roaming eyes though she hadn't said much. Blackstone always had a way with the ladies, and after they pulled off this job, he planned to pull off her tight-fitting garments.

Hearing the affirmative spoken crisply into his earpiece he spoke, "We've been cleared, let's go." The alarm tied to the loading dock door had been disabled. Blackstone turned the handle and tugged at the door – silence. *Good*, he thought, *the woman manning the security protocols on the other end knew what she was doing.*

They silently made their way through the maze that he had memorized yet he had questioned why they took this route. When reviewing the blueprints to the museum, he noted two better entry points that would have placed them closer to their destination.

"Just follow the plan," came the gentle voice of his partner. Knowing they had Molly, he thought that was her name, deactivating their path every step of the way, made the job a cinch, so he decided to simply "follow the plan".

"Pressure sensors in the next room," came the voice over his earpiece. "Give me a moment." He put up his fist to stop the movement of his partner only to find that was not necessary. She had walked over to another section in this room looking down a long corridor. He eyed her curiously.

"Sensor deactivated, proceed." Before he could utter a word, she was right back next to him – they continued. They passed through the French Tapestries and Illuminated Manuscripts followed by the German Painting and French Decorative Art. Ahead were signs for Medieval and Ancient Egyptian Art and what he had been searching for, the sign for the stairs leading to the lower level.

They padded their way across the museum with his partner continuing to scrutinize the rooms across the atrium.

"Come on this way," he said nudging her along. She gave him a long, hard, cold look. He began to reevaluate his carnal desire as he moved forward. They took the stairs without incident while Molly once again worked her magic to have the lower level door unlocked just as they reached the bottom step.

Straight ahead he could see their destination, the Exhibition Gallery. The double doors leading into the gallery were massive and recently reinforced. He knew this would be the hardest part of the journey, but again all the work was really on the shoulders of Molly.

Aside from the electronic-timed locks on the door, a retinal scanner was the second layer of security. Only three individuals within the museum could enter the room by scanning their eye.

Inside the room, the floor was broken into four quadrants. Each quadrant was affixed with randomly rotating pressure sensors. Only one sensor was active at a time and there was always one active sensor. If all sensors were off at the same time, or if a sensor stayed in one segment longer than it was supposed to, the alarm would sound. This made it impossible to deactivate the entire floor at once.

Lastly, there was a series of infrared lasers that bounced at various angles across the room. The design worked in tandem with the floor sensors to ensure every inch of the room was covered at all times.

However, the techs working at The Syndicate provided a software override that could combat most of the system. With the room broken into four segments, the software took one of the segments and broke it down into a separate quadrant. Once this was done, the pressure sensor was reconfigured to tell the software the new dimensions of the room. This being the size of the newly configured quadrant. When the sensor would activate for that segment of the room, the new configuration became the base setup for the room and only one segment was activated.

The next part was the lasers. They were set to cover the entire room and they were not broken into quads; however, they designed a plan to combat this as well. During the installation, the GIS team was instructed to mount a series of new devices nine feet above the ground. They were told they were a new batch of cameras that the company was developing. During the installation process, the cameras were mounted as instructed and brought online. The video feed worked as expected and the installation team checked the install off of their task list.

The cameras worked as an infrared refractor. When activated, once an infrared beam passed through any of the cameras field of vision, the infrared beam was immediately transmitted to another camera within the room. This process continued until the beam was transmitting through all of the connected cameras and thus keeping it nine feet off of the ground. As long as you stayed underneath it, you were undetectable.

The electronic key lock was by far the easier system to defeat. Just a simple matter of inputting a valid 10-digit code and the door lock would disengage.

Then came the retinal scan. This was an unpredictable crapshoot. During research and development, they were able to take a picture of the eye when scanned, obtain a high-resolution picture of the eyeball and present that eyeball back to the scanner. 57 percent of the time, the picture was recognized, and the system deactivated. 10 percent of the time, the picture was deemed unrecognizable and asked to try again. Upon two unrecognized readings, the system would lock down for 20 minutes.

The remaining 33 percent of the time, the system determined it was an attempt to breach the system and the alarms immediately sound. The result – a complete lock down of that area, including the gates, locking into place.

Marc and his partner arrived at the double doors leading into the Exhibition Gallery. He pulled the 10-digit code from the right breast pocket and entered the sequence. The key was accepted and Marc prepared to open the door.

"Please scan eye" displayed across the screen and the location where the eye was to be scanned glowed an ominous green.

"Please scan eye," Marc repeated out loud – confused. "What the hell are they talking about?" For this part of the mission, Marc had been left in the dark. His partner, Terri Buckley, reached into her breast pocket removing a metal cylindrical case. Marc, still baffled by the request, was astonished when he was easily pushed aside and for the first time he noticed the case in Terri's hand.

She pried the case open exposing an eyeball within. Marc could sense the bile tantalizing his tonsils and he gulped to push it back down. She carefully positioned the eyeball in front of the scanner.

While the engineers had joked that the only foolproof way the retinal scan could be defeated was to have the eyeball handy, Terri had not taken it as a joke. The failure rate was too high for her liking. She needed a sure thing.

. . .

Prior to connecting with Marc, Terri had run a side mission. Tim Saunders, who was head of security at the museum, needed a good drink in the evenings after work. He stopped in at Ray's Bar each night prior to going home to his family. He told his friends and anyone that would listen he needed a drink to calm his nerves before going home to the old ball and chain. And each night he did just that. Periodically, Tim also liked to get a little action on the side before going home. If there was a woman willing and wanting, he would take her right there in his truck.

Buckley played to his every desire while in the bar. She stroked his ego with all the words he wanted to hear – especially when she told him all the things she would do to him. However, she omitted the part about an ice pick through the ear followed up by a removal of his left eye. A standby team from The Syndicate was dispatched to dispose of the body and the car.

After a few moments of holding Tim's eye to the scanner, the light turned green.

"Molly, we're in. You're up," came the voice from Terri speaking into her lapel.

"Yes ma'am," came the response that both Marc and Terri heard. He looked at her in disbelief. He didn't know which made him feel worse. The fact that she had an earpiece on this entire time and had not said anything while he had been repeating the information from Molly as if she could not hear it.

Or the fact that she had a human eye in a metal box in her pocket. Where on earth had she obtain this eyeball and whose eye was it?

Or should he be most ashamed that as she stood there, with the eyeball in hand, bathed in green lights, he went back to his initial thought of stripping her out of all her clothes once again.

"You guys are all set," came the voice from Molly. The back-left quadrant of the room is where the pressure sensors are now concentrated. And as a reminder, do not raise anything above nine feet. I'd say eight and a half to be on the safe side. Good luck."

Buckley looked over at Blackstone, "Let's go!"

Entering the gallery Terri took the lead and moved directly to the secluded area located in the center of the room. With Molly performing her magic, the tightly secured room transformed into a walk in the park.

On their approach they saw a large metal table with three paintings, a metal cart, and three ornate wooden frames. Blackstone walked over to the cart looking through its contents.

- Emulsion Cleaner
- Varnish Remover
- Neutralizer
- Varnish
- Wooden Handle Cotton Swabs
- Surgical Gloves
- Metal Container

"Some operation they have here," he remarked. "Looks tedious." As he turned toward the table containing the paintings, he clipped the edge of the cart. One of the metal containers that sat on the second shelf of the cart began its precarious fall toward an inevitable collision with the ground.

May 20th – 9:20 p.m

AT THE BOTTOM of the escalator, the Exhibition Gallery wasn't visible to Bobby; however, he had a vague sense that he wasn't alone. He stowed away his flashlight and instinctively reached for his gun. He flipped off the leather strap holding the pistol in place and allowed his hand to hover cautiously. *Maybe it was nothing* his mind tried; however, 20 plus years of experience on the force continued to combat that thought.

He proceeded down the open atrium toward the gallery. The door was ajar, *that shouldn't be*, came the thought, but he heard nothing further. He carefully walked toward the door, ears searching for any foreign sounds, nose reaching for unknown scents.

Ten feet from the entrance he could see a faint light illuminating the space beyond. Since he had not gained entry into the room previously he didn't know if this was out of place. He slid into the opening, hand settling on the butt of the pistol, eyes focused on the source of the light. He walked, listening, smelling, peering. The fine hairs on the back of his neck began to rise warning of danger but he saw none – he heard none.

The source of the illumination, a flashlight, stood on its end at the center of the table. The alarms in his mind blared a moment too late

"Please take your hand off the pistol," came the hushed yet firm voice of a woman.

He could feel the barrel of a .45 pressed against the base of his spine. Bobby ran scenarios through his mind then decided to comply – for now. He raised both hands in acquiescence and felt his holster lighten as his pistol was removed.

"Turn around slowly," came the voice as the pressure released from the small of his back.

He did so and stood face-to-face with a barrel resting between his eyes.

"Let's be clear. I have no intention of shooting you," *in this museum*, she thought, "So do as you're told and you will be fine. Are we clear?"

He nodded wordlessly.

She pulled a pair of flex cuffs and tossed them to him. "You seem to be a capable man. Affix these to your wrist."

Bobby Cliff caught the cuffs and slid them over his wrist. He raised his hands to his mouth grabbing the long strand of the left side with his teeth – and pulled, tightening the plastic around his wrist. He did the same with the right side.

"Good. Now if you don't mind, please have a seat on the ground. This is for both your safety and ours."

Ours? He thought. He hadn't seen anyone else. *How many people were here? One more? Two more? A dozen? What have I walked in on?* He awkwardly lowered himself to the floor extending his legs in front of him.

"What are we going to do with him?" came a male voice from his left.

He could feel the intensity in the woman as she glared at the approaching figure.

In a measured voice she said, "Secure the paintings. We don't have all night."

Turning her attention back to Bobby she said, "Sit here and don't move. We will be out of here shortly."

The woman walked away, following in the steps of her accomplice. *Two perps*, he thought. As the man picked up a painting from the table, he was able to catch a glimpse. The style looked awfully familiar and he was sure he hadn't seen it before. The work looked to be that of abstract expressionism and he had the vague sense that it was a Pollock piece.

The man worked expertly, quickly, while the woman scrutinized the room. Bobby ran through his mind the avenues of escape and what to do next.

Within a couple of minutes, the first painting was secure within a cylindrical tube and the man moved on to the next. His meticulous yet efficient work continued for the next 15 minutes.

Within that span of time, Bobby watched as the man secured seven paintings.

"We're all done, it's time to go. What are we doing with him?" the man asked again.

Again, the woman ignored the question. "Help him to his feet." She turned her attention back to Bobby, "I need for you to walk out with us. You aren't going to cause us any troubles, are you?"

He shook his head.

"Good." She looked back at her partner and said, "You carry the paintings, I'll keep an eye on our guest. You take the lead, our guest will walk behind you, and I will walk behind our guest."

Marc's eyes told of his displeasure with the decision but nonetheless began retracing the route back to the loading dock.

Upon exiting the Exhibition Gallery, Terri reached Molly and advised her of their departure. The distant tech began by first resetting the quadrants across the gallery and reenabling the motion sensor patterns. Next, she one by one disabled the reflectors within the cameras allowing the infrared to return to its normal state.

Molly worked returning each security measure back to its previous state before the team entered the building. Their egress went quicker than their ingress and within a span of moments they were back outside.

The air was warm for this time of night and the moon was partially tucked behind a cloud giving off a sliver of natural light. Marc opened the panel door on the side of the vehicle placing each cylinder inside an oversized storage trunk. Marc placed the last cylinder in the trunk and turned back to Buckley, "Now, what are we going to –"

Terri, with the .45 aimed at his head, shot Marc twice and

before the body hit the ground swung the pistol and released two shots into the right eye socket of Bobby Cliff.

She activated the mic on her lapel, "We are going to need a disposal crew at the loading dock. Two subjects down. Reset the entry logs for Tim Saunders as we discussed. I'm headed to the drop with the packages.

May 21st – 6:00 a.m

VERONICA KING WOKE to the sound of her alarm for only the third time in the last month - second this week. She felt settled in her role as CEO for GIS and the incident from months prior finally seemed to be behind the staff. The FBI woman, Dabria, had not made any visits. Authorities had decided her husband had run off thus allowing for her to file for an uncontested divorce. There was a waiting period in case he wanted to contest the divorce but she was sure that would not happen. Just a formality, she mused.

The woman calling herself Bree Buckley had not made an appearance recently although she scared the shit out of her. Her daughter, Gina, seemed to be settled and slowly she was forgetting about that no-good daddy of hers.

By all accounts, King was finally getting her life back in order. Today, she'd meet with a potential client, Citi Bank, to upgrade the security across their entire footprint. Finalizing the deal secured a profitable first quarter to the tune of $6 million to the bottom line - something she was sure the board would applaud.

She finished brushing her hair, gave herself the once over in the full-length mirror - approved, and headed downstairs for her morning coffee. She would allow Gina to sleep an extra 20 minutes while she enjoyed a moment to herself.

At the bottom of the stairs, she flipped the switch, illuminating the kitchen and walked to the coffee maker. She filled the water reservoir to the two-cup line - she'd take a cup to go and measured out two tablespoons of Starbucks Pike's Place coffee. *Better make that three tablespoons,* she thought opting for a stronger brew. She depressed the brew button and turned toward the fridge. Feeling a little frisky this morning, she'd have a Danish roll with her coffee.

"I hope you brewed a cup for me too."

The strange intrusion in her house caused her to gasp audibly. She turned toward the sound cascading from her living room. The overhead light activated and there stood Buckley in the center of the room. *How in the hell does this woman keep getting into my house?*

The woman looked a little haggard, something she hadn't noticed in her before. Nonetheless, she still had the air of menace in her mannerisms.

"Relax," she said in a calm, placating voice. "No one is here to harm you or your daughter. Actually, quite the opposite. We are here to applaud you on a job well done."

We?

A figure materialized from the shadows. A woman, a tad heavy with a bob cut. It was the woman from the hologram. She stood a tad over 5 feet 5 inches with smooth, tanned skin. She had a slight waddle to her walk and a gentleness to her features.

"Mrs. Veronica King. It truly is a pleasure to make your acquaintance in person. I've looked over you for so long I feel as if I already know you." The woman offered a relatively small hand for such a large frame.

Veronica shook the proffered hand.

"I must commend you and your team on the excellent work

you did at the museum. Everything was in place as expected and operated flawlessly."

The look of shock that ran across Veronica's face was genuine. She had not known they were going to break into the museum so soon. They would now fault the system for the break-in on the morning of perhaps her biggest deal.

"Don't worry," the woman said reading her mind. "We've left enough backend clues that will lead to an inside job and we orchestrated his disappearance. By all accounts your system worked perfectly and no one will think anything different."

While that may be true, when Citi heard of this breach, they may have second thoughts. Her mind, already racing into damage control, began to discount the remainder of the conversation. How was she going to spin this with their reps?

"Oh, and don't worry about your meeting with Citi Bank," she continued. "We have already worked out a plan to resolve any potential roadblocks."

The look of shock Veronica wore on her face turned to disbelief. *How did they know about the Citi Bank deal?*

"You'll be adding me as the final seat to the board and you'll want to do so today. Familiarize yourself with my credentials," she said handing her the envelope that she had in her left hand. "Doing so fills your vacant seat and gives you some sway over the negotiations. Let's just say I have a long-standing relationship with members of their board. With me by your side the deal will go through unchallenged."

Veronica, flabbergasted, stood mouth agape. Words formed in her head but none passed through her lips. She wanted to know what sway she had on their board but decided it wasn't worth knowing.

"I do look forward to finally working with you. With me by your side, we are going to change the world." With that, she and Buckley turned toward the door to make their exit. Buckley once again, turned and eyed Veronica top to bottom. She didn't say a word but Veronica could sense her thoughts - she didn't like them.

She made her way back to the coffee pot and poured a mug. Idly she thought, *four tablespoons would have made for a much better cup of coffee after that experience.* With coffee and files in hand, she sat at the island. She opened the folder, took a sip of her coffee, and began to read. In the back of her mind she thought, *tomorrow I'm sure I won't sleep until my alarm.*

17

JUNE 8TH – 9:00 A.M

Special Agent Dabria sat in the oversized chair at Brent's Coffee Shop watching the interactions between the patrons sipping on a chai tea. The case, along with its misdirection and countless interactions, had been well crafted. She knew Buckley orchestrated the series of events - but to what end? She wrestled with this conundrum while the man standing in line nibbled playfully on the woman's ear in front of him while she giggled.

Hearing that Buckley used an alias of Bree in her unexplained interactions with Veronica King was another taunt - another jab. This news, which should have focused her mind, only made the picture more - obtuse. As much as she hated to admit it, she needed a second perspective to help lift the fog.

On cue, Detective Sampson entered the door of the coffee shop. He scanned the room intensely before laying eyes on Donatella. He recently had a haircut, she mused internally.

She stood as he approached, "Thanks for joining me."

"No problem at all. This case has me as bugged out as you. It's past time we solve this case - these cases."

Donatella nodded as they both took a seat. Pleasantries out of the way, Sampson continued.

"I say we start at the very beginning with victim number one, Samantha Young. She was shot at the hands of her lover, something forced upon him by Terri Buckley. She controlled the situation and the outcome by threatening his family. Why?"

Donatella chimed in, "Buckley has a fierce disdain for men who cheat on their significant other."

"Yea, ok. But that doesn't answer why. Why have her killed in that fashion?"

"She did it this way to ensure it caught my attention. Recall the card that you found at the scene. The sensational way in which Samantha was murdered combined with the card was meant as a message – to me."

"What was the message?"

Donatella looked Sampson squarely in the eyes, "She's saying she'll have four lavish crimes and the fifth one is meant to harm me in some way."

Sampson looked at the woman sitting across from him for a moment. He decided to press forward.

"Aside from getting your attention, is there anything crucial about the first victim?"

"No. But she did work in the same office in which Jasmyn sees her OB. Other than potentially stealing records there isn't much there for her."

"Ok," he said but there was still a thought percolating in the back of his mind. "Then you have the massacre at GIS. The entire board, save Veronica King, is wiped out. King is spared and has written a note inquiring about Bree Buckley."

"Another clear sign of intent. Bree is the first name of my goddaughter who she kidnapped to lure me into a confrontation."

"By all accounts, this woman is brilliant, you've said it yourself. We know she is responsible for the massacre but why? What did she gain?"

Donatella chewed on the question for a moment, "Leverage. She used the leverage of Adam, mainly against him, to kill Samantha. Perhaps she spared King so that she could later use her."

"To what end? If she has some sort of leverage over King. What is King giving her in return?"

"I don't know – but we need to find out. We need to look at any recent business transactions from GIS. They are one of the foremost leaders in security systems. We need to see if there are any recent transactions that could lead to a motive for Buckley's moves. I will look into this," Donatella stated.

Sampson nodded and continued, "After taking some time off, the next sign we saw from Buckley was the killing of Penny Hampton. A suburban housewife, and director of nursing that was abducted from her own garage. An abduction and murder that she didn't leave on display for the public to see, but rather in a home under development. The only connection I can see is back to Samantha Young, who also worked in the medical field. The big difference being Penny was responsible for the entire nursing operations within Atrium Health."

"There is another connection," Donatella interrupted. "Indirectly, Jasmyn reported to Penny. You have a situation in which the receptionist at her OB's office is murdered. Later, a superior of hers is murdered. I don't believe in coincidences."

"Neither do I. I've given this some thought. There is another link. Have we taken a look at her OB, Dr. Prince? Samantha reported to her and the good doctor has a relationship with the hospital."

"It's something worth investigating," Donatella stated. "Why don't you make your way to the OB's office and see what you can unearth."

Once again, he nodded. "There are two things that are bothering me. If we interpreted the card correctly, there are still two events left to unfold. One of which is meant to bring your demise. The second, what's the significance of The Thinker? Other than the first two crimes, he hasn't made another appearance."

Donatella didn't immediately respond, but the last question – The Thinker – had crossed her mind as well. What did it truly mean?

"Let's just hope we can prevent those last two, assuming the fourth one hasn't already taken place. If it has, this little dance of ours will be coming to an end really soon."

Sampson and Dabria, with a plan of action, stood and made their way to the exit. Outside, a lone figure sat in a car parked across the street. The figure watched as the two went their separate ways before turning over the ignition and exiting their parking spot.

June 8th – 9:40 a.m

DONATELLA SLID into the soft leather seat of her R8 and closed the door. She replayed an important element touched on during the conversation with Sampson. She knew Buckley wouldn't hesitate to harm others to achieve her objective. For that reason, and the fact those in the medical field continued to meet a cruel fate, she was happy that she had taken precautions when it came to Jasmyn. Precautions done without the woman's consent but done to protect her life. She continued to ponder, *Have I done enough?*

This was no time to second guess her decisions. The best way to keep Jasmyn, and those she cared about, safe was to put an end to this ordeal. The cold feeling came over her. The feeling that more blood would be shed.

She started the car looking for a contact within her phone while the Bluetooth technology connected. Once the connection was established, she placed her call. The phone rang twice before being picked up on the other end

"Special Agent Dabria, I hope the day is as beautiful as you are."

"Bryce, I need you to do something for me."

The grave tone in her voice was something unlike anything he heard before. The agent was always clip and matter of fact. On several times she was even urgent. This was expected – that was her norm. However, today she came across as pensive, worried. This caused the young man, who typically slouched as part of his normal posture, to sit up straight, hands on the keyboard, ready to provide whatever help he could.

The reality was he would do anything for the agent. She saved him from some serious jail time and had taken him under her tutelage. She straightened him out and gave purpose to his skillset. Purpose aimed at helping others. This was something he hadn't seen for his future but he was glad that he now had this opportunity. Still, he fought the urge to correct her into using his initials, BJ. Instead he simply asked, "What can I do for you?"

"I need for you to dig into the recent actions for Global Insights Security. Search a month prior to the massacre until current. I want to know of any contracts they have signed or any that are pending. I want a complete list of their clients. I want a complete list of their previous board members and a complete list of the new board members. I want to know about any cash discrepancies. I need this as soon as possible."

BJ hadn't said a word while Donatella listed off her requests.

He keyed each request mentally placing them into categories and relevance. When she was done, she said,

"BJ – thank you for your help."

There was a long pause. By this time the agent had typically disconnected the call; however, she had not disconnected today. Tentatively he said, "You're welcome." Seconds later he heard the line go dead.

During the call, Donatella had been driving with no firm destination. However, once the call had concluded, she knew exactly where she was going and exactly what she planned to do when she arrived. The destination wasn't far from her current location and she arrived in a matter of minutes.

Now, at the GIS offices, she walked through the door and entered the lobby. The same security guard, Busch, was there from her previous visit with Sampson. The stride in her step conveyed the sense she was all business and while the guard wanted to do his job, he decided it was better to let the FBI woman pass without challenge.

She pressed the up button at the bank of elevators and waited on one to arrive. After an interminable amount of time, two elevators arrived at the same time. One carrying a group of three men and one woman all dressed in business attire. They spoke in hush tones but it was clear from the few words Donatella could make out that a partnership was being sought.

The second elevator was empty and Donatella stepped into its car and pressed the button for the fifth floor. She closed her eyes, took a few deep breaths, and calmed her mind. Everything she had was supposition, but she needed to push this woman – she needed answers.

The elevator dinged, the doors slid open and Donatella Dabria stepped onto the floor. The time for niceties were over.

She strolled toward the now familiar office of Veronica King.

Along the way she garnered a number of onlookers but none stood in her way. She vaguely glimpsed at a woman reaching for the phone. *Maybe she's calling security*, she thought as she kept walking.

She spotted King walking back toward her desk from the door and she was only a few paces behind her. As King turned to sit, Donatella was closing and locking the door.

Startled she asked, "What are you doing in here? I'm going to call security."

"No need. They saw me waltz through the lobby and one of the ladies I passed on my way to you was certainly making that call. Until they arrive – if they arrive – you and I are going to have a chat. You have not been 100 percent honest with me, and that comes to an end – today."

King held a look of defiance on her face but the façade was slowly fading.

"Bree Buckley," At the sound of her name, Veronica shuttered and tried to hide it; however, Donatella caught the subtle movement.

"What do you know about her? How did you come across her?"

"I'm sorry, who? I don't know this woman you speak of. Is she important to this case and what happened to my colleagues?"

"Damn it, King! I know you have heard the name. Hell, you asked the question yourself. Who is she?"

And just how in the hell does she know that, Veronica thought.

"Let me tell you who she is. Her name is Terri Buckley – a psychopath who will destroy everyone and everything to achieve her goal. If you know who she is, it's in your best interest to tell me what you know."

What I know will get me and my daughter killed, she thought. *Plus, there's that shadowy organization she works for. Seems their reach is endless.*

"Look, Agent Dabria. I don't know this Bree or Terri person you are looking for. Now if you could please leave, I have a company to run."

Donatella with cat-like quickness was at King's side in the blink of an eye. Slamming her hands on the wood desk she yelled, "This is not a game! She has already killed several people in her path to reach her end goal. I know you're involved with her. I'm damn near certain you know about, or participated in, the death of your colleagues."

She spun the chair and pulled Veronica to her feet. "When I find the evidence linking you to the murder – the massacre – that transpired here, I'm going to bury you. After I end Buckley, you'll be next on my list!"

Distantly, she could hear the sound of rapid footsteps approaching. King responded, "Take your hands off of me. Touch me again and I'll ensure you see the inside of a cell."

The handle to the door jiggled. "Mrs. King, is everything ok? Open up this door." Another jiggle.

"Last chance, Veronica. If you don't tell me what you know, you're linking your fate with hers."

A set of keys could be heard from outside.

Veronica pondered for a moment. She could admit to knowing the woman, but with such uncertainty in the outcome, it was a chance she wasn't willing to take. Furthermore, she liked the power that she currently wielded, and she knew if she played her cards right, there would be more to come.

"I don't know who you are talking about," she said in a voice that came from deep in her core.

The right key was found, the lock disengaged, and the door flung open.

"It's alright, Charles. My guest was just leaving."

"Come on," the security guard said reaching for Donatella's arm. Before he touched her, he saw the menace in her eyes and decided it was a better option to escort her out without touching her.

Donatella gave King one last look before exiting the office that sent a chill down her spine. When the FBI woman left she took a heavy breath. Her alliance was now fully cemented with that of The Syndicate. There was no turning back because she realized she just made an enemy out of this woman and that too scared her.

June 8th – 10:00 a.m

DETECTIVE CARL SAMPSON had never been to an OB's office. The thoughts of going into the office with understandably hormonal women gave him the cold sweats. He began to wonder why he didn't take the review into GIS recent activity and Donatella take the discussion with Dr. Prince. He knew being uncomfortable was a part of the job so he needed to simply soldier on and get this over with.

"Come on, Carl. You can do this. You deal with hardened criminals all the time. You've walked into the warehouse of a drug ring where you knew the opposition would be carrying guns. You can walk into a building where women are carrying babies."

He took two more deep breaths and opened the door waiting for the barrage to hit him and then – nothing. No screaming babies, of course not, they aren't born yet. No women on edge ready to pounce. They all, the three women in the waiting room, turned and smiled and waved. Then they went back to reading their magazines or playing games on their phones. He stood there momentarily astonished. The silence was both unexpected and refreshing.

"Can I help you, sir?" came the voice from the receptionist bringing him out of his daydream. He walked over to the desk smiling inwardly at the absurdity of his reservations a few minutes prior.

He looked down at the name plate, Lucie T. Berkry – *that's an unusual name*, "Good morning, Lucie. My name is Detective Carl Sampson," he showed her his badge. "I'd like to speak with Dr. Prince."

Lucie flashed him a smile, "Well hello, detective. Dr. Prince is with a patient right now. She will be wrapping up soon. If you'd like to take a seat, I'll let her know that you are here."

His anxiety began to rise again, "Over there? In the waiting room?"

"Yes sir. I promise they won't bite," she said widening her smile.

He couldn't help but to smile back. "I guess you're right. I'll just go wait over there." Once he sat down his mind mulled over the case. They had looked at this case from every angle. This Buckley woman was constantly multiple steps ahead. He firmly believed that she was setting a trap for the Special Agent but he hadn't determined the origin of the trap. Or could it be she was trying to frame the agent for the crimes that were being committed? That was an angle he had not looked at previously.

A frame job didn't feel right. From everything he heard about this woman, framing Donatella isn't want she wanted. She didn't want to see the woman spend time behind bars. She wanted to destroy her and everything she ever cared about. So, no, it wasn't a frame job.

Furthermore, how was she staying undetected? Granted, they did not have a massive manhunt underway, but you would think she would surface somewhere with as much mayhem as she was causing. Unless she was hiding in plain sight.

"Detective Sampson," came the voice from Lucie, breaking

him once again from his train of thought. “Dr. Prince is ready to see you now.”

He pushed himself from the chair, which he had to admit was more comfortable than others he had been in, and followed the receptionist back to the doctor’s office.

“Dr. Prince, Detective Sampson is here to see you.”

“Thank you, Lucie,” the doctor said standing and extending a hand to Sampson, “Please come in and have a seat.”

Sampson shook her hand and sat in the visitor’s chair across the desk from the doctor. He couldn’t help but notice how soft her hands were.

“Detective Sampson, what can I do for you today?” she asked flashing a brilliant smile.

“First of all, thank you for seeing me on such short notice, Dr. Prince. I just have a couple of questions for you. In early December a member of your staff, Samantha Young, was murdered. A couple of months later the director of nursing, Penny Hampton, met a similar faith.”

Prince nodded in agreement with Sampson

“You’re in a peculiar situation as Samantha worked for you and you deliver babies where Penny worked,” she raised her eyebrow. “We are looking for any possible link between the two of them and –”

“And you think I have something to do with it?” she asked with a hint of irritation in her voice.

“No, not that you have anything to do with it. Just you are a link between the two.”

“A very weak link if you ask me. Samantha was a beloved member of our staff. And frankly, rehashing her death is not something I’d like to do. It was hard enough at the time and recalling how she was taken still causes me some internal pain.

Penny was well known both for her job and the work she did

in the community. I met her on a few occasions but other than that I don't know much about the woman – God rest her soul."

"I'm sorry if I gave off the impression that you were a suspect or that you had anything to do with the murders. My question is, do you know of any connection between the two of them? Do you know of anything that was out of the ordinary prior to their deaths?"

"From a professional stance, the two would not have any reason to connect. Samantha was our receptionist, a darn good one, but aside from that she would not have interacted with Penny in a professional manner.

As for anything out of the ordinary, Samantha had been the same cheerful woman up to the end. And as I mentioned already, I really didn't work with Penny. Sorry, detective, I know you would like more, but unfortunately the link you seek is not as strong as you'd like."

Hedging because he didn't have anywhere else to go, "Samantha's replacement, Lucie, how did you hear about her? From everything I heard, she was available to replace Samantha the next morning. That was a fairly quick turnaround."

It was clear the doctor had not expected this question as it took her a moment to answer. "She came to us via a staffing agency that we have used in the past. They gave us a call because they heard about what happened to Samantha and they wanted to send us a candidate immediately so that our operations were not affected."

Sampson thought this was odd. He was the lead detective on the case and, to his knowledge, information surrounding her death didn't come out until the morning. How had the temp agency reacted so fast? This was something he would need to follow up on once he returned to the office.

Feeling he obtained as much from the doctor as he could he said, "Thank you, Dr. Prince, for your assistance." He stood, handing her a business card, "If you should think of anything that would be helpful please feel free to call my cell phone listed on the card."

The two shook hands and Detective Sampson was escorted back to the receptionist desk. There he looked at the receptionist one good time before saying, "It was a pleasure meeting you Lucie and thanks for keeping me calm."

She eyed him back as well and then plastered the smile back on her face, "It was a pleasure meeting you as well, Detective Sampson."

Back at his car he thought he didn't get much from the doctor; however, he did have another thread to pull. How had the temp agency responded so fast?

June 8th – 6:40 p.m

TERRI BUCKLEY SAT on the bench outside of the GIS headquarters. While this bench originally served as reconnaissance, she liked this location. During her visits to the bench no other person had ever come to this location. She had the seclusion she desired and she was able to take in some fresh air.

She marveled at how well the plan had been coming together. The job she was tasked to run for The Syndicate went off without a hitch. Well, almost without a hitch. She had to dispose of Marc Blackstone after that fool knocked over the metal tray alerting the guard to their location. The guard who she also needed to dispose of before closing out the op. Other than that, everything ran smooth.

With that job behind her she could now focus on the auxiliary job she had been running simultaneously. After months of orchestrating events, time was drawing close. Time for that goody-goody Dabria to get what she deserved. She had all the assets in place and prepared to play their part. Now – now it was time to activate her plan.

She pulled her phone from her pocket and placed the call. After four rings the call was answered.

"It's time, tonight," were the three words she spoke into the handset before she disconnected the call. With those three words, she knew everything she planned over the last several months would be executed specifically to her prescribed plan.

June 8th – 6:40 p.m

For the second time today, Donatella found herself at Brent's Coffee Shop. She stood in line behind an elderly man as he studied the menu. He complained about the number of choices and ultimately settled on a small decaf coffee – black.

The pink-haired girl, Margaret, waited patiently while the elderly man counted out his total in change. Typically, this inefficiency and waiting would have grated her nerves, but today it was the little comedy relief she needed. Margaret, patient by nature, was letting the chink in her armor show when she reached out and asked the old man to let her help. He bristled, stating he could do it himself and then admonished her for making him miss count. Thus, he started over.

Donatella's phone began to vibrate. She reached in her left pocket and retrieved the phone.

"Agent Dabria," she spoke softly into the phone.

"Special Agent Donatella. It's Detective Sampson. Can we meet. It's urgent. I think I have a break in the case, but I'm not 100 percent sure what it means."

Awaken from his excitement she said, "I'm at Brent's. Do you want me to come there?"

"No, I'm already headed to my car. I'll see you in a few minutes."

Dabria had not seen this side of Sampson before. Normally reserved, if he was this excited, he must have something crucial.

She placed the phone back in her pocket to see the man still counting his change. Margaret stared, unsure what to do when the man finally pushed over the money and said, "Here, you count it. I lost count again."

After ringing up the old man and giving him back the unused change she looked up at Agent Dabria as if she had not noticed her standing there before.

"Special Agent Dabria! Oh my, are you hear because you need my assistance again?"

"No, Margaret," she responded with a tired yet genuine smile. "I'm here to clear my mind and I'll be meeting someone momentarily. For now, I'll have a chai tea."

"Coming right up. This one is on the house!"

After a few moments, Margaret was back with her drink for which Donatella left a tip in the jar to cover the cost of her drink in addition to the tip. The shop wasn't as crowded as she expected for this time of night and her preferred oversized chair was unoccupied. She began making her way to the chair when Sampson came rushing in.

The frantic look on his face and the hurried gait in his step made him look like a wild man. She motioned him over to the chairs and they sat.

"I found something related to our first case, the death of Samantha Young. Something that we should have caught sooner."

18

JUNE 8TH – 7:00 P.M

Special Agent Dabria sat in the oversized chair, left leg crossed over right gazing intently at Detective Sampson as he launched into his story.

"I paid Dr. Prince a visit per our discussion earlier in the day. I laid out for her the fact that she had a tangled connection with two of our victims, Samantha Taylor and Penny Hampton. She had to admit, of course, her connection with the former as she worked for the good doctor. However, she stated she only sparingly had connections with Penny. She confirmed the two women did not have any working relationship and that she didn't know of any relationship outside of work."

Donatella sat patiently, shifting her legs right over left. She felt this was a long shot, yet there had to be a connection.

"Once I finished this line of questioning, I asked her about her temp and how she was able to procure one so quickly. Her response didn't add up. She stated the temp agency contacted her offering her some assistance. The problem – the news of Samantha's death would not have given an agency enough time to find a resource and call the doctor."

Donatella began following the thread but continued listening.

"I decided this was an avenue worth investigating. During our conversation, the doctor stated she received a call from a temp agency that they typically work with, Med Staff. I called over to their office and they had no record of sending a temp to Dr. Prince's practice. I told the woman on the other end it had to be a mistake and asked her to check again. She did, and again, no records.

I decided to call the other two medical staffing companies in the area and neither of them had a record of sending a resource to Dr. Prince."

Donatella nodded, wheels turning, arranging this new puzzle piece in her mind. *Dr. Prince had been lying to them about the appearance of the temp. Did this mean she had something to do with the death of Samantha after all? Could she be part of The Syndicate and thus working with Buckley?*

Watching Sampson, she could tell he was pondering the same things. For this to be his first case, she knew he would make a fine detective. Just as Sampson was preparing to launch into his next part, her phone rang. She retrieved the phone from her left pocket and read the caller ID, "BJ". Considering the find from Sampson, she decided to bring him into this conversation.

The coffee shop was relatively empty, so she decided to place the call on speaker phone.

"Yes BJ," she said in a hurried voice. "I'm here with Detective Sampson and he will be listening in."

BJ comforted by the clip voice the Special Agent lacked in their last conversation, smiled and launched into his findings.

"I reviewed the recent GIS activity and for the most part it's legit. There are some questionable activities that do not make sense. After Mrs. King became CEO, they took on a new client, the Cleveland Museum of Art. On the surface this doesn't appear to be a problem except I looked into the security system being installed at the museum and it had to be out of their budget.

I decided to dig into the financials of the transaction. The security system was donated by GIS after a security breach was recognized by the museum. The offer to install and monitor the system, free of charge, came merely days before the museum was to send out the RFP – Request for Proposal."

Donatella interrupted, "There isn't anything criminal about giving away your services to another company."

"How right you are," responded BJ. "Nothing wrong with it at all until a crime is committed."

"What!" she exclaimed.

"The reason the museum needed to update their security in a hurry is because they were preparing for an unveiling. Rumor has it they had secured some lost work of Jackson Pollock that had not been seen by the public. They had a big reveal planned once the restoration of the work had concluded. With less than a month until the show, the artwork was stolen. They suspect, the head of Security, Tim Saunders, and one of his employees, Bobby Cliff, made off with the merchandise.

Bobby was a former cop who had a love of art. He built a close relationship with Dr. Peterson, who was overseeing the restoration. Police are going with the assumption that Bobby took the position at the museum, gained the trust of Peterson to tell him about the secret show and before the show was set to open, he and his boss made off with the artwork. Neither has been seen since the heist."

SA Dabria sat quiet for a moment. While the elements of the story could add up to be true, the pieces fit together to convey a different puzzle.

"Prior to this theft of the museum, did either man have a criminal record?"

"I knew you would ask that, and the answer is no. Both men were squeaky clean in that department. Neither man had any debt that would make you think they were bought off to commit this crime, and Bobby was a happily married man who was devoted to his wife.

Before you get too upset, I decided to dig around in the security system installed by GIS. There is some rogue code that looks to allow backdoor untraceable access – but of course I traced it. On the night of the theft a sophisticated algorithm activated, reconfiguring the pressure sensors in the room where the artwork was being held. It took me hours to find it, but it was there.

"What does all this mean?" asked Sampson.

"It means Terri, more likely The Syndicate, stole this artwork with the help of GIS. I can see Terri executing the heist but I don't see her doing this on her own. My guess is her superiors had this assignment for her."

"This explains the connection between Veronica King and Terri Buckley," Sampson stated.

Donatella pondered this too for a moment but she felt there was more, "What else, BJ?"

"I looked into their other clients. The only one that stood out worth mentioning is Atrium Health. They have supplied security services for them for well over two years, so I thought they were irrelevant. However, given the nature of our special project and the fact that Jasmyn works there, I thought this would be worth mentioning."

Donatella's body went rigid as the puzzle pieces were beginning to fit together in her mind. She looked over to Sampson with an urgency in her eyes, "What is the name of the receptionist at the doctor's office?"

Sampson wordlessly pulled his notes from his pocket

searching for the name. After a moment he spoke, "Lucie T. Berkry. Why?"

Donatella bolted from her chair, heading for the door. Into her phone she spoke, "BJ, I'll call you back." To Sampson she said, "We have to hurry, follow me!"

June 8th – 7:15 p.m

FOR THE SECOND time in the span of three hours Patti Jones received a call from Terri Buckley. The first was to let her know that "the patient" would be arriving today. The patient had been hand selected for this endeavor with a twist.

This patient had been given a Pitocin derivative concocted by the scientists with The Syndicate. Under normal circumstances, the patient is given an injection to aid in the contraction of the uterus. In many cases, it's given to induce labor.

However, the derivative this patient has received worked quite differently. First, the medicine had been synthesized to a pill form. This way, the medicine could be easily passed off as anything the supplier wanted. In this case, it was a pill to aid in morning sickness for this particular patient.

Second, the medicine gave off intense Braxton Hicks contractions. It went so far as simulating water breaking. The patient would surely believe they were in full on labor and the baby was coming at any minute. After seeing the pill in action, Patti had to admit it was genius.

The second call she had received was to let her know the patient was on the way. This was going to be by far the most dangerous part of the night. Patti, who normally orchestrated all parts of a delivery, was informed of the plan, how the night would go, and her role. She didn't like being dictated to in this manner, but she was excited.

This patient would be her first in weeks and her first out-of-town patient. Psychologically, the women she dealt with were all the same. But this was her first southern girl and she was looking forward to it.

Unlike her previous patients, Patti didn't get to spend time with this one. In fact, tonight would be their first official meeting. She'd seen pictures of her and read the write up, so she felt she knew her. However, it wasn't that intimate knowledge she liked to have of her girls. She would get some time with this one before the activities started and she figured that would have to be enough.

She realized she needed to get moving so she didn't miss the arrival. To her left sat the wheelchair she had procured earlier. She began pushing it down the hallway and out of the exit to the hospital. She turned to her left and steered the chair another 10 feet to ensure she wasn't standing in front of the door.

She reached down and pulled the hand drawn sign from the chair – "Thompson".

She was told the make, model, and color of the car. Though she wasn't a car aficionado, she was familiar enough with this particular vehicle.

After a few moments of standing outside she saw the blue Tesla turn into the parking lot, driving well above the speed limit. She held up the sign and waited patiently.

The car came to a stop, the doors unlocked, and the husband, Marcellous Thompson, hopped out of the driver's seat.

"Oh, thank you so much for being out here and ready to take her inside. Wait, let me grab her bag and we will be all set to go."

"No worries, Mr. Thompson," Patti said with a genuine smile. "We will take great care of your wife. Why don't you go and park the car, grab the bag and then come on in once you're done? We will take her up to labor and deliver located on the fifth floor. You can meet us there."

"Oh right, the car. Ok. I will go park the car and then come up to labor and delivery on the fourth floor."

"Fifth floor, Mr. Thompson."

"My bad! Fifth floor. Gotcha."

As Marcellous hopped back in the car, heading for visitor parking, Jasmyn said, "That Marcellous. You have to forgive him, this is our first baby."

Her voice was soft and sweet, Patti thought. "Don't worry, Mrs. Thompson. Like I told your husband, we are going to take great care of you." Before walking back into the entrance, Patti pulled a syringe from her pocket, removed the cap with her teeth, and pressed the needle into the neck of Jasmyn before pressing the plunger home.

The patient, raised her hands to her neck, preparing to protest; however, the sedative coursing through her bloodstream triggered an immediate reaction. She was completely out before Patti wheeled her through the entrance.

She moved with haste toward the back of the hospital using her badge to provide clearance for areas deemed off limits and not open to the public. At the southeast exit an SUV would be waiting, prepared to take them to their next destination. She moved as quickly as she could while trying to attract as little attention as possible. Terri had assured her techs working for The Syndicate would alter the video feeds, but she hadn't survived this long without being vigilant.

She made her way through the last set of doors, Jasmyn's head pressed against her chest. The SUV flashed its lights twice as it pulled up to her location. Two men exited the vehicle – one from the front passenger side and one from the rear. They sat the pregnant woman in the seat, strapped her into her seatbelt, and climbed in on either side of her. Patti leapt into the front.

"Let's go," she said with the first part of her mission now complete.

Smithville – 4 years prior

Terri Buckley awoke from anesthesia in a hospital room. Slightly groggy, she looked around noting a figure sitting at the edge of her bed. She blinked a couple of time bringing her blurry eyes into focus. Once her vision cleared, she realized the figure sitting there was her partner, Donatella.

She pressed her mind, attempting to recall her reason for this hospital stay, for this had not been her only one. The memories slowly pushed toward the front of her mind. They were at the house of Aaron Smithville. She had her gun trained on that rapist. His daughter walked into the room and cuddled up with him on the sofa. And – she shook her head trying to remember, the medicine still clouding her thoughts.

"Hey Terri," came the voice from her partner. "How are you doing?"

"Still a little out of it, but I'll live." She put on a smile while her brain continued to recall the day's events.

She could sense her partner eyeing her with interest. She could sense tension radiating from her body but didn't know why. After a few moments Donatella spoke.

"Terri, while we were at Aaron's house, he called you Becky." She paused for a moment – their eyes connected. "Why would he call you Becky?"

That's all? she thought. *That's easy enough*. Had she been lucid she may not have given a straightforward answer; however, in this instance she told the truth.

"Becky Lurtire is an anagram of my name. It's something I've been doing since I was a kid. I started with my name and came up with some interesting combinations, then moved onto famous places."

Finishing that sentence, more information came back to her about her current predicament. *Donatella was there – that's right. She wasn't just there; she had her gun drawn. The gun was pointed at... me.* A clear picture began to form in her mind. *She shot me!*

Buckley's entire demeanor shifted; a change Donatella noticed. Buckley stared at her, brows furrowing. "I'm a little tired, I think I need to get some rest. Why don't you come back later – partner." She emphasized the last word.

Donatella nodded and without another word took her leave.

June 8th – 7:15 p.m

DONATELLA, in a flat out run to her car, admonished herself for missing clues staring her in the face. Having worked with Terri Buckley previously should have helped her think through this issue earlier. Thinking back to the conversation she had with Buckley working the Smithville case it was all so clear.

Terri killed Samantha Young, called Dr. Prince's office pretending to be the temp agency, and was hired on as the new receptionist, Lucie T. Berkry. This allowed her unfettered access to Jasmyn Thompson. Getting close to Jasmyn has been her plan.

The thing bothering her, she didn't see how the death of Penny Hampton fit into the picture.

She slid into the seat of her Audi R8, fired up the engine and took off. She noted Sampson had been paces behind her and eyed his police vehicle next to hers. He could catch up.

Why would Buckley kill – "Damn it! She was the director of

nursing. She wanted to have her replaced with someone she could control. She's going after Jasmyn during the birth of her child."

She activated the Bluetooth calling function in her car willing the phone to ring faster. Finally, after a couple of rings Marcellous answered the phone.

"Hey, Donatella. I was just about to call you. We –"

"Marcellous, are you still with Jasmyn!?" She interrupted Marcellous in a huff. "Are you at the hospital?"

Alarms began to register in his head. "No, I'm not with her, I just dropped her off with the nurse at the entrance to the hospital. They are taking her to labor and delivery."

"Shit!" she said in a panicked voice. "This has all been a trap. A well-orchestrated trap. Jasmyn is in dire danger and you need to find her immediately."

She pressed down on the gas pedal reaching speeds of 95 mph. She wasn't sure if Sampson was still with her, but she had to do everything possible to save Jasmyn. She could hear a voice in the background over the in-car speakers.

"You must be Marcellous. I was told to expect you and your wife. Is she outside in the car?"

"What do you mean is she outside in the car? I just dropped her off with a nurse who was waiting outside," he stated in a high, confused voice.

A knot began to form in her chest. This cannot be happening. Jasmyn has to be ok!

"I only received the call mere minutes ago and I haven't had time to tell anyone else. I came right down so I could meet you both."

She could hear the panic in his voice when he spoke. "Donatella, they've got her. They've got Jasmyn."

"Marcellous, I'll be there in a moment, meet me outside."

She disconnected the call, immediately placing a second. This call was immediately answered before the first ring completed.

"BJ, they have Jasmyn. I need for you to activate the tracking beacon!"

For weeks Donatella had a suspicion that Buckley was working an angle that might place Jasmyn in harm's way; however, she could not find anything to prove this. She didn't want to scare the couple that she now considered friends, but she couldn't leave Jasmyn exposed with no safety net. To that end, she worked with BJ to implant a tracking device inside the spacers of the Pandora bracelet she had given to Jasmyn.

Other than activating it once to ensure tracking worked as expected, she swore she would not infringe on her privacy unless absolutely necessary – and this was an absolutely necessary case. Specifically what she had the device created for at the time.

"Absolutely," came BJ's alarmed voice. "It'll take just a moment."

Donatella swung into the lot in time to see Marcellous from a distance exiting the hospital walking toward his car. She raced through the lot skidding to a stop next to him.

A look of sheer terror had plastered his face, "Donatella, what's going on?" he demanded.

"Terri Buckley has been masquerading as the receptionist, Lucie, at Dr. Prince's office. She's been planning all along to abduct Jasmyn, for what end I'm not sure."

"How are we going to get her back?" Marcellous demanded, voice raising several octaves.

"I have BJ working on that as we speak." Looking in the rearview mirror she noticed Sampson pulling into the parking lot.

BJ's voice shot through the speakers, "I've got her! Looks like they are just entering I-277 heading west. The trace has been synced with your onboard computer."

As part of the tracking software, BJ made two additional modifications for Donatella. Using an over-the-air update, he loaded the software on her phone to track the bracelet in real time. He had also designed the software that would need to be installed on her car. Being more a software guy than a hardware guy, he sent the necessary specs to a fellow graduate from MIT to produce the hardware.

Once the hardware had been designed and the software was loaded, the package was sent to Donatella. From there she took care of having the new hardware installed. With the trace now activated, the bottom half of the windshield in Donatella's R8 illuminated. A map displaying the city of Charlotte was now present on her windshield. A red dot could be seen leaving Kenilworth Ave. taking the loop onto I-277.

"Thanks BJ," Donatella said. "I'll take it from here!"

"I'm coming with you!"

"No, you are not!" Donatella shot back. "She already has one of you, I'm not allowing you to put yourself into any danger."

"Damn it, Donatella. That's my wife. I said I'm going." He reached for the handle – locked.

"No, you're not," she said calmly while pulling off in a flurry.

Marcellous, standing next to his car, leapt into the driver's seat and took off behind her.

June 8th – 7:15 p.m

FOR DETECTIVE SAMPSON, chasing Donatella on foot from the coffee house was not an easy feat. Her long, athletic legs propelled her across the concrete at a much faster rate than he could move.

He reached his squad car, old Betsy, 20 seconds after Donatella had taken off. "Come on, old girl, start up for me." He turned the key in the ignition and for the first time in ages, the car started on the first turn. He yanked the car into drive giving pursuit.

He was able to make out her black car against the blackness enveloping the city. She was tearing down the highway, her car moving as gracefully as she had done. Old Betsy on the other hand had her work cut out for her. As the needle edged closer to 80 mph, the car began to shake. He was afraid to push her any harder, but realized he was losing ground so pressed his luck.

"Come on, old girl. We can do this."

He could sense himself losing track of her as the brake lights continued to grow in distance. His cop intuition told him she was headed toward the hospital, so that would be his aim as well. He had a chance to learn more about Donatella over the last few months and this was the first time he had seen her this animated, this intense. He sensed this episode coming to a climax and he was worried how it would all end.

Betsy groaned as he edged the car closer to 85 mph and he was happy to see the exit for the hospital was approaching in one mile. By this time, he had lost all contact with the Special Agent and he hoped his guess was correct. He thought about activating the red and blue lights along with the siren but the streets were clear enough for him to navigate.

After a few minutes he pulled into the hospital lot and could see Marcellous standing outside of the Special Agent's car. As he inched closer, watching out for passing pedestrians, he noticed Marcellous becoming more animated.

He pulled in behind Donatella's R8 shifting Betsy into park. "Good job," he said patting the dash. Reaching his hand toward the seatbelt latch, he saw the brake lights in front of him register white for a moment. He looked up in time to see Donatella's black R8 pulling off and Marcellous jumping into his blue Model S. By the time he shifted his car into gear, Marcellous had already taken off trailing the agent.

"Alright, old girl. Looks like our night is about to get more exciting!"

FIRING out of the parking lot, Donatella made a left onto Blythe Blvd – accelerating at a dizzying speed. "BJ, best guess on where they are headed."

"They are still heading west on I-277 and they don't appear to be speeding. Heading that direction there are a number of under construction or abandoned buildings."

"Terri didn't go through all of this to end up in an abandoned building. She still has plans for Jasmyn – and me."

Speeding toward the intersection, she slowed slightly to make the right onto Kenilworth. Checking her review mirror, she saw the unmistakable blue Tesla belonging to Marcellous turning the corner right on her bumper. *He's going to get himself killed*, she thought, but she pressed forward.

"Guess it depends on which way they go once they approach I-77. Going north they could be attempting to leave the city or to the home of Veronica King."

Donatella thought the latter was highly unlikely.

"Continuing west, they could be heading toward the airport."

"Well let's hope they turn north," she said entering the highway. Now free of the constant stop lights and cross traffic, she opened up the 562 horsepower V10 engine with the 0-60 acceleration of 3.4 seconds. She ate up concrete and cars like Pac-Man and the pellets.

Checking her review once again, she saw Marcellous keeping a car length distance, desperate not to lose track of her and his wife.

Donatella watched the windshield navigation display as she weaved her way through traffic. She had made up plenty of ground and was still closing in.

The vehicle carrying Jasmyn made a right and headed north on I-77. Donatella pondered what could possibly be this way and she got the answer over the in-car speakers.

"Wreck on 74. They may be making a run north to circle the airport, if that's where they are going."

Donatella blew past the Panthers stadium less than a mile from 77. She peered up at her rearview to see Marcellous still fast on her tail. At the speed she was traveling, making the quick right to exit onto 77 could be dicey.

Peeling her eyes from the rearview, she checked the side mirror to see a four-door sedan accelerating onto the highway. She depressed the gas pedal pulling more horses from her engine before yanking the steering wheel to the right.

She cut in front of the sedan, looked like a black Honda, and immediately onto the exit. She fought with the Audi to stay on the ground as she rode the berm taillights whipping past in a blur.

"In another 10 seconds you should see them," came the frantically calm voice of BJ. "Unfortunately, all we have is her location. I don't know what kind of car they are driving."

"I've got them BJ," came her clip response. The SUV Jasmyn had been tossed in was cruising down the center lane. As if they sensed Donatella nearing, they jumped onto the express lane and accelerated.

Donatella, who had to cut her speed slightly once she hit traffic, maneuvered her vehicle to the express lane and gave chase. The SUV that the abductors were in was no match for the speed of her car and she knew that. The problem was, how did she stop the vehicle without harming Jasmyn, or the baby?

She covered the distance in five seconds before seeing an arm reach from both backdoor windows. In the ever-fading darkness she immediately recognized "gun" and realized she was pinned in on the express lane. Instinctively, she slammed on the brakes as gunfire showered the ground where she would have been had she continued her course.

Ahead she could see the SUV pulling back into the main traffic as she pressed forward again. As she accelerated, she thought she heard the sound of a helicopter in the distance but was not sure. What she needed was a plan. The good thing is she had the bastards in her sight. The problem was if she spooked them too much, they may just harm Jasmyn right now and cut their losses.

Closing in on the vehicle once again she realized the arms were back in the window, but their speed had increased dramatically. She was nearing 90 in her vehicle and was barely making up ground. She pushed the car to go faster while formulating a plan in her mind. She knew she only had one chance if she was going to make this work.

She methodically looked for her opening while accelerating into triple digits. The SUV was a mere 10 yards in front of her when she realized the out of place lights shooting from her left.

She heard the indistinguishable sound of hot metal crunching together. She felt the body of her car lift into the air before seeing the back of the SUV rotate from left to right. She felt the immediate impact of the car hitting the ground, heard the gas ignite from the airbag deployment before being smacked in the face and entombed in a protective bubble.

Her vision was immediately skewed but for a moment, her ears still worked. She felt her body being roughly jostled, glass shattering, and more metal crunching. She had the sensation that she was upside down. She heard BJ yell her name several times before losing consciousness.

MARCELLOUS WAS FAST on the tail of Donatella as they approached the Panthers stadium. He was furious with the agent for not taking him along, but that didn't mean he too could not give chase. He took a quick glance in the rearview mirror to see the beat-up clunker police vehicle that Detective Sampson was driving. He put his focus back on the road just in time to see Donatella accelerating and making a right to exit onto 77 north. He prepared to do the same when he noticed a car, looked like a black Honda Accord, flying onto the highway within the space he had left between himself and Donatella. He pressed on the break quickly lowering his speed from 91 to 60.

Free from any additional incoming traffic, he maneuvered toward the exit picking up speed again. In doing so he was able to reach the exit ramp a few moments after the Special Agent. Just in time to see her flying down the berm to avoid the slower moving traffic exiting I- 277 the proper way.

He decided he would follow in her wake when a white F-150 also decided the berm was the quickest way to escape this traffic. Again, Marcellous had to hit the brakes in an effort not to run up into the back of this truck. Idly he thought, *at this speed I may have killed myself.*

His frustration mounted as the truck who seemed to be in a rush when he jumped onto the berm was now moving at a snail's pace. Marcellous smacked the steering wheel and for good measure, laid on the horn. He was losing precious seconds that he didn't have and he needed for them to move – now. He saw a sliver of an opening and slammed on the accelerator. The twin engines of the Tesla whined back to life and he took off again in trailing position.

The three second delay from the Honda entering I-277 and that five second delay caused by the Ford entering I-77 resulted in Donatella being nearly a mile in front of him. From his vantage point, he could see her car entering the express lane trailing an SUV that too was gaining speed.

He made a straight line toward that lane sliding through the pedestrian-like speed of traffic continuing north. He noted the sound of automatic gun fire erupting in front of him as he entered onto the express lane. The red brake lights of Donatel-la's vehicle shone for a few moments before they went dark and she sped off again. *Good, I'm gaining on them.*

In the distance he heard the *thwap-thwap* of helicopter blades as he picked up speed. He could now see the SUV Donatella was pursuing exit the express lane shortly followed by the agent.

He glanced at the speedometer, realized he had crossed the century point and pressed harder. The only thought racing through his mind was catching up to these fiends and saving his wife. He had no clue how he was going to do that, but he damn sure knew Donatella would have a plan.

Suddenly, less than 100 yards in front of him he saw it. A dumpster truck which had been coasting down the express lane veered through the standing cones and broadsided the rear corner panel of the agent's car. The impact immediately flipped her car in the air. The car smacked the concrete on its right side before flipping over, and over, and over again. Glass and metal flying everywhere as the car decelerated from its 100-plus speed to nothing.

Marcellous watched in horror as the scene played out in front of him. The car lay in a crumpled heap on the right side of the road. He quickly glanced up at his rearview mirror to see the beat-up clunker of Sampson approaching. At that point he decided to continue the pursuit and he would allow Sampson to stop for Donatella.

He pressed down on the accelerator once again, keeping his head on a swivel for any more surprises as he chased after the vehicle carrying his wife.

While he knew the vehicle was an SUV, he had not seen the vehicle up close. There weren't too many vehicles on the road ahead of him and probably less SUVs. He continued to plow forward when the *thwap-thwap* of the helicopter that he heard earlier sounded as if it were right on top of him.

He saw a stream of light jutting from the sky and focusing in on a vehicle in front of him. To his surprise, and astonishment, the light was focused on an SUV. He figured this was the one he was meant to follow.

Once the SUV was illuminated, it picked up speed and yet again, Marcellous did the same. Again, he was further away than he liked but he threw caution to the wind and floored the accelerator. The speed, while dizzying, was necessary and he continued to press forward.

However, this was short lived. As he drew closer to the SUV, he saw a fleet of similar vehicles entering the highway and forming up with the one he was trailing. He could still make out the vehicle in question as the light was still shining brightly in its direction.

Marcellous continued to close the gap when the light on the vehicle disappeared. *Shit, an overpass!*

In a rehearsed motion, the surrounding vehicles all adjusted spots and to his chagrin, he didn't know which vehicle was the right vehicle. The vehicles cleared the overpass and the light was shone on a vehicle but he wasn't sure it was even the right one.

Each vehicle, now acting independently, set off at different speeds. Two took the next exit while three carried on forward.

"Shit!!" he yelled out loud smacking the steering wheel once again. He decided to stay on the highway trailing one of the vehicles no longer illuminated by the helicopter.

SAMPSON PUSHED old Betsy up the I-277-entrance ramp watching the speedometer slowly climb from 55 to 70 mph. He could feel himself losing contact with the more superior vehicles but he wasn't going to stop his pursuit. An idea crossed his mind.

"Dispatch. This is Vanessa," came the subdued voice from the other end.

"Vanessa, this is Carl."

"Hey Carl, sugar. How –"

"Vanessa, I need a bird in the air immediately. I'm in hot pursuit of an abduction vehicle traveling west on I-277."

He could sense the dispatcher sitting erect in her chair as she responded, "We have one a couple of miles away aiding in a drug bust."

"Get them here pronto, old Betsy isn't built for pursuit."

"What type of vehicle is the assailant driving?"

"I'm not sure, the vehicle in question is being chased by an FBI agent in a black Audi." He didn't dare mention the fact that there was also a civilian chasing the black Audi. Surely the bird would spot that without his confirmation.

"10-4. I'll let the bird know."

The steering wheel began to shake violently in his hand as his speed reached the 90 mph mark. Approaching the Panthers stadium, he saw the brake lights of Marcellous as he aimed to exit onto I-77. He noticed a black Honda slip between Special

Agent Donatella's vehicle and the blue Tesla driven by Marcellous.

He immediately jumped back on with dispatch, "Vanessa, suspect has turned north on I-77. I repeat, north on 77."

He yanked Betsy's steering wheel to the right slowing slightly to enter the ramp for 77. The 19-year-old Chevy caprice was holding up under the strain but he didn't know for how much longer. Traffic had slowed considerably on the ramp, so he was forced to take the berm to track the lead vehicles.

As he completed the entry onto 77 north he could spot Marcellous' vehicle crossing the highway heading toward the express lane. He checked his sideview mirror looking for an opportunity to merge gracefully when he heard the report of a semi-automatic weapon fire cascading through the night's air.

He pressed the pedal down to the floorboard and crossed through the flow of traffic at a reckless speed. Shots being fired on a busy highway didn't bode well and this chase needed to come to an end.

He jumped back on the horn, "Vanessa, damn it, where is that bird? Shots fired; shots fired."

"Bird incoming, ETA one minute."

"Tell them to hurry the hell up. We need to bring this chase to an end."

As the phrase left his lips, he realized he didn't know how he was going to end this chase. Entering the express lane, he could see the faint signs of Marcellous' vehicle in the distance. Betsy was holding steady at 90 mph and he was squeezing every bit of horsepower out of her that she could manage.

The time to cover the entrance of the express lane to the next exit passed in a flash. As he approached the exit he pondered why the traffic on the main portion of the highway had slowed. Looking to his right, he had his answer.

There were several large trucks blocking the flow of traffic.

He didn't have time to resolve this in his mind at the time, but later would realize this was part of the overall plan.

When he exited the express lane and hopped back on the main flow of I-77, he heard the unmistakable sound of a high impact collision ahead of him. Lord, now what? Twenty-five seconds later his question was answered. The beautiful black Audi R8 that he rode in just days prior had come to a rest, on its hood, on the right side of the highway. Glass and metal were strewn across the highway while smoke reached skyward from the wreckage.

"Officer down!" he yelled back at dispatch. "Send paramedics and fire." He brought Betsy to a stop and jumped out of the car. Idly, he heard the helicopter fly by as he ran to the upside-down vehicle. Upon approach, he could see all the airbags had deployed inside the car. "Lord, let her be okay!" He reached for the driver side door handle and pulled. The door wouldn't budge. He placed his foot on the frame of the car for leverage and pulled as hard as he could – all of the muscles in his back and biceps bulging under the stress. Laying his head back and pulling with all of his might, the door finally opened. He pulled the knife from his pocket, flipped the blade open and deflated the air bags.

"Donatella!", he yelled into the cabin, but received no response – at least no response from her.

"Who is that? Is Agent Dabria ok?" came a voice from the speakers.

Donatella, upside down from his viewpoint, had lost consciousness. He cradled her head while he released the latch to the seatbelt. Her lifeless body fell into his arms and he gingerly removed her from the vehicle. Unaware if the vehicle would explode at any moment, he continued to carry her away to what he felt was a safe distance.

Sampson dropped to his knees and lay Donatella on the

ground. She was still breathing which was a good sign. He visually inspected her for any other impalements – he didn't see any. Another good sign. She had a number of bruises covering her exquisite face, and though he was no doctor, it didn't appear she had any facial fractures. Gazing at her, she looked as if she was sleeping peacefully.

Sampson reached into his pocket excavating for a vial of smelling salt. Finding what he was searching for, he opened the package and placed the object under her nose. "Come on, Donatella," he said willing her to arouse. "Come on, I know you are in there!" After a few moments she was awake – groggy – but awake.

"Jasmyn," she said with an intenseness in her voice. "Where is Jasmyn?" To this he had no answer. She stood unsteadily to her feet and he began to protest, "You're in no condition to be standing. We need to have you checked out at the hospital."

The cold glare from her hazelnut eyes abruptly put an end to any additional protest. She began walking back toward her car with Sampson walking aside her.

"I need to find out where she is, and we need to rescue her."

Sampson realized she was heading toward her car – a bad idea he thought, but he realized the smoke he initially saw had stopped. Without hesitation she climbed back into the wreckage that was once her Audi. To Sampson it seemed like she was in there for 10 minutes, but in reality, it was roughly 20 seconds.

She emerged from the wreckage with her cellphone in hand.

"BJ," she spoke urgently into the handset. "Where is she?"

"Agent Dabria! My God! Are you ok?"

"I'm fine BJ, where is she?" I see her tracker stopped roughly two miles from your location. It hasn't moved for a while."

Dabria could feel a tightening in her chest. "Detective, to your car. Fast."

Sampson, still playing catch up to the entire situation, did as he was bid. He silently prayed as he turned the ignition for the car to start. Once again old Betsy came through.

"Continue heading north," she said, still fearing the worst. She could sense the detective eyes shifting her way while he drove but she paid him no mind. Her focus was on Jasmyn and the baby. "Where is she BJ?"

"In another 30 feet you should be right on top of her."

Donatella didn't see any trucks and she didn't see anyone standing by. *Lord, let her be ok.* She didn't know what she would do if Jasmyn and the baby were harmed because she failed to protect them.

"You're there. You should see her."

"Stop the car," she urged jumping out before it came to a complete stop. She looked around anxiously, but she didn't see a body. However, something a few feet from the road glinted in the moonlight. She rushed over and to her dismay, and relief, lay the bracelet and no body. "Damn it, they found the tracker."

Detective Sampson appeared next to her side. "Bad news. The helicopter I called in to trace the vehicle you were chasing lost contact with the vehicle. Sounds like they had a number of similar vehicles converge on the SUV you were chasing. When they emerged from the overpass the helicopter lost track of the correct vehicle. They gave chase to the one they felt was the correct vehicle and it turned out to be empty, aside from the driver."

Donatella pounded a fist into the ground. Her mind raced on what to do next and she didn't have a clue. Her phone rang, it was Marcellous.

"Yes, Marcellous?"

"They have loaded Jasmyn onto a plane. They are preparing to take off."

19

Donatella sat in silence as Detective Sampson pushed his ancient vehicle toward the airport. With the loss of adrenaline coursing through her system, her body felt the effects of the high-speed crash with each jostling of the car. However, the physical pain she felt was minor in comparison to the mental anguish she endured knowing she let Jasmyn and Marcellous down. She didn't have a clue where they had taken Jasmyn or what they planned to do with her. She knew she had to get her back and she would stop at nothing to see that done.

She had BJ trying his best to determine which plane they boarded and where the plane was headed. They were able to narrow the plane down to five private flights that had left the terminal, but they couldn't chase all five. They needed a break, and they needed one now.

Sampson pulled into the cellphone lot next to Marcellous' blue Tesla. Pulling old Betsy into the parking spot, she gave one final grunt and died before he could even turn off the ignition. *You did good old girl* was his passing thought as he opened the door for the last time.

Marcellous bolted from the car calm, yet intense. The worry was written within each wrinkle creasing his forehead. His eyes had narrowed, not in an accusatory fashion, but one laden with determination. A determination that pulsated from his skin into the atmosphere. He waited patiently as Donatella gingerly lifted herself from the sagging seat, using the doorframe to steady her movements. Before he could speak, the agent's phone began to ring.

She peered down at the display, searching for the caller ID, *Private*. She answered.

"Well if it isn't my favorite FBI agent."

Donatella squeezed the phone, instantly recognizing the voice.

"The famous Donatella Dabria. Seems you and I have some unfinished business."

"Where is Jasmyn –"

"Don't you interrupt!" Buckley fired back in a rush. "Your job is to listen and not talk. You claim to be good at your job, yet, I continue to get close to the people you love most. How is that? It doesn't matter. Everything you need to find me, and your precious Jasmyn was given to you long ago. You're just too dense to figure it out. But I'm a good sport and simply killing Jasmyn would not be any fun. So, to that end, I'll give you one final clue, but this clue comes with strings attached. Once I give you this clue you will once again be on the clock – for your hour of reckoning has come. But I'm giving you more than an hour – in fact, I'm giving you four hours."

Donatella began to grit her teeth as the others looked on anxiously. She activated the speaker on the phone and placed it on the roof of the car while the other two circled around.

"Undoubtedly you know we have boarded a plane, we knew Marcellous was following us, but he posed no threat. Travel time has already been factored into the four hour window I'm graciously giving you, but if you plan to save Jasmyn, you cannot afford to make any mistakes. Now," she said with an exaggerated pause.

"I'm only going to say this once as I do not like repeating myself. One of these things is not like the others."

The phone went dead on the other end as Marcellous, Sampson, and Donatella all looked at each other. Donatella set the clock on her phone knowing how maniacal Terri is about her timeframes.

"Just what in the hell does that mean?" Marcellous blurted out. "One of these things is not like the other! That's the biggest load of shit I have ever heard."

Sampson chimed in, "Does she mean one of the crimes is not like the other? The massacre at GIS is certainly different. All of the other crimes had only one victim while this one wiped out a number of people."

Marcellous finding his ground again, "Jasmyn is the only one they abducted and moved to a new location, could that be the meaning of her ambiguous clue?"

Both men looked over at Donatella. She had both eyes closed in intense concentration.

"Donatella, what is it? Do you have an idea?"

Silence endured for another 30 seconds. She sat there motionless with the intensity still evident. Suddenly, she opened her eyes and retrieved her phone from the hood. She found the number from her call log, pressed the green phone key and waited.

"BJ," she said when the other end was connected. "Did one of the planes fly to Cleveland, Ohio?"

BJ, used to the curt manner, immediately pulled up his data. "Yes, one of the planes filed a flight plan to land in Cleveland –"

Donatella disconnected the call. "Marcellous, we need to

take your car to hangar 33. Let's go, we don't have any time to waste."

"What, what is it?" he asked, opening the door and sliding into the driver's seat. Donatella ambled to the passenger's side and with the grace of a bear, fell into the seat. Sampson sat in the back behind Donatella.

"Leave from this lot and head toward the terminal. Take the back-access road off to the right, this will take you to where the private planes are located. Hurry."

Marcellous placed the car into gear and proceeded as directed.

"Buckley is correct, we had a major clue sitting in front of us the entire time. Detective Sampson, the night Samantha Young was murdered you found a card left in the picture frame. On the back there was an image."

"Yea," he responded. "It was an image of The Thinker."

Donatella continued, "On the bottom of the canister at the GIS headquarters, there was an image."

"Yea, it was the same image."

"That is the key."

"What," Marcellous said incredulously, "What does the image of The Thinker have to do with the abduction of my wife?"

"One of these things is not like the other," she responded. "On March 24, 1970 in the early morning a politically radical group calling themselves the Weather Underground set off a bomb. This bomb was placed on the pedestal of a famous statue that sat outside the Cleveland Museum of Art. When the bomb detonated, it didn't destroy the intended artifact, merely damaging it beyond repair. The museum decided that they would not replace the statue and it still sits outside of the museum to this day. That statue –"

"The Thinker," Sampson finished.

"Yes. This is one of the things that's not like the others. It's the only one that has been damaged."

Marcellous approached a gate being manned by two guards. Donatella rolled down her window and the guard on the right-hand side looked into the window.

"Agent Dabria. Didn't expect to see you this evening."

"Miles," she said wincing. "Need to make an emergency departure."

"Absolutely. Open the gate and let them pass," he said to the other man.

The mechanical arm raised and Marcellous gave SA Dabria an inquisitive look as she rolled the window back in place.

"You'll want to make a left at the second row and go to the far end. Hangar 33 is the last one on the right."

The trio sat in silence, each for their own reasons, as Marcellous once again followed the provided direction. He was worried out of his mind about his wife and their unborn baby. He was also firm in his stance that they would not be leaving him behind.

Detective Sampson wondered if this was spiraling out of control and if they needed back up. He damn sure knew he would not let the Special Agent tackle this problem alone, but he worried they didn't have a game plan.

Donatella had one thought. One simple unregulated, unflinching thought – Destroy everyone that gets in my way.

Marcellous pulled the vehicle next to the hangar where two men in pilot attire stood like sentries at the entrance. Donatella, stiff yet motivated, extracted herself from the passenger's side followed by Sampson and finally Marcellous.

She eased over to the pilot on the right, "Are we prepared to take off?"

"Yes, Agent Dabria. The flight plan has been filed and we are free for immediate departure."

"Good. Waste no time getting us in the air."

Sampson and Marcellous followed in her wake through the entrance into the main areas of the hangar. Inside they saw a Gulfstream G550 awaiting their arrival. Donatella led the trio up the stairs into the cabin of the aircraft. Both Marcellous and Sampson had not been on a private plane before and were struck by the pure opulence that lay before them.

Two plush leather cream captain's chairs sat facing each other on the left side. On the right sat a bench with the same upholstery that looked as if it could seat four comfortably. A table with place settings for three sat further back in the cabin next to a drink station that had an assortment of bottled waters, sodas and wine chilling on ice. A TV was mounted on the wall against the back of the entrance.

Marcellous found that his mouth had involuntarily dropped open and he had to consciously work it closed. He found himself thinking he could never fly commercial again.

Donatella sat in the chair facing the other two place settings, followed by Sampson and then Marcellous.

"Gentlemen, I'm not going to tell you you're not coming on this trip because I know it's a waste of time. But," she said wincing in pain, "this will be extremely dangerous." She turned and lay her piercing hazelnut eyes on Marcellous.

"I know you want to save your wife, but it does her no good if she's saved and you're dead. I'm allowing you to come along only if you play by my rules."

Marcellous, steely-eyed, never lost contact with her glare, simply nodded in agreement.

She turned her head to the left focusing in on Detective Sampson. "Carl, Terri plays for keeps. She has no compunction about killing to get what she wants. If you go along, you will be forced to use your intuition, experience, and gun. There will be death and you will be the arbiter of it or the recipient of it."

Sampson involuntarily straightened in his chair and nodded his acquiescence.

A flight attendant materialized, handing Donatella two capsules and a freshly poured glass of water.

"Emily, let the captain know we are ready to depart. Once we take flight, we will need a light meal, please see to it that we are served once we level out."

Emily agreed and took her leave.

Donatella popped the capsules into her mouth and chased them with a long drink from her glass. "If we have any chance to succeed," she said picking up the thread, "we need to have a plan and we are going to need some help. Let's get started."

20

Donatella strode gingerly toward her pending conflict with Terri Buckley. She realized Buckley held all the cards and the plan she devised was a dangerous gamble. From day one, the murder of Samantha Taylor, Terri has been manipulating events to lead to this moment.

She stepped on the first step – she would need to immediately hone her senses to the surrounding. Knowing Terri's propensity for surprises, she was sure to encounter her fair share.

She stepped on the second step – although she was entering the building alone, she had backup and support. She needed to trust that they could perform their task for this gamble to stand a chance. She wasn't used to working with or trusting a partner since the destruction of her partnership with Buckley. Now, she was entrusting her life with an author, a fellow law enforcement officer, and a computer genius.

Stepping on the third step – she mentally walked through the gear she carried on her person. Her FBI issued Sig Sauer P226 9mm semiautomatic handgun, slots for two extra clips, her set of 12 Japanese Shinobi throwing knives, and an ASP 21" expandable baton.

She stepped on the fourth step – when this episode came to its end, she would need to rededicate her focus on tracking down The Syndicate. Her closest link to this shadow organization was Buckley in this cat and mouse game. She needed to keep her alive, at least long enough to extract the needed information.

She stepped on the fifth step – she worried about the condition of Jasmyn. Marcellous said she was in labor when they arrived at the hospital. Could the baby already be born? Is she even here in this museum? There was only one way to find out.

She took the sixth step – the landing, at which stood the statue of The Thinker. His legs horribly mangled while he sat in deep contemplation. She looked at him, pondered her mission, and said to herself, *stop at nothing to save Jasmyn. If they are in the way, they will be dealt with quickly and efficiently.*

She bypassed the statue and continued her ascent toward the pillars and the south entrance into the museum. Although it was well past closing, Donatella was not surprised to find the entrance to the museum was unlocked.

She pushed her way into the foyer of the 1916 building, ear tuning and eyes adjusting to the light. The interior of the building was illuminated only by dim light dully shining from the long vertical sconces adorning the walls. She glanced down at her watch – 55 minutes remaining.

With no patrons in the building, she was sure she could search the entire building in that amount of time; however, the lack of patrons didn't equate to a lack of formidable foes that were undoubtedly spread throughout the interior.

Stilling herself, she passed through the foyer into the rotunda. Donatella had to admit to herself that she didn't know much about art so she dispassionately passed by each piece without giving it a second glance. Furthermore, she had more pressing concerns she needed to deal with at the moment.

Upon entering the rotunda, the PA came to life. "Agent Dabria, welcome," came the sharp clip voice of Terri Buckley. "I'll dispense with the melodrama and get straight to the point. You've twice robbed me of the vengeance I rightfully deserve. That prick Smithville deserved what I had planned for him, but you ruined it. And, well – you simply won't die. So, if you won't die, then your mental anguish is the next best thing."

Her voice deepened in pitch, "I told you that I will destroy everything and everyone you love. Make no mistake, I fully plan to make good on my promise. Now, to why you're here. The prissy Mrs. Jasmyn Thompson. I must say it was a pleasure getting to know her over the last several months. It's a shame that after this evening she will – let's just say forever be changed."

Donatella winced inwardly while outwardly balling her fist.

"As you can guess, she is somewhere in this building. For the moment she, and the baby, are both unharmed. But as I mentioned on our brief call, you are on the clock. And according to my clock you're now under an hour. I suggest you get moving, but beware of the building and its patrons."

The PA went silent. She was effectively on the top floor which logically meant Jasmyn was on the bottom floor. However, Terri likes to go off script. Therefore, she could very well be on the second floor – but certainly not this one. Nonetheless, prudence meant she needed to clear this floor prior to proceeding to the next.

Donatella turned to the right preparing to go through the Armor Court when a sound emanated from the ceiling. A gate as wide as the entrance began to descend from the ceiling in a slow methodical fashion. She idly thought, guess I'm not meant to go this way. In that same instance, the pathway leading back to the foyer from which she came began spewing a gate from the ceiling. Straight ahead or down the escalator seemed to be the only paths forward. She could see clearly into the room straight ahead which meant the escalator was the only path.

Donatella stepped onto the escalator heading down to the next level. Undoubtedly, Terri had something planned for her and she would need to stay focused. The movement of the escalator stopped once she was halfway between floors. First thought was a power outage, but this was quickly dismissed as the escalator going in the opposite direction was still moving up. Her next thought was – trap.

At the bottom of the escalator stood a barrel-chested man with a head two times the size it should be. His eyes and muscles bulged, almost in a strain and he wore a crooked smile across his face. He balled both meat cleavers, placed them against each other and pressed, causing his knuckles to break the cacophonous silence.

Behind and above her she heard a muffled chuckle. She quickly turned around to see a man standing at the top of the escalator that could have been the twin brother of the man at the bottom. Instead of balling his fist to make his knuckles pop, he took each finger, bent them sideways one by one to generate a cracking sound. She turned back to see that the man at the bottom of the escalator had stepped on the first step.

The escalator could be heard restarting; however, this time it too was going up. Jolted by its sudden movement, Donatella knew she needed to think quickly. The two burly men had her trapped. She knew she could not take them both on at the same time so without a moment's more hesitation she decided to become the aggressor.

She charged down the upward moving escalator toward the man ascending from the bottom. It was clear by the shock that registered on his face that this was not what he expected to happen. As she ran, she quickly calculated her options, high or low.

High she ran the risk of being caught in midair and being flung like a rag doll. Or she could land awkwardly on the metal teeth of the steps.

Low she ran the risk of the ape falling on top of her and thus pinning her to the metal stairs until they reached the top. Both options had their downfalls, nonetheless, she must act.

The moment of indecisiveness from the burly giant at the bottom resulted in his downfall. Donatella leapt into the air raising her knee in time to connect with his nose. The bone gave an audible crunch and she immediately knew the nose was broken. Her momentum carried her another foot forward causing the man to fall over backward while he reached his hand up to cradle his broken nose. This simple, involuntary action meant he could not brace himself for the pending impact as his head cracked on the metal step. A trail of blood immediately oozed from the impact, but she didn't stand around to admire.

The other man, frozen in his steps, now had the higher ground and a theoretical advantage. Again, Donatella decided she would press the issue. She turned around and began racing up the escalator. With both the escalator and her momentum headed in the same direction she was gaining more speed than if she were simply running up a flight of stairs. She reached to her belt grasping for her ASP 21" expandable baton.

In one fluid motion, she removed the baton from its pouch and snapped her wrist parallel to her right leg as it extended on the step. The moment the baton became completely expanded, with as much force as she could muster, she curled the baton upward in an uppercut motion and connected with the chin of the man. The motion that took all of two seconds left little time for the assailant to defend the baton's arc.

This rocked him on his feet, but he still stood. Jugular still exposed from the initial blow, she backhanded him in the neck, once across his left temple, and again on the back of the neck as he fell forward – unconscious or dead, it didn't matter to her. As his body hit the ground, his twins' body was deposited next to him from the escalator.

Donatella began to chide herself for not checking the room directly in front of her in the first place. No doubt this is where the man came from and she could have disposed of him first. She retracted the baton, placed it back in its holder and eyeballed the escalators. The one on the left that was originally going up was now going down. She stepped on the escalator and instead of waiting for it to reach the bottom, she took the liberty of running down to the second floor.

DETECTIVE SAMPSON WAITED the agreed upon five minutes before he approached the north entrance to the Cleveland Museum of Art. His task was to breach the museum from the opposite side with the expectation that all eyes and attention would be on Donatella.

During the planning for this infiltration, the trio of Donatella, Detective Sampson, and Marcellous conducted reconnaissance of the museum. They observed the locations for ingress and with the assistance of BJ a plan began to materialize.

While Donatella and Sampson would operate as the boots on the ground, Marcellous and BJ would operate as their support. Marcellous would act as support for Donatella – a support she knew she didn't need, but an activity used to keep him safe and out of the way. BJ on the other hand had the more crucial job of guiding Detective Sampson.

While Donatella and the crew were on the plane making

their way to Cleveland, Ohio – BJ was hard at work. He managed to break into the servers at GIS and obtain the plans to retrofit the museum with the updated security system. The plans helped by providing a layout of the museum. Going through the layout he was able to ascertain two probable locations for where they were holding Jasmyn.

Sampson would be responsible for searching those two locations and at this moment he was on his way to the first one.

"When you walk through the entrance, your first destination will be around the corner to your left. There doesn't appear to be any traps along the corridor, but I urge diligence."

Sampson nodded his head but kept silent as he pulled open the door to the north entrance. The corridor entrance was wide, cold, and dark. The partitions to aid in the control of traffic had all been moved to one side in the corner. There were a number of seating areas strategically placed, presumably to provide a much-needed rest for the elderly or children just learning to walk. The only light came from the floor-to-ceiling windows circling the area.

Sampson listened hard but heard nothing. He began to wonder if this was a good thing or a bad thing. A properly planned trap is always silent before its sprung. Exposed in the center of the room, he moved over to the right pressing himself against the wall. He felt better having his flank covered and thus one less concern he needed to deal with.

He reached the corner, preparing to make a left to his destination but decided to take a look to the right first. There, facing the opposite direction, was a sentry patrolling. Sampson evaluated the terrain and realized he could not make it to his destination without the sentry being alerted to his position.

The adversary was roughly 15 feet away and gaining more distance with each step. Sampson decided to make his move. He pulled his gun from his holster as a precaution – if his foe turned before he could make his move, he would put two rounds into his chest.

Silently, and with haste, Sampson accelerated. The sentry took four more steps and began to pivot on his left heel. Sampson, noticing this deviation, broke into a sprint to cover the remaining distance and with a cobra-like strike, hit the sentry with the butt of the gun across the exposed left temple.

The crunch of the impact was loud in the empty space and he prayed it didn't alert anyone else. He stretched out both arms and caught the man as his unconscious body began to cascade to the floor. He dragged the body over against the wall placing him in the shadow overtaking that half of the space.

Sampson checked to the right, left and behind him for any additional immediate threats. Satisfied by the still in the night, he cautiously stalked forward. After 20 seconds he stood in front of the double doors leading to the ArtLens Gallery. On the left-hand side of the door sat a keypad.

"BJ, I'm at location Alpha and there is a touchpad awaiting some type of entry."

"Touch the display to activate the screen."

Sampson placed his hand against the display and a light illuminated from underneath his palm. Moving his hand, he saw a number pad.

"When you're ready enter the following digits: 9-7-8-2-7-2-3-0."

Sampson quickly inserted the numbers as he heard them through his earpiece. Upon pressing the final number, the words 'Access Granted' appeared on the screen and the mechanical lock disengaged. *I don't know who this BJ is, but he is coming in extremely handy*, he thought.

When he entered the room a motion sensor light activated and he pulled the door closed behind him to keep from illuminating the corridor. Conducting a quick survey of the room, he realized the motion sensitive light only illuminated a portion of the room. Weary, he began to move forward. At the edge of the first beam another overhead light illuminated providing more visibility ahead.

The room itself seemed empty as the silence engulfed him. He continued deeper into the room scanning left to right, right to left. As he turned his focus back in front of him, off to the right he perceived a slight motion in the darkness. He turned and froze. He stared into the darkness but didn't see any additional movement. He continued to move forward.

At the back of this room BJ had discovered a secondary room that was not on the original blueprints. They rationalized this could be the place that Jasmyn was being held captive. This would serve as Sampson's first stop in the search for Jasmyn Thompson.

If memory served him correctly, the interior room would be visible when the next light illuminated. As he neared the termination of the light's beam, he was certain he was no longer alone. The aura of the room had shifted. Within the three steps it took to cover the distance between him and the end of the beam – he dropped to the ground just in time to hear a shot fly overhead.

There stood a man in full black attire with both arms extended. The assailant was only 10 feet in front of Sampson, who scrambled to his feet and tackled the foe before he could fire another shot. The impact of being tackled and then hitting the ground was not enough to cause the assailant to lose his grip on the gun.

He tried several times to aim the pistol at Sampson; however, Sampson had him by the wrist and the battle of strength and will was on full display. Laying on top of the man, Sampson took his right elbow and shot it into the midsection of his foe. The blow had no impact as the man on the ground wore a Kevlar vest covering his upper body.

In pursuing this failed attempt, Sampson had released the left arm of the attacker who now used his free hand to connect with the kidney of Sampson with two brutal punches. Pain racing through his side and back, he began to loosen his grip on the man's other arm. He closed his eyes and shot his head forward into the lower half of the other man's face. The impact caused him to feel an instantaneous daze, but it also took out several teeth of his foe.

He could tell that he now had the upper hand and he was determined to continue pressing forward. He elbowed the guy in the forehead as he maneuvered his right hand toward the gun. In doing so, he also shifted his weight across his torso looking to gain leverage. The assailant brought his left hand up toward the gun and both men struggled to gain control as all four hands wrestled for the best spot.

During the struggle another shot fired harmlessly into the empty space and the battle ensued. Sampson knew this next attack would be useless, nonetheless, he shot a knee into his attackers left side. Once, twice, three times. Although he knew the pain would be minimal, the body tends to protect itself against harm and the man buckled slightly on each impact. This provided the window Sampson needed.

He dropped his right hand down to his side and retrieved his pistol. Rolling to his right and off of the man, he raised his gun up, pressed the barrel to the side of his assailant's neck and pulled the trigger. All fight instantly left the man whose body went limp and the gun fell harmlessly to the ground.

Sampson's face made contact with the cool ground and he let out several pants attempting to catch his breath after exerting so much energy during the conflict. He quickly took inventory of his body – no major issues, just some bruising. He quickly thought – *three shots fired. Still no one came barging through the door.* He pushed himself from the floor, oriented and continued in the direction of the interior room.

The exterior of the room looked to be 30 feet in width and 10 feet high. From his vantage point he could not determine the depth. The onyx room had no windows – just a door situated in the middle of the structure. Sampson walked to the door, turned the handle and pushed the door open. Inside the room was fully lit – and empty.

"Shit," he said activating his mic. "Location Alpha is a dry hole – an empty room." Frustrated, but not surprised, he followed up with, "Making my way to location Beta."

AT THE BOTTOM of the escalator, Donatella did a quick survey of her new surroundings. In her immediate vicinity she didn't spy any adversaries, but her intuition told her they were nearby. Moving through the cavernous space she recounted the fact that Sampson should be breaching the museum. She had to trust he would achieve his task while she pushed through hers.

With each step she thought through how she would end this conflict. Terri would not allow herself to be arrested – she would fight to the bitter end. Donatella was willing to do whatever was necessary and would match her adversary's level of intensity.

She heard a motor in the distance engage followed by another. No doubt another trap, but she moved forward. The short hairs on the back of her neck stood erect when she eyed what sat in front of her.

The gates to both her left and her right had been closed leaving a narrow corridor leading into the library space. There was a low illumination being produced within the space. Upon entering the library, she was amazed by the sheer size. The width of the library reminded her of the width of a football field. The length was roughly double the size of a basketball court. In all the space was nearly 30,000 square feet. Undaunted, she continued walking into the room with her senses on high alert, eyes darting side-to-side.

The door to the entrance sprung closed with an echoing thud; however, the sound didn't break her stride. Directly in front of her four men dressed in black head to toe stepped from behind sliding bookshelves. To her right four additional individuals appeared – two appeared to be women. On her left, three men stepped forward.

Although she didn't sense any movement directly behind her, training told her she needed to check. She quickly looked over both shoulders – empty. Satisfied, she realized 11 assailants surrounded her. She could not see their faces; however, the intent to kill poured from their body language. She took a moment to look over each person and the immediate scenery surrounding them. Within each individual view, a plan began to materialize.

She spoke into her throat mic, "Library, lights."

On the other end of the connection, Marcellous Thompson had been pacing back and forth both furious and anxious. Special Agent Dabria made it clear he was not to enter the building. Instead, he would be on the other end of the comms directly connected to the special agent. He was to keep the line open and only speak if confirming a command. So far, the comms had been silent and he was left to stew.

In the room they secured a block away from the museum he couldn't help but to feel useless. His wife was in peril and he was told to sit still and wait. He could be of some assistance, but the agent hadn't even given him a chance. Hell, he was the one that tracked them to the airport and knew they were on a plane.

When the voice from the comm awoke in his ear, he was

momentarily shocked. He froze in his tracks and quickly replayed the transmission in his head. Then he repeated, "Library, Lights. Confirmed."

He took the three steps back to the computer and began to recall the directions he received from BJ as they were going over the plan. From wherever he was located, BJ managed to hack into the security system for the museum. Understanding he would need to be in continuous contact with Detective Sampson, BJ quickly wrote a program that would allow Marcellous some rudimentary control over different elements within the building. Once such thing had been the lights.

Typically, there was a complex set of commands needed to operate the different sections of the building; however, BJ simplified the interface that Marcellous would be interacting with for this mission. Utilizing the floorplans that he had secured, BJ mapped each room to only their corresponding lights forgoing the section configuration developed by the engineer.

Marcellous scrolled the alphabetical listing of rooms and quickly found 'Library' sitting in the middle. He placed his finger over the touchscreen and pressed the button. The button which had been colored green turned red once depressed.

Back in the library Donatella waited like a coiled cobra for Marcellous to extinguish the lights. During her training with Master Yoshida, her Krav Maga sensei, they trained for scenarios in which they would be greatly outnumbered by their enemies. One of the most grueling training sessions she endured was the blindfolded battle royale.

During this intense one on seven session you were blindfolded against heavily armed combatants. Your task was to defeat them utilizing your senses and familiarity with the environment. Donatella found this to be a challenge of her mental and physical fortitude; however, like all of the training thrown at her, she soon mastered this discipline as well.

Outnumbered, 11 to one, she decided to even the playing field – and once again she would be the aggressor. The lights flickered once and then plunged the library into darkness.

Donatella sprung to her right concentrating on the last known location of the assailant closest to her. With a speed born through violence she hit the combatant squarely in the solar plexus with an open palm. Most of the blow had been absorbed by the vest he wore across his chest; however, the force of the blow was enough to cause him to stumble. She followed up the attack by sweeping his legs, knocking the assailant to the ground. She swiftly pulled a Shinobi throwing knife from its sheath plunging the tip of the blade through his carotid artery. A warm spray of blood shot from his neck as his heart continued to push blood through the arteries.

She extracted the knife from the dying man's neck and in one fluid motion while perched on one knee she flung the throwing knife through the darkness encompassing the library. The blade arched through the air, silent in its flight. Donatella didn't wait for the impact, instead she rose quickly and ran to her left.

Just before she heard the initial volley of gunfire, she heard a body hit the ground, two down she thought. She recalled a table roughly five feet from her starting position. She slid through the table's opening extracting her Sig Sauer P226. Ears tuning for the slightest sound, she heard the sound of gun brushing against leather 30 degrees to her left. The sound was consistent in his movement thus the enemy was stationary. She turned the requisite 30 degrees and fired two shots in quick succession.

She was rewarded with the sound of metal clanging against the floor followed by a muted thud. The intensity in the gunfire continued to fly harmlessly above her with only a couple making contact with the table.

She could hear the footsteps of the remaining two men on the left. They were attempting to regroup – mistake on their end. Silently, she army crawled from underneath the table, stood from her prone position and ran toward the direction of the sound. Not wanting to give away her location, she pulled the retractable baton from its holder, popping it open with a quick flick of the wrist. She heard the sound as it shot to its full length; however, with the chatter of gunfire she was sure the two men close to her position had not noticed.

To their detriment, they began speaking much too loudly to accommodate the sound of the overpowering gunfire. Donatella, in a backhanded motion, connected the baton with the kneecap of the man closest to her. The metal on bone made an audible crunch. The unsuspecting foe yelled out loud from the surprise and brutality of the impact against his knee. Instinctively, he brought his hand down to his affected area. What started out to be a backhand, turned into a forehand coming back toward her body. This motion connected with the extended elbow shattering the articular capsule and the lateral ulnar collateral ligament.

The arm hung useless next to his body as he screamed in pain once again. The quick violent attacks finally materialized within his brain and his body crumbled to the ground. He would be out of the fight. His partner realizing they were under attack struggled to extract his sidearm. Similar to their elevated voices, this delay in extracting his weapon aided in his demise.

During her evaluation of the room, she realized this particular combatant was taller than his buddies with an abnormally long torso. As a result, the vest he wore was poorly fitted. His chest was covered; however, his left and right kidneys were slightly exposed. Donatella swiftly rotated to his left side.

Sensing her aiming point, she swung the baton with a ferocity that nearly lifted the agent from her feet.

As the yell of anguish left his lungs, his body trying to protect itself arched backward exposing his windpipe. Unrelenting, she bounced the baton on the jutting Adam's apple, silencing the yell and probably compressing the windpipe. She thought, *five down – six to go.*

The remaining assailants, realizing they were firing in the wrong direction, trained their fire in the location of the yells. She quickly flattened herself to the ground as bullets riddled the still elevated body of the last man who was probably near death already. Their fire discipline and regard for their comrades had been displaced with fear and self-preservation.

After a few moments the constant gunfire in the library ended abruptly and Donatella could sense the landscape within the library shifting.

From her earpiece, she heard Detective Sampson say, "Location Alpha is a dry hole – an empty room. Making my way to location Beta." SA Dabria let her frustration dissipate and once again focused on her task at hand.

In the distance, directly in front of her starting position, she could hear the sound of the stacks rolling on its wheels. With her eyes closed, even with the room cast in darkness, she reoriented herself in the three-dimensional space. She listened for the slightest sound and felt for the slight shift in air current.

She quickly moved up the left side of the room, now empty of potential danger, in a wider arc than probably necessary. Before coming level with the stacks, she heard a slight rustling. It was the sound of a man crouching and grappling for a table or a chair to presumably use as a shield. The sounds of his breathing would be faint to others; however, to her finely tuned ears it was a natural beacon. She extracted another throwing knife while listening to catch the rhythm of his breaths. Within two more inhalations, she had a bead on his location. The knife exploded from her hand and a second later the breathing had stopped. Later, when the body would be examined, the medical examiner would find the knife protruding the bridge of his nose directly between his eyes. Six assailants accounted for, now headed for the homestretch.

She had expelled two rounds from her 15-round cartridge. With five enemies remaining, she liked her chances of disposing of them quickly. "Marcellous, library lights. Give me a three second countdown."

She kept her eyes closed knowing the initial burst of light would temporarily dazzle anyone with their eyes still open. She pulled her Sig Sauer from its holster crouching with the anticipation. The countdown began in her ear. When Marcellous hit one, she waited an extra second and then opened her eyes.

Partially hidden by the stacks was a man crouched with his head slightly visible. Donatella fired two-shots and quickly shifted her gaze looking for another target. A woman caught in the middle of the room, obviously moving from the right side of the library back toward the stacks, had her arm covering her eyes. Donatella took aim at the arm and let off two more shots. Nine bullets remaining, three foes.

Gunfire erupted from behind her and she fell to the ground. The shots whizzed by harmlessly and she had not been hit. She turned toward the threat realizing the man was simply firing and did not have a target in sight; however, this made him her next prime target.

From her prone position, she could only see the lower half of his body. She fired a shot directly into the groin violently knocking the man from his feet. When his body hit the ground, head facing her, she fired off one more round and then rolled to her left and jumped back to her crouched position. One man and one woman remaining.

She scanned the room darting her eyes to the stacks and then back to the right side of the library. She saw no forms and felt no movement. The last two were either better at hiding than their comrades or they had been taken out by friendly fire. Though she would appreciate the latter, she wouldn't count on it.

She walked back closer to the stacks. She played back their configuration from when she entered the room and thought back to the sound she heard of them moving when in the darkness. The ones in the middle had been drawn closer together.

She sprinted to the end of the stack closest to her and began traversing the remainder, one by one, until she reached the middle two. She momentarily paused and then with her gun extended she stepped out from behind the covering aiming down her sights – an empty row. She ran the calculation quickly through her head, this had to be right. She felt the movement coming from above her all too late.

The man crashed into her with enough force to send her gun spinning under the stacks causing her to fall to the ground with him landing next to her. She scrambled to her feet as quickly as she could realizing he too was on his feet at the same time.

He was quick sending a jab toward her face, which she parried pushing aside the blow with her right hand and countering with her left. The blow missed as he ducked and spun to his left. They faced each other, Donatella feeling exposed as her back was now to the opening of the room though momentarily covered by the stacks.

He charged, deciding he would be the aggressor in this dance, looking as if he would try to sweep her leg; however, at the last minute he reverse pivoted and connected with her rib. She'd had worse impacts to her ribs; however, she had saw those coming and was always able to soften the blow. Admittedly, he caught her off guard and though the power behind the kick was lacking, she received 100 percent of the impact causing her to crumble slightly.

She sensed his left fist moving toward her head and not wanting to take the full impact, continued her fold to the left down to the ground. He missed causing him to slightly go off balance. She aimed a straightforward thrust kick to the knee, but he shifted his leg at the last second, so she caught him with a weak attempt to the shin.

Get up, she thought as she completed the roll to her left, the two now separated by a couple of feet. The report of a handgun filled the library as she saw the book next to her head shred to pieces. She ducked, receded and tried to calculate the location of the shot. Certainly still ground level and likely the stack to her left.

She ran top speed down her column searching for another Shinobi knife. The woman appeared 10-feet in front of her, gun at the ready. Donatella could see her knuckles flex as she prepared to pull the trigger. With two knives on either side of her middle finger, she let loose while diving headfirst to the ground.

The round exploded from the gun and this time impacted her left shoulder, spinning her 180 degrees. She slid on her back, blood oozing from her wound as the woman fell face first to the right of her. Donatella tried to move her left arm and the signals firing from the brain were not being received by the arm. "Shit!" she said out loud in a low voice.

She could hear the footfalls of the man preparing to enter this column. The gun the woman was carrying was now tucked slightly under her lifeless body. She tugged at the barrel of the gun, praying it didn't go off as the footsteps grew near. She extracted the weapon and spun it on the ground until the handle hit her palm.

The man stood over her, triumph in his eyes, her Sig Sauer

in his hand. With a smirk he leveled the pistol at her head. He opened his mouth to say something and Donatella placed two rounds through the opening before he could formulate a word. His head, and his body blew backward as her gun fell to her lap. Eleven down, she thought and let her head fall to the ground.

21

As Detective Sampson rode the down escalator, he realized how deep he was infiltrating the museum. If Jasmyn Thompson was not in location Beta, they would have to search the entire building. He looked down at his watch. Fifteen minutes left. He didn't know what would happen when the time limit expired and in everything he learned about this Terri Buckley – he didn't want to find out.

At the bottom of the escalator he made the turn leading him toward the Exhibition Gallery. BJ warned breaking into this location would take some work. As part of the security mechanisms, a retinal scanner had been installed. He had a couple of theoretical ideas to defeat this security measure, but his confidence level was low.

"I'm at the door," came a hushed, harsh voice from Sampson.

BJ, as always, was prepared and read off the 10-digit sequence for Sampson to enter. Before entering the final digit, Sampson muttered a silent prayer. The electronic lock disengaged and he let out an audible sigh of relief. He needed something to go right because up to this point so much had already gone wrong.

This next part, the retinal scanner, was the biggest crapshoot he ever saw in his life. Even when BJ explained the plan, Sampson thought it was risky.

"What we will do is take a high-resolution picture of Sampson's eye – in fact, let's do both to be safe. Images are stored as their ASCII values which have been encrypted before resting at the database. Within the hour, I will have cracked their encryption and will have the key necessary to store the images supplied by Sampson."

"What's the probability of this being successful?" Donatella inquired.

"Roughly 32 percent."

"That's it?!" yelled Marcellous. "We are risking the life of my wife on a 32 percent chance of success?"

"Given the situation we are in, that unfortunately, is the best we can do. This security system is pretty airtight. If we make it that far, under any other circumstance, this would be considered a win.

The moment of truth was now staring him in the face. "Please scan eye" was written across the screen and the location where the eye was to be scanned glowed an ominous green.

Sampson muttered another, yet slightly longer, prayer and positioned his eye next to the scanner. His mind raced as the laser raced across his eyeball and imminent failure began to register in his mind. Three seconds later the light turned green and again, he let out a sigh of relief. He pulled his sidearm from the holster, opened the door and stepped through the entrance – he was in.

Inside the Exhibit Gallery Sampson spotted a freestanding

white structure about 20 paces diagonal from his current position. Bright lights were bursting from the seams of the structure as if it was hastily thrown together. This feels right, he thought as he stalked forward.

Suddenly, he heard footsteps moving toward the entrance of the structure so he slid behind a vertical pillar just to his right. A woman in a full set of green scrubs walked through the exit followed by two armed guards. The guards didn't seem to be interested in the woman as they gazed the horizon for pending threats. The woman pulled down her mask and extracted a cell phone from her pocket. Sampson was close enough to hear the numbers report with each press on the phone. The woman put the phone to her ear.

"We are all set here. The patient is still sedated and per our plan she will be awaken after the procedure." A pause ensued and then she continued, "Confirmed, we will start immediately."

She placed the phone back into her pocket and turned to head back to the room.

In that moment Sampson knew he had to make a decision – and he decided. He stepped from behind his hiding spot, leveled his gun at the mullet cut being sported by the man closest to him and squeezed.

The back of his head exploded in a red mist as Sampson swung his pistol to take aim on the other armed man. The sound of the gunshot echoed in the space and was enough to get the other assailant reacting. Before Sampson could line up his shot the man flattened to the ground and searched for cover.

The woman ran back to the entrance as two more guards came filing out of the structure.

"Shit!" he said out loud and into the mic. "I think I have found Jasmyn in location Beta. Being engaged by hostiles. One down, three more present."

He fired at the second man coming through the entrance clipping him in the neck.

"Two down."

He ducked back behind cover as two shots flew by. He realized he was being reckless. If Jasmyn was in there, he couldn't fire weapons freely. He needed to be careful. Furthermore, he didn't have time to allow this gun battle to carry on.

Two more shots hit the pillar taking chunks out with each impact. This pillar is not going to hold at this rate. The second enemy on the scene ran across the opening while his partner laid down suppressing fire; however, Sampson decided to take his chance.

He spun from his cover while simultaneously hitting the ground in a prone position. He stitched a trio of rounds progressively moving from ankle to torso. He thought he heard to shots penetrate cloth prior to seeing the adversary hit the ground.

The man laying down suppressing fire turned momentarily to see his partner hit the ground and Sampson continued to press his advantage. He crab-walked with as much speed as he could muster. Once he reached the location the assailant was using for cover, he dove around the corner firing two more shots. Both bullets caught the man in the abdomen and he slouched over dropping the weapon in his hand.

Sampson wasted no additional time – he hopped to his feet and ran to the entrance of the structure.

Inside the room he saw Jasmyn stretched out on an operating table. The woman he saw outside just a few moments prior stood over Jasmyn's lifeless body with a scalpel in hand. Fear gripped him, *Am I too late?* Then he recalled the conversation the woman had with the faceless voice on the other end.

"The patient is still sedated..."

"Drop the scalpel," he demanded pointing the pistol directly at her head.

In a remarkably calm and poised voice the woman spoke, "I suggest you drop the gun. You're likely too stupid to know that this scalpel is resting on Ms. Jasmyn's carotid artery. With a small amount of pressure this extremely sharp instrument will splice through her skin and sever the artery. She will die and there will be nothing you can do about it."

"I can shoot you between the eyes if I see one muscle flex in your body!"

"You could but it – "

Sampson fired three shots, planting each one between the eyes. He quickly surveyed the room for any additional threats and saw none. He ran over to Jasmyn and pressed two fingers against her neck. Her pulse resonated and for the third time he sighed with relief.

"Jasmyn is secure. I repeat, Jasmyn is secure."

DONATELLA HEARD the report over the earpiece from Sampson. He had Jasmyn, and that meant their primary mission was now complete. However, her job was not done. She had only been laying on the floor for 30 seconds before the all clear came in from Sampson. The feeling in her arm began to come back yet the bleeding had not stopped.

She sat up and looked over at her left shoulder. She saw the entry and exit wound which was a good sign as the shot was a through and through. She could move the pinky, ring, and middle finger, but her pointer and thumb were still giving her fits. She tried to raise her arm and was met with less than 10 percent in mobility. This will have to do, she thought pushing herself to her feet with her good arm while holding on to her Sig Sauer.

As she began to move away from the stacks, the room was pitched into darkness.

"I wondered how long you would lay your sorry ass on the floor," came Buckley's voice from the PA. I have to admit, the trick you did with the lights – I never saw that coming. Seems like you had some assistance. Strange for a woman who kicked her partner to the side because she preferred to work alone. Kudos to your tech on the outside. He – or she – was able to dip into our system undetected and managed to keep us out while you went on your little killing spree. Seems like killing is becoming easier and easier every time I see you."

"The only person I want to kill at this moment is you," Donatella said through gritted teeth. "Why don't you show yourself so we can settle this once and for all."

"There, there. No need to be hostile. All you had to do was ask." A light illuminated in a room elevated roughly 20 feet from the floor. In the room behind a curved glass stood Terri Buckley. She stared down at Donatella with her arms placed behind her back.

"Seems to me all of your efforts are about to come up short. You see I just gave the go ahead to extract your newest godchild from your newest friend. It's too bad you will not be there for the birth. I haven't decided what to do with the baby, but rest assured the mother-to-be will never meet the baby. Once the precious bundle of joy is delivered, let's just say the mother will be dealt with swiftly."

Donatella realized Buckley did not know about Sampson and the fact he had just rescued Jasmyn. This was good as they could hopefully escape unnoticed.

"I figured the least I could do before ending your miserable existence was to let you know the fate of yet one more person you swore to protect. You seem to be a constant failure, it's a wonder how you still have a badge."

Donatella snapped the Sig eye level and emptied it in the direction of Terri. She wasn't surprised to see Terri, still standing with a smirk on her face. There was no way she would be in the same room unless she had some sort of protection. Donatella released the empty clip, placed the gun under her left arm and retrieved a new clip with her right hand. She slid the clip into the butt of her Sig and then banged the gun on her hip to lock the clip into place.

"Seems like that left shoulder of yours always gets in the way. No worries, you will not live long enough to deal with the pain." The emergency lights illuminated around the room. Circular sections of the floor around the room opened and long cylindrical containers began to elevate from the floor.

"Let me officially introduce you to 'TDK' – The Donatella Killer. No doubt you've seen the effects of its handy work in the aptly named GIS Massacre, and once again in the Penny Hampton case. The scientists worked to perfect its effects for months after our last encounter at Orbitz Technology. It received its debut at GIS and I have to admit, it performed well. However, death came too soon. There was not enough – agony. So, they tweaked the formula once again and the excruciating time it took for Mrs. Hampton to expire met the desired goal."

"Now, before you decide to go all Rambo and shoot the containers, I'll tell you that would be a grave mistake. You see, the faster the mist is dispersed, the longer it takes for the effects materialize. Counter intuitive, I know, but a design requirement I had from day one. The longer it takes, the more agony you feel, so I suggest you leave my canisters just as they are," she mirthlessly chuckled.

"Now, I have a plane to catch. There is a certain someone I need to go and pay a visit." The elevated room went dark and the lights to the library were once again fully lit.

Donatella spoke calmly over the comms, "BJ, I'm in the library. Find me an alternative route out of this room."

She visually searched each corner of the room. The canisters were strategically placed so that the mist would reach each corner of the library at precisely the same time.

BJ came back on the comms, "Two of the four walls are load balancing and thus have been reinforced. The door looks to have been locked remotely and the encryption for this lock has been changed. I don't have the key and it'll take a few minutes for my software to break the code."

The mist from the canister to her immediate left began to hiss and a lavender colored haze began to creep across the room.

"How much time do you need?" SA Dabria asked BJ.

"Five maybe six minutes," came the reply.

"Hurry then, BJ. Hurry."

Donatella took inventory of the room once again and went into action. She quickly removed her shirt, wrapped it around her head covering her mouth and nose. She pulled the binding tight and began moving.

She pulled the body of the girl that lay closest to her toward the canister. Working with one good arm, she pressed the body against the right side of the canister.

The mist coming from that side slowed as it pushed against the body but continued to blast in full force out the left side.

Satisfied, she moved toward the next canister. Five feet from the canister lay the body of another for who expired during the battle. Although his stature was small, he was compact – dense. It took more exertion than she would have expected but she finally had him in place.

She could feel the effects of the poison already coursing through her body. She had an unbelievably warm sensation running across her skin as if it was on fire. She did her best to ignore this feeling and the pain in her shoulder.

She ran in the direction of the next canister. There was a man lying on his back close to the canister, but he was nearly twice the size of Donatella. If she had the use of both arms, she could move him. However, with one being out of commission, she opted for the woman who was further away, but smaller.

As she dragged the woman, she lost her balance, and fell. Struggling back to her feet, she could feel a sensation tugging at her esophagus. The feeling made her want to clutch at her throat and with her bare hands attempt to rip out the pain. She blocked out this newest distraction and propped the woman in place.

"BJ, update," she croaked barely recognizing her own voice.

"Another three minutes."

Donatella began to run the mental calculations. Time was running short and her options were dwindling. The haze generated by the spewing canisters had covered roughly 70 percent of the room. She ran through a cloud of the poison closing her eyes and holding her breath until she reached the one closest to the door. There she realized two hard realities.

The first - the door didn't have a keypad on the inside. Breaking the encryption would not do her any good.

The second – her legs had gone completely numb and she could not move them anymore. She fell to the ground, throat closing, skin burning. She thought to herself, before her world went dark, *at least Jasmyn and my godchild are safe.*

EPILOGUE

The sound of machines chiming and the smell of disinfectant filled the air. The temperature felt abnormally cool, but somehow comforting. Hushed voices could be heard deep in conversation, but no discernible words could be made out.

Special Agent Donatella Dabria opened her right eye and then the left. The owners of the hushed voices stood in front of her in a white haze hiding all pertinent features. She tried to lift her left arm to find it had been immobilized. Her mind pressed for answers, though none were forthcoming.

Where am I? How did I get here? Why am I here? She blinked a couple of times to bring her eyes into focus. The person in front of her, she still couldn't tell who it was, must have noticed some movement as they came rushing to the Special Agent.

"Donatella," came the soft reassuring voice. "My name is Dr. Emily West."

A few more blinks of her eyes and her vision began to clear. Standing next to the bed stood a mid-30s woman with auburn hair straightened to shoulder length. She wore what appeared to be frameless rectangle glasses but upon later inspection turned out to be silver.

"Welcome back," she said picking up with the conversation. "We've been waiting for you to rejoin us."

Us? Donatella turned her head back toward the foot of the bed. For the first time she noticed Detective Sampson and Marcellous Thompson standing there.

"You gave us quite a scare there for a while; however, you're expected to make a full recovery. You'll need to do some rehab for your shoulder to regain full range of motion, but other than that I think you'll be good to go."

She began to recall the gunshot wound she took to the shoulder and the fight that took place within the museum. Many of the details were still a little fuzzy as she tried to bring them to the forefront of her mind.

"I promised your visitors they could stay for only a few minutes. One or both of them have been here every day since you were brought into the hospital. I'll leave you all alone."

Dr. West began toward the door and as she passed Sampson and Marcellous she reminded them not to agitate the patient. They both agreed and she walked out of the door.

Both Sampson and Marcellous filled the vacant space left by the doctor. They pulled chairs that were sitting a few feet from the bed and sat so that they were all at eye level.

Donatella cleared her throat and with a raspy whisper asked, "Where am I?"

"You're at University Hospitals Cleveland Medical Center," Sampson stated. "We brought you here directly from the museum. Do you recall what happened?"

Donatella fought once more with her brain, but the memories were slow – disjointed. "No, not all of it. Fragments of a fight in the museum are trying to resurface but I cannot make sense of it all."

"The doctor said your memory may be spotty for a while; however, it will come back. Let's see what we can fill in.

Once I secured Jasmyn within the Exhibition Gallery, I began my exfiltration. Just as I exited the building, your transmission for an alternative exit from the library came over the comms. Although your voice was calm, the request came across as dire. Marcellous," he said nodding at the younger man, "heard the request as well. He left from his location and hastily approached the museum. In the meantime, BJ continued to work on the new encryption for the library door. At the three-minute check, your voice was haggard and Marcellous here burst into the museum searching out the library."

Donatella looked over at Marcellous – he averted eye contact.

"He reached the library as BJ was able to break the encryption. He entered the code, opened the door, and saw you laying on the floor. A purple haze sat like a dim fog in the room, nonetheless, he rushed in, scooped you up in a fireman's carry and bolted out the room."

Donatella's hazelnut eyes were still locked in on Marcellous. He looked back in her direction and this time he did not break eye contact.

"Dr. West said had you been exposed to the poisons circulating throughout the room any longer, the damage may have been irreversible. Had it not been for the quick feet of Marcellous," he patted the younger man on the back, "and the fast fingers of your computer genius, BJ, we would have lost you."

Donatella contemplated this for a moment, "Marcellous," she said in the still low raspy voice, "Thank you! Thank you for risking your life to save mine."

Marcellous, unsure of what to say, simply nodded his head and said, "You're welcome."

Donatella turned her gaze back to Sampson. More of the

puzzle pieces were connecting in her memory. "What happened with Terri Buckley?"

"She escaped and has not resurfaced. It's been nearly three weeks and we have not heard a peep from her."

Three weeks, she thought, *how long have I been out?*

"The woman, nurse, in the room with Jasmyn when I found her was Patti Jones."

The name sounded familiar to Donatella, but she was having a hard time placing it.

"She was the one recently hired as the director of nursing at the hospital where Jasmyn worked. I'm sure there is some connection to Buckley, but we have been unable to link the two – other than the fact she was holding Jasmyn captive."

The door to the room swung open; however, Donatella didn't look to see who had entered. She was still studying Sampson and the meaning behind what he hadn't said.

"Dr. West made it clear you were to have no more than two visitors at a time. Seems like my time is up. That's ok, I have another case I've been asked to lead. A young college coed was found with her skin filleted and I need to be return to Charlotte. It's good to have you with us again and be sure to look me up when you are back home."

Sampson stood and clasped Marcellous on the shoulder one more time. Awkward in what he should do with Donatella, he just nodded and made his way to the door.

Donatella was surprised when her next visitor sat down in the chair. In front of her sat Jasmyn Thompson and in her arms, she held her newborn.

"Donatella, I would like you to meet your godson, Sebastian Xavier Thompson."

TERRI BUCKLEY, a notoriously light sleeper, was partially awake when her phone rang. Picking up the handset and eyeballing the clock, she realized it was just after 4 a.m. Upon answering the phone, the voice on the other end started immediately.

"As you are aware, Donatella survived your latest encounter at the Cleveland Museum of Art. We've given you the leeway to deal with her as you have seen fit; however, it's time we properly plan for her demise. In your normal drop, you will find the outline of the plan we have developed. See to it that it's executed flawlessly, or we will be forced to step in."

The line on the other end went dead and Terri was left holding the phone in her hand. She was unaccustomed to being spoken to in such a manner and did not take to kindly to the tone or the threat. She squeezed the phone in her hand until it snapped in half.

The voice next to her spoke, "What is it?"

"Nothing I can't handle. Turnover and go back to sleep."

"I can't, I'm awake now. I think I will go downstairs and make some coffee."

Terri watched as Veronica King stood from the bed, wrapping herself in the robe Kyle bought her many Christmas' ago. Veronica pulled her straightened hair from underneath the collar of the robe and let it fall past her shoulders.

When Veronica exited the bedroom, Terri turned, dropped the pieces of the phone in the trashcan and made her way to the shower.

SHE BARELY ESCAPED with her life and the battle has drawn even. Signup for my newsletter to be notified when **Annihilation** releases, and witness how Donatella brings this conflict to an explosive end!

Note from the Author

THANK you for the purchase of Hour of Reckoning and the continued support of the Donatella series. For this installment of the series, it was important for me to round out the backstory for Terri Buckley. I firmly believe when you have feelings invested in characters, good and bad, you find yourself caring what happens to them. Even though Terri is the antagonist, you begin to find yourself conflicted about how you feel about her. Are you on her side because of what happened to her, or are you against her for everything she is doing in the present? It was key for me to build that conflict within the reader.

I DECIDED to team Donatella up with a partner for this book, Carl Sampson, as an introduction into the next series he will play a major role in. As a new detective he has a lot to learn and being paired with Donatella is no easy feat. Along the way he starts to find his footing and will be prepared to step out on his own... we hope.

AGAIN, thank you for reading book #2 in the Donatella series. To stay connected to the series and my future upcoming series, sign up for my newsletter by clicking on the link.

SINCERELY,
Demetrius Jackson

Excerpt from Annihilation

DONATELLA RAN, arms pumping, lungs burning. Her mind told her, *you still have time*; however, her heart warned her, *you're already too late.*

She blocked out the competing judgements and instead focused on the fury emanating deep within her core. She should have seen this inevitable outcome - she should have prevented it.

She conquered the last corner moving at top speed to witness black smoke billowing skyward. This, the first sign her heart was correct. tugged at her emotions and she ran harder. A building normally present in the landscape was ominously missing.

Wordlessly she internalized a prayer, outwardly a tear began to materialize. Distantly she heard the horn blaring from her left as she ran through the intersection.

The smoke previously in the background now gave glimpses of its origin. The normally smooth concrete structure of the building lay crumbled and tangled with its invisible metal skeleton.

Upon later reflection she would recall hearing the screams and pleas amidst the rubble, but in this moment, she could only hear her failure. She could feel her mind beginning to side with her heart as despair began to settle.

Fire trucks and EMS crews raced past her seeking the reason for the frantic calls. Donatella knew the reason and she knew the arbiter of this heinous act.

Arriving at the scene of what was once a five-story building, she now saw smoke, rubble, ash, and destruction. Resigned to the fact she had failed those she swore to protect, her mind and heart agreed at last.

With one final look, her eyes took in the destruction, while her mind and heart became resolute in their agreement - *Terri Buckley would not live to see the sun rise tomorrow.*

This book is a work of fiction. Names, characters, places and incidents are products of the author's imagination and are used fictitiously. Any resemblance to actual events or persons, living or dead, is entirely coincidental.

Hour of Reckoning

First edition: August 2020

ISBN 978-0-9771133-3-0 (Paperback)

ISBN 978-0-9771133-4-7 (Hardcover)

Created with Vellum

Made in the USA
Columbia, SC
07 May 2024

34999692R00193